Under the Waterfall

Have Body, Will Guard Adventure Romance

by Neil S. Plakcy

Copyright 2013, 2020 Neil S. Plakcy. This book is a work of fiction. Names, characters, places, and incidents either are products of the author's imagination or are used fictitiously. Any resemblance to actual events or locales or persons, living or dead, is entirely coincidental.

All rights reserved, including the right of reproduction in whole or in part in any form. This book was originally published by Loose Id. Maryam Salim did an awesome job of editing this book, and the rest in the series.

Reviews for Neil Plakcy and the Have Body series:

"Never slows down" – Literary Nymphs Reviews on *Three Wrong Turns in the Desert*

"Plakcy's characters... charm" – Kirkus Reviews

"An engrossing writer" - Publisher's Weekly.

"Plakcy's Tunisia is the perfect exotic locale for your fantasy summer vacation, if you don't mind dodging an assassin or two along the way." – Dick Smart, reviewing for the Lambda Literary Review

"If you're going to walk under the waterfall, don't complain if you get wet." - Corsican Proverb

DEDICATION

A love-struck Romeo sings the streets a serenade—for Marc.

1 – Mountain Hideaway

The narrow two-lane road climbed steeply through the Corsican countryside, lined with trees as straight and slim as toothpicks that towered above ferns and the fragrant, low bushes called *maquis*. Those strong, determined bushes had given their name to the French resistance, and thinking of them inspired Michel Perreau as he leaned forward, gripping the handlebars of his bright red motorbike.

Behind him, his boyfriend, Cris, had his hands clasped together around Michel's waist, his feet solidly placed on the bike's footrest. Tiny blue butterflies darted alongside them as they zoomed around the switchbacks that climbed the mountains.

For a while there was no one else on the road, and Michel relished the feel of Cris's body so close to his, daydreaming of the pleasures that awaited them at their secret place—an oceanfront cave nestled beneath a sparkling waterfall.

He zoomed through a hairpin turn, feeling Cris lean into it with him, as if they shared one body. He looked over his shoulder and smiled. When he looked back at the road, he was startled to see they were coming up fast on a truck carrying huge tree trunks down from the high mountains.

Michel leaned back and applied the brakes quickly. Gravel scattered beneath the front wheel, and he had to grip the handlebars to control the sideways motion.

"You're crazy!" Cris yelled, but Michel could hear the exuberance in his voice. As soon as he could, he accelerated the bike and passed the truck, both of them waving at the driver as they shot forward.

The dry air was cool, but the March sun was hot, and Michel felt it baking into his body, warming him for the lovemaking to come. His balls had pulled up, and his dick pressed uncomfortably against his tight jeans. A tiny trickle of sweat began in each armpit. He knew Cris would like that—he loved to nibble at Michel's pits while teasing his ass with a long, slim finger.

Cris leaned forward and kissed the back of Michel's neck, and Michel's body quivered. He had never met anyone who made him feel the way Cris did—so fully alive that every nerve in his body tingled. Not just when they kissed or made love; he felt that way any time he thought of his handsome, sexy boyfriend. Now with their bodies touching at so many points, his dick pressed against his pants and his heart raced and all he wanted to do was ditch the motorcycle, rip off his clothes, and offer his whole body to Cris.

They zoomed past a cluster of small stone houses, then a bar with two outdoor tables and a sign advertising Pietra—the local beer made with chestnut flour. Michel slowed the bike as they approached the tree that signaled the entrance to Cris's hometown of Cargése.

Michel followed the curving road down to the marina: a long stone breakwater that protected the harbor, and rows of slips for pleasure and fishing boats. The air smelled like salt water and motor oil, overlaid with the fresh, briny smell of fish. "You're sure your father won't be here today?" he asked Cris over his shoulder as he slowed the bike.

"He's supposed to be in Ajaccio, leading a demonstration," Cris said. His father was a fisherman, but in the past few years he had become an environmental activist as well.

Michel pulled the bike to a stop at the far end of the marina, where he shut it down and removed his helmet, shaking his hair free.

Cristoforu Aquaviva hopped off the bike behind him, tugging Michel's extra helmet from his curly black hair. He was darker than Michel, more muscular, with eyes as black as cured olives, and he wore a T-shirt, denim cutoff shorts, and bright yellow track shoes. He moved with the easy grace of a born athlete. "You are a wild man," he said. "The way you drive!"

"I'm wild in more ways than that," Michel said, smiling and moving toward his boyfriend.

"Not here," Cris said. "We'll have plenty of time to play when we get to the waterfall."

Michel unhooked the day pack from the back of the bike and shouldered it as Cris led the way to a small flat-bottomed boat that swayed in the gentle current. It belonged to his father's best friend, the man he called Uncle Andre, and he'd told Cris he was free to use it whenever he wanted. He grabbed the rope to pull it close and jumped in, holding it steady for Michel. Cris untied the rope, and the boat drifted from the pier as he revved the outboard.

Michel sat facing him, his back against the gunwale, and opened his pants so that his stiff dick sprang forward. Cris laughed, then looked up to steer the boat out of the harbor. "Shit!" he said. "My father's here."

He pointed ahead of them to a fishing boat painted light blue, with a red stripe just above the waterline. *L'Ange de la Mer* was twenty meters long, with a heavy-duty winch attached to the bow for lowering and raising the lobster nets. A handsome man in his forties stood at the bow. He was an older, more weather-beaten version of Cris—the same black hair, stocky build, chiseled features.

He was talking to a pretty young woman who stood on the dock beside the boat. She wore high heels and a bright green dress that clung to the curves of her body, and her dark, curly hair spread across her shoulders.

"Isn't that Vanina Andreadi?" Michel asked. "What's she doing here?"

"She's part of that group, you know, Students for a Green Corsica," Cris said. "She must have followed him back from that protest."

"Not exactly dressed for a rally, is she?" Michel muttered. He barely knew the girl, only that she liked to hang around the football team, flirting with the coach and some of the better-looking players. He was jealous that she could get away with that behavior just because she was a girl.

Cris steered the small boat into the shelter of a large cabin cruiser. "How will we get past your father?" Michel asked. Neither boy was out to his family, and neither wanted to admit to a parent that they were on their way to a protected cove to have sex.

"We'll have to skip the waterfall," Cris said. "You can jump out here, and I'll put Uncle Andre's boat back. Then we'll meet up at your bike."

"Crap," Michel said. "That's going to ruin our day."

"Can't be helped," Cris said.

Michel looked up and saw the girl on the dock wave at Nic and turn toward the parking lot. "See there, Vanina's leaving. Maybe your father will too."

Vanina looked back toward *L'Ange de la Mer* and noticed the two of them in the small boat. She laughed and pointed at Michel's open pants, his dick swaying like a tree in the wind.

"You idiot!" Cris said. "She's such a gossip. She'll tell everyone at school that she saw us."

"She doesn't even know who I am," Michel said as he scrambled to close his pants. "And all she saw was the two of us in a boat with my pants open. I could have been ready to take a piss."

"I'll talk to her tomorrow in class," Cris said. "See what she thinks she saw. There's no way she could suspect anything about me."

Cris played football for the University of Corsica Pascal Paoli, and none of his friends or teammates knew he was gay. He wanted to keep it that way.

They watched Vanina walk to a small red car and get in. As she drove out of the lot, Nic Aquaviva ducked into the cabin of the fishing boat. "Hold on," Cris said, and he gunned the engine of the small boat.

Michel grabbed the gunwale and felt the spray on his face as they zoomed past *L'Ange* and out beyond the breakwater. "I'm not the only crazy driver," he said when they were away from the marina and Cris had slowed the boat.

"Yes, but I'm crazy when I have a reason to be." The coastline around Cargése was steep and rocky, but Cris knew every inch of it from years of fishing with his father. After a few minutes, he turned inland and slipped through a crevice in the tall stone walls, to a secret cove he had discovered years before.

A shallow lagoon was ringed by cliffs of twenty to thirty feet high. To the west, a small river cascaded over a tumble of red rocks, splashing into the cove. Cris steered the boat up to the shore, and Michel jumped onto the narrow strip of sand. Cris cut the engine and tossed the line to Michel, who held it until Cris jumped out and took it, tying it around a spike of rock.

Then Cris grabbed his boyfriend by the waist and pulled him close. Lips pressed against lips, groin against groin, hands moving eagerly under T-shirts to find bare skin. Cris's lips tasted like a mix of strawberries and wind.

"My dick is raw from pressing against your ass all that way on the bike," Cris murmured into Michel's ear.

"I'll have to be especially nice to it, then." Michel kissed Cris's jaw, rough with a few days' stubble, and pressed his hand against his boyfriend's stiff cock through his shorts.

Cris pulled away. "Race you to the cave," he said, and he took off down the shore to the waterfall.

"No fair! I have to carry everything!" Michel called. He grabbed the pack from the boat and hurried after Cris. By the time he reached the steppingstones that allowed them to climb up to the cave's entrance, Cris was standing by the water's edge, one leg resting atop a boulder speckled with mica.

"I win!" he said. "You know what that means."

Michel knew. It meant he would have to do anything Cris wanted for as long as they were at their secret hideaway.

"Yes, sir," he said, smiling. "What would you like me to do?"

Cris pulled his football shirt over his head in one smooth movement, exposing his muscular chest covered with a layer of dark hair. Only two round pink nubs stood out against the black coat. Saliva pooled in Michel's mouth as Cris slowly undid his leather belt and unzipped his denim shorts.

"What are you waiting for?" Cris asked. "Get out of those clothes."

Michel couldn't stop staring as Cris's pants hung open, exposing a V-shaped patch of white jockey shorts and a slim line of pale flesh above the waistband. Cris liked to wear his pants and shorts tight, and he had to shimmy to get them down over his massive footballer's thighs.

"Snap to it!" he yelled as he kicked off his sneakers and dropped his shorts. Then he stood there, with the waterfall behind him, like a marble statue come to life. His arms hung loosely at his sides, one foot just in front of the other.

"I'm enjoying the view." Michel pulled his polo shirt off over his head. He was slimmer than Cris, and his skin was several shades lighter than his boyfriend's, spotted with occasional freckles. He kicked off his running shoes, and when he undid his pants, they fell to the ground, slipping easily past his hips.

He had a dusting of hair between his pecs and a neatly trimmed bush around the base of his dick. He shaved under his arms and plucked stray hairs from his nose and ears. But as much as he preferred his own body smooth, he loved the hair on Cris's.

Cris moved toward him, and Michel met him halfway, his stiff dick pressing against the nylon of his bikini briefs. Michel reached up, grasping the hard bones of his boyfriend's back, while Cris's fingers snaked beneath Michel's briefs to cup his ass. Pressing their bodies together, they kissed.

Michel's heart raced, and he felt short of breath as his tongue dueled with Cris's—both eager to explore the other's open mouth. Then Cris pulled back. "Come on, let's go. I can't wait to make love to you."

He slid his briefs down his thighs, and his half-hard dick popped free. Forests of curly pubic hair sprouted from his groin and under his arms. He turned to pick up their clothes, and Michel admired the crack of his ass, lined with silk.

Michel dropped his briefs, then opened the day pack and removed a couple of beach towels. His dick was achingly hard, swinging free between his thighs, as he imagined the pleasure that was to come. Then Cris took his hand and led him over the rocks to the barely visible path that sneaked behind the waterfall.

He remembered the first time Cris had brought him to this place, a few months before. Cris had been very mysterious but told Michel to bring towels and food for a picnic. The waterfall was glorious, and the tiny lagoon at its base beautiful. But the best part of the place was the small cave behind the cascade.

The spray chilled them as they stepped carefully over the wet, mossy stones. Michel's naked body tingled, and his dick pulsed. Cris stepped into the cave, the size of a bedroom, and turned to face him.

They had built themselves a bed of a sort—a pile of twigs covered with layers of worn comforters, with a couple of old pillows at one end. They embraced once more, then fell onto the bed in a jumble of long legs and arms and hard dicks. Cris pressed Michel down on the bed and climbed on top of him.

He kissed the curve of Michel's neck, then arched his back and pressed his body down on Michel's, grinding his dick against his boyfriend's. They both enjoyed this way of making love—the friction of Cris's hair against Michel's skin, the weight of Cris's football-trained body pressing down on Michel, sometimes making it hard for him to breathe.

The tiny droplets of water on their skin turned warm, then dried in the friction of their bodies. Michel wrapped his hands around Cris's back, pressing him on, pushing his own body up to meet him. He dug his short fingernails into Cris's skin and began to pant as his orgasm rose. Cris matched his passion and force, and then Michel's dick erupted, spewing its geyser against Cris's body hair. Cris followed just a moment later, rubbing his dick savagely against

Michel's skin as it erupted.

Cris turned on his side and slid next to Michel on the makeshift bed. He rested his head on Michel's smooth chest as Michel caressed his back. "I want to be able to do this whenever we want," Michel murmured. "Not have to sneak away for an hour or two."

"Your father would kill you if he found out about us." Cris lifted his head so that it rested on a pillow and faced Michel. "Olivier Perreau would not tolerate a homosexual son."

"Your father would kill both of us," Michel said. "If he knew you were friendly with the son of his sworn enemy. He'd never even get to learn about the sex."

"So what do we do, my little cabbage?" Cris asked. "Is there any way you can convince your father to abandon this project of his?"

"As easily as you could convince yours to discard his principles," Michel said. "There is nothing we can do about those two old men but ignore them. And make love together as much as we can."

It was only a temporary measure, Michel thought as Cris leaned over to kiss him again. But it was all they had.

2 – Cosmopolitan Flavor

Aidan Greene woke on a Monday morning in March to sunlight streaming in through the east-facing bedroom window. Though he had been happy to live in a small house in Tunis with threadbare rugs over concrete floors, a collection of mixed furniture, and an outdoor shower, because Liam McCullough was there, at heart he enjoyed his creature comforts.

A month before, they had given up their home and their small business as bodyguards to visiting diplomats and wealthy tourists so that they could both take positions with a company in France that provided similar close protection services.

Liam had pushed for the move because he thought Aidan would be happier in the more cosmopolitan and liberal atmosphere in Europe. Aidan appreciated the gesture, and as a Jew, a gay man, and an American, he was glad to have left behind the Muslim fundamentalism that was sweeping through the Arab world. He would have stayed in Tunis forever, though, if that's what Liam had wanted.

Their boss's wife had found and furnished for them this apartment in the heart of Nice, with wall-to-wall carpeting, sleek Scandinavian furniture, and modern appliances. As Liam had predicted, Aidan loved being in Europe, and he particularly loved the apartment.

Liam hated the place, though. He complained that the lobby was too glitzy, with gilt-trimmed paintings and marble floors. He preferred bare concrete to plush carpet, a simple futon to a king-size bed with thick pillows, the freedom to come and go without a concierge keeping track. There were too many mirrors in the apartment, and the furniture was too new to be comfortable.

Hayam, their small mixed-breed dog, had adapted as well as Aidan had. The day Aidan landed in Tunis, fleeing from the pain of being dumped by his boyfriend of ten years, she had shown up at his apartment door as if carrying a message that he would love again. Hayam had a soft, fluffy coat the color of very light coffee, a square head with a patch of white around her black nose, and another white patch under her neck. She weighed about twenty pounds and still had the endless energy of a puppy.

Hayam loved the small garden just outside the French doors, and she had already found her favorite places in the sun and on the couch. That morning she was sprawled on the floor next to Aidan's side of the bed, snuffling through her flat nose.

Aidan sat up and stretched. Liam slept on his back beside him, a fluffy, down-filled pillow below his head. His partner could sleep anywhere, under any conditions, even on a pillow-top mattress covered with high-thread-count Egyptian cotton sheets.

As often happened when he watched Liam sleep, Aidan's heart swelled. He found it hard to imagine he could love anyone so much, that anyone could make him feel so complete. He had believed that in any relationship there was the lover and the one who was loved. With his last partner, Blake, Aidan had always been the lover. He looked after Blake's every need, forcing down his own desires when they conflicted with Blake's.

But now, with Liam, Aidan luxuriated in both roles. He made sure their daily life ran smoothly. He bought and prepared Liam's favorite foods, kept the apartment neat and the clothes clean, and always had a bottle of their favorite wine chilling in the refrigerator. In a dozen small ways every day, he expressed his love.

Liam, on the other hand, rarely paid attention to domesticity, and he was not one for small gifts. But the very fact that he'd been willing to give up everything for Aidan's happiness spoke volumes about the depth of his love. He'd never once complained about losing the independence of choosing his own clients or fitting into the bureaucracy of an established company.

The night before, they'd received an emergency call from their boss, requesting that they meet with him that morning. Aidan didn't know what it was about, but he worried nonetheless. Had a client complained? France was more liberal than Tunisia, and he and Liam did their best to keep their personal lives separate from their work, but suppose someone had objected to being assigned a pair of gay bodyguards?

Aidan turned to his partner, ready to plant a kiss on Liam's forehead to wake him. But then a naughty impulse overtook him, and instead he tweaked the small gold ring in Liam's left nipple. Quick as lightning, Liam's right hand grabbed Aidan's before he could sneak away.

"You're never going to be faster than I am," Liam said, his eyes still closed. He had the ability to be completely awake in a fraction of a second, a result of his SEAL training.

"Maybe I don't want to be." Aidan leaned over to kiss Liam on the lips. He had morning wood, and he pressed his groin toward Liam, then gently rubbed his stiff dick against his partner's thigh.

"You are such a horndog," Liam grumbled, even as he turned toward Aidan and pulled him close.

When they'd met, Aidan had been the more experienced lover. Liam's sex life had consisted mostly of hurried encounters with strangers or casual acquaintances. During their two years together, Liam had gained technique to match the amazing control he possessed over his body. He could flex muscles Aidan never knew existed, regulate his breathing, and multitask in creative and entertaining ways—sucking Aidan's dick while penetrating his ass with a finger with one hand and using the other hand to tweak a nipple.

Liam seemed to enjoy having sex as much as Aidan did, which Aidan found a refreshing change from his old life with Blake, who had always made sex seem like a chore he performed only to keep Aidan happy.

Aidan always slept in the nude, and he had gradually converted Liam to the same habit. He loved the feel of his partner's mostly smooth skin, interrupted by a thatch of dark blond hair beneath his arms and around his dick. He ran his hand along Liam's arm, feeling the bulge of his biceps.

The pressure on Aidan's dick was exquisite as the sensitive head rubbed against the fine blond hairs of Liam's thigh. His pulse raced, and his breath came fast and shallow. He leaned down to take Liam's left nipple in his mouth, pressed the cool gold against Liam's skin with his tongue, then nibbled at the nub of flesh. Liam's body stiffened, and he took a deep breath. "You know it drives me crazy when you do that," he said.

"In a good way, of course," Aidan said, releasing the nipple and looking up.

"In a very good way." Liam put his hand on Aidan's head and pressed Aidan's lips down onto his, forcing him to breathe through his nose.

The pressure of the kiss and the lubrication provided by his precome pushed Aidan toward orgasm, but he pulled back, unwilling to shoot so soon. He squirmed out of Liam's embrace and leaned back against his pillow. He pulled his thighs up and exposed his puckered ass.

Liam took the hint, shifting position so that he could run his tongue over Aidan's balls and tease his perineum. Aidan shivered, knowing all he had to do was touch his dick and it would explode, but he resisted, prolonging the pleasure as long as he could.

Liam folded his tongue and penetrated Aidan's ass with it, pushing forward so his nose was buried in Aidan's wiry pubes. He flexed his ass muscles and rubbed his dick against the bedsheets as he worked his tongue around Aidan's hole.

It was finally all too much, and Aidan's body shook as an orgasm ripped through him. A moment later, Liam gasped as he spurted against the sheets.

Aidan slumped back against his pillow, and Liam pulled up beside him. "Big mess," he said and yawned.

Though he'd have preferred to go back to sleep, Aidan slid out of bed and returned from the bathroom with a wet washcloth, which he used to clean up his partner. "I'll have to wash these sheets," Aidan grumbled. Liam's sperm had soaked a big oval—conveniently more on Aidan's side of the bed than his own.

Hayam woke and yawned deeply. Aidan went back to the bathroom as Liam rolled onto his side for a few more minutes of sleep. Then Aidan pulled on a pair of sweatpants and a long-sleeved T-shirt and retrieved Hayam's leash from the kitchen counter.

The little dog danced around, her toenails clicking on the tile floor, as Aidan tried to get the leash attached to her collar. She was accustomed to running free in Tunis, and she didn't appreciate the need for a collar and leash in Nice.

He finally wrestled the little fur ball into submission and then led her out into the hallway of the apartment building. She hurried forward, eager to get outside. It was barely seven o'clock, but with the morning meeting ahead of them, Aidan wanted to get a head start on the day, and he let her scamper.

The March morning was a good ten or fifteen degrees cooler than Aidan had become accustomed to in Tunis, but the brisk, ocean-scented air was refreshing. Hayam immediately nosed her way under a rosebush, heavy with pinkish-red blossoms. "Watch the thorns!" Aidan said.

She looked up at him quizzically as she peed, and he laughed. The streets around the Place Massena were already buzzing with delivery trucks and early morning commuters. A middle-aged woman in a bright pink business suit bent down to pet Hayam, saying *"Quelle mignon!"* and Hayam wagged her fluffy tail eagerly.

Aidan loved the cosmopolitan flavor of the city, so different from Tunis. Ancient stone buildings shouldered in next to modern glass colossi. Chic women in the latest Parisian couture shared sidewalks with elderly ladies in black pushing rickety metal carts. Because his French was good, he could understand the street signs and banter with the shopkeepers.

He smiled and nodded at the old man washing down the sidewalk, and at the gendarme at the corner. When he reached his favorite *boulangerie*, he tied Hayam's leash to a tree while he went inside for his regular order—two croissants and a *boule*—the round French loaf Liam favored.

On their way home, they stopped at a tiny park where Hayam had already expressed an interest in doing her business. Aidan examined a massive aloe plant as she squatted, remembering the much smaller aloes his mother had raised on their glassed-in porch back in New Jersey. Had she dreamed of these monsters, nurturing her little ones?

A sudden tug on the leash told him Hayam had finished and was ready to move on. Keeping a firm hold on her, he cleaned up with a plastic bag from his pocket, then deposited it in a trash can that read *merci* on the lid.

When they returned to the apartment, Liam was outside on the small paved terrace, in the midst of his morning exercise routine. He'd always worked out in the nude back in Tunis, the way the ancient Greeks had, but here in the heart of the city, visible from a dozen apartment balconies above, he donned a pair of loose shorts. Aidan stood by the French doors for a moment, watching him. But a sidelong glance at the clock forced him to head for the shower so he'd be dressed and ready by the time Liam needed the bathroom.

He stripped the bed, then took off his own clothes and tossed everything into the laundry basket. He wondered again what the emergency was that had brought the regional manager of the Agence de Securité from his office in Marseille to meet with them in Nice. They had worked with Jean-Luc Derain on a job that brought them from Tunis to France, and Derain had been impressed with their work—enough to woo them to join his firm and relocate.

They were free to turn down any job, but so far they hadn't— the apartment was expensive, and the cost of living in Nice was a lot higher than in Tunisia, and even though they had plenty of money stockpiled, they both felt it was necessary not only to keep the cash flowing but to make a good impression on their new employers.

By the time Aidan was showered and dressed in khakis and a polo shirt, Liam had finished his routine and was in the kitchen, still wearing only his skimpy shorts. He was the more mechanically minded and could figure out any machinery within minutes. He had quickly mastered the complicated cappuccino maker and appointed himself house barista. Aidan smelled the brewing coffee as he walked into the kitchen.

"Morning," Liam said as he poured milk for frothing into a small metal pitcher.

Aidan gave his partner a quick kiss on the lips. "Morning. Sleep well?"

"That bed is like quicksand," he grumbled. "You fall right into it."

"You can always sleep on the floor if you prefer," Aidan said as Liam stuck the pitcher under the frothing wand, and the sound of the noisy steam filled the room.

Aidan laid out bread, butter, jam, and cheese for their breakfast. He loved French cuisine and had been delighted to try again the foods he had learned to love the last time he lived in France, when he was younger, teaching English at a private academy in Aix-en-Provence and traveling through Europe whenever he had vacation. *Confiture de groseille* was one of those. "Any idea what this meeting with Jean-Luc is about?" he asked, putting the red currant jam on his croissant.

Liam finished off the coffees and brought them to the table. "Not a clue," he said, ripping into the boule.

They had seen Jean-Luc only occasionally since their relocation. He had operatives in several cities along the Côte d'Azur, where celebrities congregated and often needed the services of a close protection agency. Most client bookings came through the Marseille office.

The Agence de Securité had required them to obtain French

driver's licenses as well as to renew their CPR credentials. They were regularly sent updates on trouble spots in Europe and had spent many hours familiarizing themselves with the area around Nice—the hospitals, police stations, major highways; the elegant hotels and high-priced restaurants where their clients might stay and dine. They had rehearsed the drive from the airport into the city and spent time among the luxury yachts at the Port Lympia, on the edge of the old part of the city.

Other bodyguards, a mix of retired cops, young bodybuilders, even a former Mossad agent, were stationed in Cannes and Monte Carlo. Liam and Aidan had met them and worked together on a series of ordinary cases that required multiple operatives. They had escorted the family of a sheik from one of the oil-rich emirates and a paranoid American lottery winner and kept an eye on the party-happy teenage daughter of a Russian oligarch.

"Must be a new client, don't you think?" Aidan asked.

"Don't start speculating. It could be anything."

Aidan wanted to kick him. His partner was too grounded in reality—when Aidan wanted to engage in flights of fancy, imagining hidden meanings in ordinary conversation or elaborating on casual comments from clients, Liam always pulled him back to earth.

"What if he's not happy with something we've done?" Aidan asked. "Suppose a client complained about us."

"Aidan," Liam said, breaking off a second hunk of the boule. "Don't go crazy. He's our boss; he wants to meet with us. End of story."

Aidan grumbled as he picked up his coffee cup. "You're no fun."

Liam lifted his coffee cup and clinked it against Aidan's. "While you, on the other hand, are a circus monkey. Now eat your breakfast."

3 – A Troubled Island

Aidan cleaned up and made sure Hayam had water in her bowl and her favorite chewy toys handy while Liam showered and dressed. It was just before nine as they walked out through the lobby, waving good morning to Madame Serroli, the Italian-French concierge, who lived in an efficiency apartment adjacent to the building's front door. She spent her days behind a wooden desk in the lobby, accepting packages and vetting visitors.

She was a heavyset woman with garish red hair and a welcoming smile, and she had taken quite a liking to Hayam. The little dog had already stayed with her several times when Aidan and Liam were tied up on assignments.

They stepped out onto the sidewalk as a tiny Smart car zipped past them, around a delivery van with its back door open. A French pop song floated past from a newsstand, cars beeped, and in the distance they heard the high-low whooping of a police siren. A breeze swirled through the fronds of a palm tree, bringing the scent of the ocean with it. Aidan beamed with pleasure at the surroundings, and the chance to be there with Liam.

The temperature had already risen a few degrees, and they quickly walked to the office, located in a modern, glass-fronted building on the Rue Dubouchage, sandwiched between an ancient stone church and a garage specializing in luxury cars.

They climbed the stairs to the second floor. Victoire, a widow in her mid-sixties who habitually wore black, sat at a desk in the office's reception room. Aidan suspected she chose the color more for its flattering aspects than as a nod toward mourning, because she looked so stylish. She was addicted to paperback romances, and there was always a garish-covered book at her desk, beside her jewel-encrusted reading glasses.

Victoire kept in touch with Liam, Aidan, and the other agents based in Nice by e-mail and cell, and once they had completed the paperwork for their *cartes de séjour*, work permits, they rarely saw her.

When they arrived at the office, Jean-Luc was sitting on the edge of Victoire's desk, flirting with her. He was a tall Frenchman with tousled black hair, a former flic who had retired from the force at fifty and returned to work after his wife tired of having him underfoot. He switched to English when they walked in. "Good morning. I always like to arrive here early, so I can spend some time with your beautiful secretary. But now we must attend to business."

Victoire giggled, tucking a loose strand back into her pixyish cap of black hair, and told Jean-Luc that if he didn't stop flirting, she would call his wife. As they walked into the conference room behind Victoire's desk, Jean-Luc said, "I hope you have been adjusting. The apartment, it is fine?"

"It's very nice," Aidan said.

The room contained a simple round table and four chairs. Framed photos of the Côte d'Azur hung on the walls. A floor-to-ceiling window along one wall afforded them a view of the rising foothills of the Alpes-Maritimes.

"I'm sorry to ask you to leave Nice so soon after you arrive," Jean-Luc said as he took a seat, "but we have a job that I must fill, and you are the men to handle it."

Aidan sat across from Jean-Luc and turned on his netbook so that he could take notes or use the Wi-Fi in the building for research. Liam slid into the chair beside him.

"The job is an emergency," Jean-Luc said. "I spoke with the client last night, and that's why I asked you here this morning. He has received an escalating series of threats and needs bodyguards in place immediately."

Jean-Luc passed a manila folder toward them. Liam opened it, and Aidan saw that it contained the standard client information form, with only a few items filled in. "I haven't had time to put together any research, but I'll tell you as much as I know. Our client, Olivier Perreau, is a businessman in Ajaccio, the capital of Corsica. Do you know it?"

Corsica, Aidan thought. When they were just starting to get settled in Nice. He had never been to the island off the southern coast of France, so he shook his head, but Liam said, "I was there once. Years ago. Just to Ajaccio, though."

"Monsieur Perreau is a mineral engineer who worked for many years for Outremer, a large French mining cooperative. Ten years ago, he left Outremer to become a consultant and purchased an abandoned silver mine on the northwest coast of Corsica. He has been in negotiation with Outremer for some time to fund the reopening of this mine, now that the price of silver is very high."

As he listened, Aidan opened an Internet browser and began a search for Olivier Perreau.

"The deal is to be signed next Monday," Jean-Luc continued. "But a week ago, Monsieur Perreau received a threatening letter at his office, demanding he cancel his plans to reopen the mine. He reported the letter to the police, who were unable to trace it. A second was delivered to his residence a few days ago, which included a threat against all his property. Perreau again reported the letter and demanded protection from the police."

"Sounds like a standard pattern," Liam said. "Did he make any adjustments to his plans?"

Jean-Luc shook his head. "He tells me he must complete this deal on time." He sighed. "Then yesterday a third letter arrived at his wife's office, with specific threats against Perreau, his wife, and their son. He has demanded his son return from the university campus in the center of the island—circling the wagons, I believe is the American expression."

"Why are you sending us?" Liam asked. "Don't you have people in Corsica already?"

"I have a man in Ajaccio I call on now and then for small jobs. But this is too big for him—it requires two operatives to live with the Perreaus until next Monday. My man can only provide occasional support as needed."

Jean-Luc leaned forward. "Corsica is a troubled island. It has been a part of France for over two hundred years, yet it has its own culture, even its own language—an Italian dialect. There is a history of criminal gangs, and in the 1970s a nationalist movement took hold, with bomb attacks against the police, the government, and the property of non-Corsicans. Such attacks have continued sporadically."

"Could these threats be from one of those groups?" Liam asked.

"Perhaps. The letters express resentment that a Frenchman, and a French company, may exploit the island's natural resources. But no one group has claimed responsibility."

Aidan looked back at the laptop and saw the picture he had been waiting for had loaded. He turned the computer so it faced Jean-Luc and Liam. "Here's the client," he said. "From the Web site of an organization of mining engineers."

The man on the screen was in his mid-fifties, a solid-looking Frenchman with dark hair touched with gray, a strong jaw, and steely dark blue eyes. Aidan downloaded his biography to the laptop's hard drive, as well as a copy of the picture.

Jean-Luc's cell rang, and he said, "I must take this call. I will return quickly."

When he was out of the room, Liam looked at Aidan. "What do you think? I know you're just starting to get comfortable in Nice."

"I can manage. We've only been here a short time; let's not set a precedent by turning down jobs. If we get a reputation for that, we might wind up on our own again."

"Which might not be a bad thing," Liam said.

Aidan looked at him. Did Liam long for the independence he had enjoyed in Tunis? Had this move been a mistake?

"Earth to Aidan," Liam said. "We need to make a decision."

Liam was happiest when he had a mission to accomplish, Aidan knew. The Agence needed their help, and so did this client, whose family was in danger. "It sounds like something we could handle," he said.

Liam nodded as Jean-Luc returned to the room. "We're in," Liam said to him.

"Very good," Jean-Luc said. "You have Perreau's phone numbers and his address on the form there. The man in Ajaccio is called Paul Dubois. I will e-mail you his phone number and let him know the details of the assignment."

Liam passed the piece of paper to Aidan. Perreau's wife's name was Agathe, and his son's was Michel. Aidan typed as Liam and Jean-Luc continued discussing the assignment.

"How soon do you need us to go?" Liam asked.

"As soon as you can. There are several Air France flights per day." He stood up. "I have someone in my office preparing a dossier. I will forward it to you as soon as I have it. Call me once you are in Ajaccio and let me know what you think."

They both stood as well and shook hands with Jean-Luc. "We have no way of knowing at this point whether those threats are credible, but you must consider this a case that requires great vigilance," Jean-Luc said. "Perreau may have exaggerated the danger—but he may not have. I would not like to lose either of you so soon after hiring you."

"We won't be lost," Liam said.

4 – Excitement of the Journey

Aidan e-mailed the photo of Olivier Perreau and a smaller one of the man and his wife at a charity affair to Victoire to print out. While Liam made a phone call, Aidan opened Perreau's biography and ran it through an online translation Web site. Though his French was reasonably strong, he wanted to have the English ready for Liam, who spoke fluent Arabic but only basic French.

They stopped at Victoire's desk and picked up the photo and the printed bio, and she also handed them a schedule of the Air France flights to Ajaccio. As they walked back to their apartment, Aidan asked, "What do you think?"

"Hard to know much without a chance to see the client and assess the situation," Liam said. "But I called Louis and asked him to get me whatever he can on Corsican nationalists."

Louis Fleck was a CIA agent stationed at the American embassy in Tunis under the guise of a cultural attaché. He and Liam had a long history and had often worked together and shared information. Over the last few months, they'd had dinner regularly with Louis and his partner, Hassan, a Tunisian architect. One of Aidan's regrets about leaving Tunis was putting so much distance between them and their friendship.

"I'll make sure Madame Serroli can take care of Hayam while

we're gone," Aidan said as they neared their building. "Then I can handle the packing."

"I'll get us tickets to Corsica and then go online and see if I can fill in some of the holes in the client form," Liam said.

Aidan stopped in the glitzy lobby to wait for the concierge to finish a phone call with a dilatory plumber. Once she had thoroughly reprimanded him for his poor performance, she hung up and smiled at Aidan. He made the arrangements for Hayam, then walked down the hall to the apartment.

He would have preferred a higher floor, one perhaps with a view of the Mediterranean, which was only a half-dozen blocks away. But the ground floor was simpler—no elevators to worry about, and the ability to open the French doors to the garden and let Hayam out when they needed to.

Liam was on the phone and the computer simultaneously. Aidan plugged both devices into their chargers, then began packing. Liam was much broader in the chest than Aidan, but he liked his shirts tight, and Aidan preferred his loose. That meant they could share those, as well cargo shorts, with multiple pockets for phones, flashlights, guns, and other necessary tools of their trade. Since Liam was several inches taller, the only clothes they couldn't switch off were slacks.

He loved the way he and Liam worked together. When he'd lived with Blake, Aidan always walked on eggshells—would Blake approve of the flowers on the dining room table or Aidan's dinner preparation? Blake was mercurial and demanding, and Aidan had found it hard to anticipate him.

The day he returned home from a teaching job to find Blake at home, two years before, was one of those unexpected moments. *"I want you to move out,"* Blake had said, destroying an eleven-year relationship in a single sentence. The need to flee from Blake and Philadelphia had led Aidan to Tunis, where he met Liam and turned his life around.

He had joined Liam on a wild chase through the Sahara, falling in love with the big, handsome bodyguard. He had experienced depths of passion and romance he hadn't thought himself capable of.

He believed he owed Blake a debt of gratitude. If Blake hadn't kicked him to the curb, he might still be back in Philadelphia, living a mundane and loveless life. The last two years had been amazing, he thought as he packed boxer shorts for himself and jockstraps for Liam, who preferred as little restraint under his clothes as possible. Not just the sex, which was still passionate and fun, but the day-to-day life with a man whose company he enjoyed. From their boring assignments protecting tedious clients from imagined threats, to the moments of high adventure and danger, he had loved being by Liam's side.

When he decided to join Liam in his personal protection business, Aidan had taken a weeklong course in Georgia on the basics of the job. He'd come home with lists of items to have on hand for a wide range of assignments, including a long-handled inspection mirror used to look under vehicles for bombs, two-way radios and a charging station, folding knives, and an emergency medical kit.

He couldn't take everything with them, but there was still a wide range of items to pack into the two big duffle bags and the matching backpacks they used for travel. Since they might have to accompany the Perreaus to social events, he packed dress clothes for both of them as well as outdoor gear.

"We've got tickets on the 2:30 flight to Ajaccio airport in Corsica," Liam said, coming into the bedroom. "Fifty-minute flight, then a fifteen-minute drive into the city. I figure we'll take a taxi, and if it looks like we need a car to get around, we can pick one up tomorrow."

They worked together to finish preparing for their departure and then took a cab to the airport in Nice. After passing through security at terminal two, they waited at the gate for the Air Corsica flight. The turboprop Aerospatiale/Alenia ATR 72 was only about half-full, so they each got a two-seat row.

Aidan leaned back in his seat as the plane soared down the runway and out over the bright blue Mediterranean. Below he saw the crescent-shaped pebbled beach along the Bay of Angels, yachts and sailboats just tiny specks. The verdant hillside of Mont Boron towered over the city with its Parc du Chateau, waterfall, and the ruins of an ancient fortress.

As the small jet curved out over the ocean, Aidan stared at the water, remembering other flights—first, the one he had taken from Philadelphia to Tunis, shaken and despairing, heading toward the vague promise of a teaching job he had found on an online Web site.

He pushed aside that memory for the charter flight he and Liam had taken from Tunis to the resort island of Djerba, off the Tunisian coast. It was their first real assignment together, protecting a young pop star who had received death threats, and Aidan remembered the mixture of apprehension and excitement he had approached that job with.

Then another flight, this one from Tunis to Marseille, Aidan on his own for the first time on a job, chaperoning a thirteen-year-old girl to meet her father. With each trip, his confidence had grown, and his love for his partner had deepened. He looked forward to what each new assignment would bring.

"Aidan? Earth to Aidan."

He looked over at Liam. "Sorry, I was daydreaming."

"You've been doing that a lot lately. Did you read the bio of Perreau? There's nothing much there, but at least we can start to get to know him."

Aidan took the piece of paper from Liam and read it once again.

Olivier Perreau had been born in Nantes, France, in 1960. After his graduation from the École Nationale Supérieure des Mines in Paris, he had worked for Outremer, a French mining conglomerate, at several locations in Africa. He had been stationed in the African republic of Gabon for several years, then returned to Paris to work at the company's corporate headquarters in Paris in 1988. He had married Agathe Lecolombier in 1990, and had one son, Michel. He had continued to work for Outremer in Paris. In 2002 he formed his own corporation, Argentum, bought the mine in Corsica, and relocated his family to Ajaccio, where he worked as a mining consultant while experimenting with new technologies. Though Outremer was his primary client, he had also worked for several other firms, both large and small.

"Why do you think Perreau left a solid career in Paris to move to a backwater like Corsica?" he asked Liam. "Maybe he was forced to leave? There might be something in his background that relates to the threats—a hidden secret, a vengeful ex-employee?"

"You're doing it again," Liam said. "Jumping ahead before we have all the facts. Slow down and wait until we get more information before you start spinning stories."

"Yeah, yeah," Aidan said, but he smiled.

The rocky island of Corsica was shaped like a teardrop, with a mountainous spine and sparkling water in shades of blue, purple, and navy surrounding it. They had a good view of the harbor and the city as the plane approached for a landing. Aidan felt a surge of adrenaline and enthusiasm as they hit the tarmac and taxied to the gate. A new assignment in a new place, with Liam by his side.

They landed late on Monday afternoon, Aidan surprised that only that morning they'd awoken in Nice with nothing more on their agenda than a meeting with Jean-Luc Derain, and now here they were on an island they knew nothing about, ready to start a job that could be dangerous. They retrieved their bags from a scrum on the tarmac, then had to wait in a long customs line for non-French citizens.

Aidan stepped forward first when the agent motioned them, holding out his passport and his French *carte de sejour*, with the

Agence indicated as his sponsor. Liam was right behind him with the same documents.

The agent, a skinny, pimple-faced boy who couldn't have been more than eighteen, didn't know what to do with a pair of Americans with French residency. "Why are you not in the other line, if you live in France?" he asked.

"Because we have US passports," Aidan said.

The boy cocked his head in confusion, and Aidan was reminded of the way Hayam approached anything new and potentially dangerous. The boy picked up his phone and had a mumbled conversation with someone on the other end. "You will wait," he said when they were finished.

"Do you want us to step aside?" Aidan asked.

He shook his head. "Just wait."

Aidan sensed the impatience of the tourists behind them as the line stalled. The supervisor, a dark-skinned woman with a crisp uniform and an equally crisp manner, arrived after a few minutes. She quizzed them on the reason for their stay, suspicious that foreigners had to be imported to do such a simple job as watching a family, and she scrutinized their documents carefully.

"What's the holdup?" a portly man in a Hawaiian shirt called from the line. He had a heavy New York accent. "I've got to use the can!"

The supervisor glared at him and held up her hand, palm out. It was a few degrees warmer in Corsica, and Aidan felt the tickle of sweat beneath his arms as they waited for her to complete her evaluation. Finally she nodded curtly to the teenager, and he stamped their documents and waved them onward.

Liam hefted his duffle and Aidan did the same, and they swam through the tide of passengers, past a group of bored-looking teenagers in matching T-shirts that read "Mission Corsica" beneath a stylized crucifix. Then around an Arab family that had staked out a square of tile as a makeshift camp and through the sliding glass doors to the taxi ranks.

The Campo dell Oro airport was on the south side of the Bay of Ajaccio, and the cab took them along the waterfront on the N193 highway, with the glittering Mediterranean to their left. Aidan leaned forward to look at the view, the mix of old and new buildings, the flowers and the tumble of traffic.

The Perreaus lived off the Rue des Magnolias on the north side of the city, up a long and winding road lined with low-lying plants and spotted with occasional bursts of red and yellow flowers. Aidan was so pleased to be there.

"Don't like this," Liam said, looking out the taxi window.

Aidan was surprised. How could he be so happy, and yet Liam not? "Why not?"

"Only one road from the house into the city. No chance to vary Perreau's route."

The street was lined with eucalyptus, chestnut, and lemon trees as it wound up the hillside. The taxi turned into a cul-de-sac and then into the semicircular driveway of a two-story stucco house set back against the mountain, flanked by tall date palms, with a roof of corrugated red tiles and matching brick-red shutters.

As the taxi coasted to a stop, a man Aidan recognized as Olivier Perreau stepped out of the front door. He looked agitated, with bags under his eyes as if he had been sleeping poorly. He waited there as Aidan paid the driver, and Liam lifted their bags from the trunk.

"Monsieur Perreau?" Aidan said, addressing the man in French as the taxi drove away. "I'm Aidan Greene, and this is Liam McCullough. We're from the Agence de Securité."

"Very good." Perreau managed a weak smile. "I will feel much better now that you are here."

He led them inside. "There is a guest room to the right," he said, pointing. "Only one bed, I am sorry to say. But there is a couch as well, or perhaps you will sleep in shifts?"

"We can share the bed," Aidan said. "Is there a bathroom on this level as well?"

Olivier pointed to a closed door ahead of them, under the staircase. "There. And that is my office beside it." He hesitated, then added, "My wife and I will await you in the dining room. She has been very upset by these letters, and I am sure your presence here will help her greatly."

Aidan and Liam carried their bags under the arching staircase and turned right, into the spacious guest room. The wallpaper was faded and the carpet worn, as if no one had bothered to decorate it or update it during the years the Perreaus had lived there.

"He looks stressed," Aidan said as he dropped his backpack on the bed. He patted it; it wasn't as firm as Liam liked, nor as comfortable as Aidan preferred. But it would do.

"If they weren't upset, they wouldn't have hired us." Liam scanned the room, then stepped over to the French doors that led out to the backyard patio and pool. "I don't like being this isolated. I wish we could convince them to go to a hotel somewhere until the contract is signed."

"We can bring that up." Aidan hoisted his duffle onto the bed beside the backpack. A tall wooden armoire stood along one wall; there was a single painting on the other side—a view of Paris in the rain. Not the most welcoming of guest rooms, but Aidan and Liam had stayed in many places less comfortable. "We should go out there now, and unpack later."

"Agreed. And I'll take a walk around the property after we talk to the Perreaus." He looked over at his partner. "Are you nervous?"

Aidan shook his head. "Intrigued, maybe, but not nervous. Should I be?"

"Nerves are good," Liam said. "They're the body's preparation for the fight-or-flight response. As long as you don't let them get the best of you, they can be helpful."

It was a variation of the kind of mini-lecture Liam often provided, a role reversal Aidan secretly found humorous. "Fine, I'm nervous. Hold my hand. I'm scared."

He reached for Liam's hand, but his partner jerked it away. "I keep telling you, Aidan, in this job you're either serious or dead. And I much prefer the former option."

He turned to walk out to the dining room, and Aidan followed.

5 – Behavioral Approaches

Aidan liked the proportions of the dining room, which was to the left of the front door and led out to the kitchen at the rear of the house. It was classically furnished—a dark wood table and six chairs, and a glass-fronted armoire to one side, displaying a collection of glass statues, among them pieces of Lalique, Baccarat, and Daum. The Perreaus sat side by side at the table, facing toward them.

Agathe Perreau was a slim, dark-haired woman in her early fifties who still retained the smooth-skinned beauty of her youth. Like her husband, she was visibly upset, nervously toying with the clasp of a gold bracelet.

After introductions, the four of them sat down, Aidan and Liam facing Olivier and Agathe Perreau. Aidan was surprised that Olivier did not sit at the head of the table; his somewhat imperious manner led Aidan to believe that was his usual position. But perhaps he felt the need to comfort his wife.

Aidan led the conversation, as his French was much stronger than Liam's. He gave them a quick recap of their background and skills, and assured the Perreaus that they had the full backing of the Agence de Securité. "Our job is to make sure nothing happens," he said. "We'll do everything we have to do to keep you safe."

"What can you tell us about these threats you have received?" Liam asked.

Olivier slid a manila folder across the table. "These are copies of the letters we received. The first came in the mail to my office."

Aidan and Liam looked together at the first letter, which had been printed from a computer. It was written in simple, straightforward French, a demand that Perreau break off his negotiations with Outremer and give up developing the mine, or there would be unspecified "consequences."

"Who knew about this deal?" Liam asked, looking up.

"At the start, my family, my secretary, my young apprentice, and my attorneys. At Outremer, I cannot say." Olivier reached over and clasped his wife's hand.

Liam nodded and flipped to the next letter. "The second was delivered here to the house," Olivier said. "Slid under the front door during the night. Maria found it when she came to work and left it on the kitchen table for me."

Agathe said, "Maria is our housekeeper. She comes every weekday morning to prepare our meals and keep the house clean."

The second letter was also computer generated. It repeated the same demands as the first, but also included a direct threat to Perreau and his family. "We know where you live," it concluded.

Aidan looked up. Both Perreaus were watching him closely. "When did you contact the police?"

"After the first letter arrived," Olivier said. "I thought they would be able to pursue the matter and stop whoever was sending them."

"Were they able to discover anything?" Liam asked.

Perreau shook his head. "No fingerprints on the letter or the envelope. No indication if the threat came from an individual or from one of the nationalist groups."

"Why would you consider those groups?" Liam asked. "Have you had problems with one or more of them in the past?"

"There is one group, Citoyens pour la Côte, which has been writing letters to *Corse Matin*, the newspaper in Ajaccio, against my plans to reopen the mine. The man in charge is a fisherman called Aquaviva. He often protests against companies trying to do business on the northwest coast."

"Anything more than letters to the newspaper?" Liam asked.

"He recruited some students from the university and staged a rally outside the mine entrance a few weeks ago. I called the police then, and they said as long as he was on public land, he could remain." He glared. "He was arrested once, I know, when he chained himself to a tree to stop the construction of a *hypermarché* in Porto. I told the officer who was investigating the letters about Aquaviva, but he said they had no evidence to bring him in for questioning."

From the look on Perreau's face, it was clear he believed the police were not doing their duty. "And then?" Aidan asked.

"And then the third letter," Perreau said. Aidan turned the second letter over, and he and Liam looked at the third. "That was delivered to the clinic where my wife is a pediatrician. That is when we called the Agence de Securité. We no longer had any faith in the gendarmes."

The letter left at the clinic indicated that the sender knew where both Perreau and his wife worked, and where they lived. The threat was more explicit this time. If Perreau wanted to keep himself and his family safe, he had to cancel his agreement with Outremer immediately. The mine was to be permanently closed, the property ceded to the government so it could be rehabilitated.

"I assume there's no possibility you can cancel this contract—or at least put it on hold?" Aidan asked.

"No," Perreau said. His fear appeared to fade, to be replaced with anger. "In the last two years, as my research became more positive, I began to invest more heavily in development. Everything I own is tied up in this. If it fails, we may lose our home and fall deeply in debt. Outremer is interested in the project now, because the price of silver is high. If that changes…" He leaned forward. "I must sign this deal on Monday or risk losing everything."

"We'll talk about all that soon," Aidan said. "First we'd like to get some information."

He opened the folder containing the client form. He had printed out blank ones for Agathe and Michel, but began with Olivier. "Is everything here correct?" he asked, showing the form to Perreau. It listed his age, home address, and phone.

Perreau nodded.

"What exactly do you do, Monsieur Perreau?" Aidan asked.

"I am a mining engineer by training," he said. "I have been a consultant for Outremer as well as other mining companies. In my spare time, I investigated new methods for removing silver from lead. I was finally able to secure a patent for my process, which I hope to use at a mine I own in Ménasina, on the north coast. But to do so requires more capital than I have, so I have arranged a partnership with Outremer."

"Do you work in the field? In a laboratory? Or an office?" Aidan asked.

"I have an office here in Ajaccio—you have the address there. And a small laboratory at the mine site. I spend roughly half my time in each place."

They discussed his routine—how he traveled between locations, who knew his schedule, and so on. Aidan opened the laptop and took notes as Perreau spoke.

"Will you be able to stay away from your office for the next week?" Liam asked. "It would be easier for us to protect you if all three of you remain at home, or better yet, at a hotel."

Olivier shook his head. "I cannot. I have many things to accomplish before the deal is signed, and much of it must be done at the office or out at the mine. I also have materials here I could not take to a hotel. You must do what you can to stop these people immediately."

Gently, Liam said, "I'm afraid that's not how we work, Monsieur Perreau. We are not investigators or counterterrorism experts. We are bodyguards—we stay close to you and your family, and we intervene when there is any threat to your safety."

A corner of Perreau's mouth turned up in a sneer. "So you will just sit here? Wait for these animals to attack me or my wife or our son?"

Aidan jumped in. "We do more than just respond. We evaluate

your home, your office, and your routines and suggest how you can make small changes to reduce your vulnerability. We often work closely with the police."

Perreau crossed his arms over his chest and set his mouth in a grim line.

Liam turned to Agathe. "How about you, Doctor? Will you be able to remain at home?"

"I have many young patients who need care," she said. "Though I work with other physicians at a clinic in Ajaccio, I cannot shift the burden of my patients to them."

Aidan was no longer surprised that clients resisted changes to their lifestyles in response to danger, and he had come to believe that the best strategy was to make the client aware of both the threats and the possible alternatives, and encourage rather than enforce behavioral changes.

He stole a glance at Liam, who took a stronger approach, sometimes scaring the clients more than Aidan thought necessary in order to achieve the correct level of security. For the moment, though, his face remained impassive.

Aidan began a new sheet for Agathe, listing her work hours, the address of the clinic, and the names of the other employees there. She had her own car and drove herself to and from work.

It was slow, tedious work, and Perreau's obvious nerves didn't make it any easier. Aidan was a bit surprised; when a family was threatened, it was often the woman who broke down, while the man remained stoic. What made the Perreaus different? Could there be a clue to the danger in their behavior—perhaps Agathe knew more than she was letting on? Could she be involved somehow in the threats?

Aidan caught himself. Once again, he was jumping ahead without waiting to collect all the facts. He went back to the details of Agathe's professional life, and once they were finished, the four of them turned to the Perreaus' social life. Olivier and Agathe had a circle of close friends with whom they often dined out, French nationals transplanted to Corsica or Corsican-born professionals who identified more with France than with their native island.

Olivier admitted that several of them knew about his impending deal. None had expressed disdain, however. He had not mentioned the threats to any of them. By the time they were finished, the intensity of the questioning appeared to have drained them all. Then Aidan heard the roar of a motorcycle pull up in the driveway.

"That is Michel," Agathe said, smiling for the first time. "Our son. He is a student at the university in Corte, in the center of the island."

"I told him he must come home for the week," Olivier said. "He is unhappy to do so."

"It's a good idea," Liam said. "You don't want someone to be able to use him to pressure you."

Michel Perreau walked into the living room, a backpack slung over one shoulder. He was a handsome young man, favoring his mother more than his father, with her grace of movement. His jeans and T-shirt hugged his slim body, and he wore heavy leather boots.

"These are our bodyguards," Olivier said. He was about to introduce them by name when Michel shrugged and continued out of the room.

6 – Negotiations

Liam watched the boy stride across the room. He looked younger than Liam had expected—barely out of his teens. And clearly angry.

"I'm sorry," Agathe said. "He can be a very moody boy."

"We'll talk to him," Liam said. "But for now, if he prefers to ignore us, that's fine." He had often dealt with the teenaged children of clients and had learned it was best to speak to them without their parents present. Teenagers were such a bundle of angst, resentment, enthusiasm, and fear, and were less likely to act out when removed from parental oversight.

"No, he must speak to you now." Olivier got up and followed his son out of the room.

There was a family dynamic going on, Liam thought. Not unlike the one he'd been through as a teenager—although it didn't appear that Olivier Perreau was a mean drunk who lashed out at his child with his fists the way Liam's father had done.

He turned to Agathe Perreau. "There is no way we can convince you to remain at home, Doctor?"

"I must go into the clinic tomorrow, at least. But I have no interest in taking any risks. I have seen what happens." She looked from Aidan to Liam. "Do you know much about these nationalists?"

"We received this assignment only this morning," Aidan said. "But we learn quickly."

"I was born in Oran, in Algeria. My family were called *pieds noirs*—both my father's and my mother's family were French people who had lived there for a century or more."

"Albert Camus and Yves St. Laurent," Aidan said.

"Yes, they are two of the most famous. My father's family were *grands colons*—big landowners," Agathe said. "They did not want to leave everything behind. But when the terrorists destroyed their home in Oran, burned their fields, and murdered people they loved, they had no choice."

Liam listened politely, though Aidan was clearly more interested. His partner was always fascinated by people who had intersected with history—his great-grandparents, who had left Russia; college friends who had fled violence in Africa; a cousin of Sephardic Jewish descent who had been born in Cuba. Liam had heard all the stories and seen the way they colored Aidan's worldview.

"My family were among the lucky ones," Agathe continued. "We were relocated to Marseille, and we began with nothing. My father, a doctor in Algeria, worked at the dock until he could validate his credentials. My mother cleaned toilets. It took them many years to recover their position."

Liam admired the woman's steely determination. No wonder she was less worried than her husband; she had already lived through danger and survived.

Somewhere else in the house, Liam heard raised voices, Olivier arguing with Michel. He watched Agathe's eyes turn toward the door through which her son and husband had exited; then she looked back at them. "I grew up listening to stories of the terror the Muslims forced on the pieds noirs. Many of my people came to Corsica," she continued. "This small, sleepy place began to buzz with French people and French culture. The nationalists were angry."

"These same nationalists who have threatened your husband?" Liam asked.

"There is one large group, the FLNC," she said. "But under that sheltering umbrella there are many smaller cells, like the one my husband mentioned."

Michel walked back into the dining room, followed closely by his father. Liam stood up and held out his hand. "I'm Liam, and this is Aidan," he said. "We're here to protect you, but you're going to have to work with us."

"We do not need protection," Michel said, refusing his hand. "All my father has to do is give up his plans to desecrate the Corsican countryside."

Without warning, Olivier slapped his son hard on his right cheek. "I knew we should have sent you back to France to study. You have learned only nonsense in Corte."

Michel turned to his father, anger flashing in his eyes. Liam's reaction was instinctual, based on all the times he had protected his mother and his sisters from his father's rage. He stepped between father and son, momentarily determined to make the client regret his actions. But his years of training kicked in, and he took a deep breath and said, "Let's sit down, please."

Olivier stalked back to sit beside his wife. Michel slumped into the chair at the end of the table. Aidan and Liam returned to their original seats.

Aidan seemed to sense the emotion bubbling up inside Liam, and he took the lead. "What are you studying at the university?" he asked Michel. "Political science? Sociology?"

"Civil engineering," Michel muttered.

If Aidan was surprised, he didn't show it. He continued in an even voice. "So you must understand the specifics of your father's plan. What is it that you feel bothers the nationalists? Just the fact that you are French, rather than Corsican?"

"You are American, aren't you?" Michel asked. "You have ruined your own country. You wouldn't understand how the Corsicans feel about their land."

Olivier glared at his son, and Liam resisted the urge to jump into the conversation.

Aidan kept his voice calm. "Then educate me. This silver mine, it was open once, wasn't it?"

Michel kept his arms crossed over his chest and said nothing.

"Not for over one hundred years," Olivier said. "Do you know how we mine silver, messieurs?"

Both Aidan and Liam shook their heads.

"Argentiferous galena is a kind of silver-bearing lead. Much of it rests in the hills of the western coast. Silver has been known and prized by humans since prehistoric times, and the mining of silver has changed little since then. The ore is roasted, and the resulting oxide is smelted to separate the silver from the lead."

He leaned forward. "Nearly a dozen years ago I began to work on a refinement to the process of removing silver from galena. I researched the places where I might find this ore, and ten years ago I bought an abandoned mine here in Corsica and relocated my family. Since then I have conducted tests on my process with ore from the mine."

He stood up and began pacing around the room. "Two years ago I was confident that I had achieved success. I approached Outremer and found them a willing partner who could invest in the necessary production facilities. We believed we had been negotiating in secret—until these threats began."

Liam understood Olivier's anger. He had a plan to take care of his family, and his son resisted. If Liam's father had ever had such a plan, Liam had never seen evidence of it.

Aidan turned back to Michel. "Now that I understand the process, please tell me, in your own opinion, why this is a bad thing for Corsica and its people. Doesn't it mean new jobs and prosperity?"

"For French people." Michel sneered.

"Like you and your family!" his father thundered.

"Please, monsieur," Aidan said. "I would like to hear Michel's opinions."

Liam was proud of the way Aidan had transferred his ability to manage a classroom into a talent for handling clients. Small moments like this one reminded him how lucky he was that Aidan had stumbled into his life—and how smart he had been to grab hold of Aidan and refuse to let go.

Olivier growled but returned to his seat beside his wife. Aidan looked back to Michel.

"The profits from this mine will go to this French company," Michel said. "Yes, there will be jobs—but most likely the company will bring French engineers in, and the only jobs for Corsicans will be low-paying ones in the mine."

"I have tried to…" Olivier began, but Aidan looked at him. Aidan had been a teacher of English as a Second Language for years before meeting Liam and joining him as a bodyguard, and he had long since perfected a glare that would silence any recalcitrant student. Liam hid his amusement.

"I understand," Aidan said. "Suppose the company were to promise to set aside a certain number of high-paying jobs for Corsicans. Surely there must be qualified candidates among your classmates at the university?"

"There is also the environmental cost." Michel uncrossed his arms and rested them on the chair.

"Monsieur Perreau?" Aidan asked.

"The primary income for the area around the mine comes from tourism," he said. "Yes, there is much unspoiled beauty there, and bringing in mining equipment, digging in the hills, and creating traffic on the roads will definitely change the environment."

Michel smiled, as if he'd won a major point.

"But my process is significantly less harmful than what has been used before," Olivier continued. "My partner company is committed to minimizing emissions as well. The mine is in an isolated area, not easily accessible to tourists, and its operation will be camouflaged so as not to disturb the view of the ocean."

Aidan looked over at Michel, who was sulking again. But at least, Liam noted, he was not as violently combative as he had been.

Agathe stood up. "It is almost dinnertime. Will you eat with us, messieurs?"

"However you wish, madame," Liam said. "Aidan and I are happy to take our meals on our own or to join you."

"I will speak to Maria," she said. "Two more places at the table. We eat at six, if that is well with you."

Michel backed his chair from the table, stood up, and stalked across the room to the stairway to the second floor. Aidan and Liam nodded to the two elder Perreaus and then returned to the guest room. Aidan began unpacking, and Liam watched him for a moment, noting the way he had to find the right places to put everything away, beginning to make the unfamiliar room into his own territory.

While Aidan worked, Liam called Paul Dubois and introduced himself. "You're another freelancer?" Liam asked.

"I am a private investigator here," Dubois said. "From time to time I do small jobs for the Agence. If you need anything from me, you have just to call."

"Thanks. I will." Liam made sure Dubois had the necessary information on himself and Aidan, and on the Perreaus, and then hung up. Aidan had already put their clothes away, and Liam watched him organize their equipment on the wooden bureau.

"You really have a talent," he said. "Good job calming things down and getting Michel to talk."

Aidan smiled and looked up at Liam. Liam knew Aidan appreciated the praise. He was not as strong, and he didn't have Liam's extensive background as a Navy SEAL or his ability in hand-to-hand combat. He knew he was the weaker one, and Liam took any opportunity to reinforce his partner's specific skills.

"Come here, you," Liam said, opening his arms.

Aidan leaned up and kissed Liam's mouth as they came together. He wrapped his arms around Liam, his hands reaching upward. Liam's lips were dry, and he pulled back for a moment, licked them, then kissed Aidan again.

Liam loved the feel of his partner's body against his—the warmth, the softness, the subtle aroma of clean sweat mixed with lavender soap. His dick swelled, and he pressed it against Aidan's belly, feeling his partner's dick pushing against his thigh. It had to be some animal instinct, he thought as he leaned down to kiss Aidan's cheek, this urge to have sex in a new place. Maybe that was his way of marking his territory.

"I want to go outside and examine the grounds before it gets dark," Liam said into Aidan's ear. "But we'll continue this later."

"We'd better. Otherwise I might be forced to look to a younger man for some fun."

Liam backed off. "What do you mean?"

"Michel. Couldn't you see it?"

"See what?"

"Liam, he's gay." He held up his hand, palm out. "No, I'm not going to romance the client. I know that's against the rules. I was just teasing you."

"You think everyone is gay," Liam grumbled.

"No, I just have better gaydar than you do. I'll walk around outside with you and finish unpacking later."

Though it was true that Aidan's gaydar was much more finely tuned than Liam's, he still felt his partner had a tendency to assume too much about people without enough evidence. "Bring a notebook," Liam said. "We'll add what we see outside to the instructions we give to the Perreaus."

Outside, he noted that five large homes clustered in a semicircle off the main road to Ajaccio, backing up against a rocky hillside. The Perreau house was the second in, with local fieldstone on the first floor and around the doors and windows. The rest of the house was stucco, painted a faded mustard yellow.

"Tell me what you see," Liam said as they stood at the street, looking back at the house. He liked to test Aidan this way, teaching him to see a place not for its beauty or convenience, but for its defensibility.

Aidan looked around. "You mentioned the location as we were driving up in the taxi. One road, and if we were leaving the property, we could only go up or down. The way the road twists and turns, it would be easy for someone to set up an ambush as Perreau was on his way in to work."

"Good point," Liam said. "How do we work around that?"

"If the route can't change, then we change something else. Leave the house at a different time. Sometimes take his car, sometimes hers." He made a note of that.

Liam nodded approvingly. "Now the house."

Aidan looked up at the rocky hillside that surrounded the cluster of houses. "Sniper on the hills," he said. "You could probably get a good shot from up there—one of the Perreaus as they leave the house. Maybe even shoot someone through a window."

He looked at Liam. "So we have them keep the curtains closed, right?"

"Yup. And if we have them both park over there, by those pines, the trees will provide some cover for getting from the house to the car."

"The nationalists, if that's really who they are, have already escalated their threats—from office, to home, to Dr. Perreau's office," Liam said. "The next threat will be something more serious."

"What do you mean, if that's who they are?" Aidan asked. "Who else could it be?"

"We don't make any assumptions until we have the facts. Perhaps another company wants to develop that mine, for example. Maybe some relative or acquaintance who resents Perreau's success. The nationalists Dr. Perreau was talking about could be a convenient cover."

"We can't discount the possibility that Michel might be involved," Aidan said. "You saw how resentful he is. He knew the details of the deal, where his father and mother both worked. He could belong to that group at the university his father mentioned—

without his father's knowledge, of course. That would explain why the first two threats weren't specifically dangerous. He wants his father to stop, but he doesn't want to hurt him."

"Interesting idea. But let's hold off on presenting that to the Perreaus for a while. They've got enough stress as it is."

They continued around the perimeter of the property, checking for closeness to neighbors, for doors that could be jimmied or windows that could be broken. "The FLNC—or whoever they were—haven't threatened the house, but they have indicated that they can get close."

The sun was beginning to sink behind the hillsides, and the air cooled considerably—dropping below fifty degrees as they walked. "Time to go inside," Liam said. "We'll have dinner and then do some research afterward."

7 – Pressure Points

Aidan brought his notes with him to dinner when they joined the three Perreaus at the dining room table, assuming they'd talk after the meal was over. Olivier sat at the head of the table, Agathe to his right, with Michel to his left, his back toward the hallway. Aidan took a seat next to him, and Liam sat beside Agathe.

Always an acute observer of seating dynamics in the classroom, Aidan noticed the shift from their earlier positions. Previously there had been a balance—Aidan and Liam on one side, Agathe and Olivier on the other. Michel's arrival, and his taking a place at the foot of the table, had disrupted that equilibrium. Now it seemed that a kind of balance had returned, Olivier like the classic statue of Justice holding the scales, one family member and one bodyguard to the right, another pair to the left. Aidan thought it a good sign that he and Liam had been integrated into the family so easily.

Olivier welcomed them to the table and poured liberally from a bottle of chenin blanc from the Loire valley.

The wine and the delicious aromas emanating from the kitchen relaxed the atmosphere in the room, though Michel didn't seem to feel the difference. "There are excellent wines made here on the island," he said. "But my father insists that real wine must come from France."

Olivier's response was forestalled by the arrival of a petite thirty-something woman with a white apron over a skirt and blouse. She emerged from the kitchen with a platter of small, well-cured, link-size sausages resting beside cured olives and a long loaf of fresh-baked Italian bread. "The *saucisson*," Olivier proclaimed. "We have many wild boar on this island, and the local sausages are quite a specialty. This one has quite a sweet flavor."

"Thank you, Maria," Agathe said, and the woman returned to the kitchen.

"You mentioned she comes every day during the week?" Liam asked.

"Yes. She arrives each morning around seven, cleans the house, does the laundry and so on, and then leaves after serving dinner."

"We'll need her full name and address," Liam said. "Just to run a background check."

"Maria has been with us for five years," Agathe said.

"We're looking for pressure points," Liam said. "Could someone convince her, or pay her, to provide a key to your house? To explain your domestic routines?"

"She is a member of the working class," Michel said. "Of course she must resent those who rule. That is the way things work."

Aidan heard the sarcasm in his voice but knew as a college student Michel was vulnerable to any ideology that challenged his parents. He speared a piece of the aromatic sausage and raised the fork to his lips. "No one is accusing her—or anyone—of anything. But the sad fact is that when something like this happens, everyone must be investigated." He popped the morsel into his mouth and savored its tangy richness.

"Even us?" Michel demanded.

"Is there something about you we should know?" Liam asked.

Michel was immediately wary. "What do you mean?"

"Do you belong to any groups at the university? Associate with Corsicans?"

"We are all Corsicans," Michel said. "It is impossible not to associate."

"You know what he means, Michel," Olivier said.

"I belong to the engineering society," Michel said. "Would you like a list of the other members?"

"I don't think we'll need that right now," Liam said mildly. "Could you pass the platter of saucisson?"

As they ate, they talked about the island of Corsica. "It is a beautiful island," Agathe said. "Deep forests in the interior, glacial lakes, gorges, maquis-covered slopes, and snow-capped granite peaks." She looked at them. "Do you know the maquis?"

"Only as the nickname for the French resistance to World War II," Aidan said.

"It is what you would call the scrub brush," she said. "Many kinds of low-growing, scented plants—different ones at different altitudes. Corsica is called the scented isle, you know, because of this."

When they finished the appetizers, Maria delivered a platter of roasted chicken surrounded by root vegetables. "You must have studied a lot about the island when you were in school," Aidan said to Michel as he served himself. "What can you tell us?"

"Do you want to hear about the history of occupation? Corsica has seen the Greeks, the Carthaginians, and the Romans. Then the Vandals, the Goths, and the Moors, until the Genoese took over in the 1400s. Then they passed the island off to the French as the spoils of war."

"The French have brought much prosperity to this island," Olivier said. "And the Corsicans cannot complain. They have a university now, and their language is taught in the schools."

"Do you speak it?" Aidan asked.

Olivier shook his head. "Just a few words. Michel can speak a little, though it is not really necessary for living here."

"Of course not," Michel grumbled. "The peasants should speak the mother tongue."

"Everyone in Corsica speaks French," Olivier said. "There is no need for someone like me to speak the local patois."

Michel snorted.

They drank more wine, though Aidan and Liam were careful not to imbibe too much. "I'd like to hear more about Corsica," Aidan said to Michel.

"Nearly fifty percent of the houses on the island are vacation homes for rich Europeans," he said. "The government now wishes to change the classification of miles of coastline to allow more development. Soon you will not be able to tell Corsica from the concrete high-rises of Majorca or the Côte d'Azur."

Aidan speared a roasted potato. "But doesn't that mean jobs for civil engineers? Opportunities for young people like you?"

"Now you come to the conflict between my son's liberal ideals and the reality of the practical world," Olivier said. "A lesson I have been trying to teach him for many years."

"There is an ecologically sound way to develop," Michel said. "One that does not mean digging vast holes in the hillsides, polluting the groundwater, or overwhelming the mountain view with concrete."

"Many of the attacks by the local terrorists have been against new construction," Agathe said. "Vacation homes, hotels. I wish Michel would choose a less dangerous profession."

"Do the police have any idea who is behind these groups?" Liam asked. "Is the FLNC a political party or merely a terrorist group?"

"They are nationalists, not terrorists!" Michel insisted. "There is a difference."

"Perhaps in goals," Aidan said. "But often not in the means they use."

"There are several politicians in the Corsican assembly, as well as local officials, who support nationalist goals," Olivier said. "The man I spoke of earlier, for example, Niculaiu Aquaviva. He is often in the news, leading protests or speaking with legislators. As if such a rude, unschooled man could have anything important to say."

Out of the corner of his eye, Aidan noticed Michel stiffen at the mention of the name. Was he somehow involved with the man's group?

"I have spoken with Monsieur Aquaviva," Agathe said. "He is a reasonable man, from a very old Corsican family. He is not so rude as you think."

"You spoke to him about his daughter's health," Olivier said. "Of course he would be polite to you." He turned to Aidan and Liam. "My wife will not tell you, but she is one of the best pediatricians in all of Corsica. People often bring her very ill children when no one else can help them."

Agathe smiled. "My husband exaggerates. But I did treat the youngest Aquaviva child—a little girl with a persistent series of breathing problems. I was able to diagnose a defect in her lung." Her face darkened. "Sadly, the operation she needed was beyond our capacity on the island. I referred them to a hospital in Nice, but Laurenzia died before they could perform the procedure."

"That's sad," Aidan said.

"It's criminal," Michel said. "The French government should improve our medical facilities so that such things cannot happen. But they do nothing but authorize the building of more holiday homes."

It appeared Maria had already left by the end of their meal, because it was Agathe who brought out a plate of cheese. The first was a sheep's milk *brebis*, firm and ivory colored, yet with a smoothness and a grassy, almost caramel taste. It was paired with a soft white cheese called *brocciu* that reminded Aidan of ricotta. Olivier insisted that they try snifters of the local Corsican brandy.

It was close to nine o'clock by then. Michel drained his brandy and demanded another, and his father refused. To forestall the brewing argument, Liam shifted the conversation to the results of his walk around the house with Aidan. The Perreaus listened to the ideas they had come up with.

Michel was resistant, but Liam was quiet and patient with him, until he finally capitulated. He finished the last of his cheese, pushed the plate away, and stalked out of the room.

"I apologize for my son," Olivier said. "He is a young hothead, and he often speaks about things he knows nothing about."

"I try to explain to my husband that Michel says these things to provoke him," Agathe said.

"It's the arrogance of youth," Aidan said. "We all go through it to some degree. We feel that we know so much more than our parents, that we see the world more clearly."

"Right now," Olivier said, "I only wish to see the conclusion of this agreement. After that there will be time for Michel to come to his senses."

"That's what we're here for," Liam said. "Aidan and I will walk around the house once more and make sure everything is secure. Good night, *monsieur-dame*."

8 – WITHHELD DESIRE

Michel stood at his bedroom window looking out at the hills. The room had been his since the family's relocation to Corsica ten years before, and it was still furnished the same way—a single bed, a desk, and an armoire. Over the years he had switched out the posters on the walls, from sports heroes to pop stars, now to the flowing art nouveau designs of Mucha and Toulouse-Lautrec. He knew they were silly and pretentious, but he loved being surrounded by their beauty.

The shelves overflowed with his schoolbooks—heavy engineering texts interspersed with a few of the classics of French literature from required courses. His desk was always covered in papers; he had to move several piles to make a place to set up his laptop whenever he came home for a weekend.

It was a cozy den—his refuge from his parents—with the added advantage that the big window overlooking the backyard was easy to slip through. For the moment, though, he stood there and watched the two bodyguards walk past, speaking in low tones. There was something between them, he decided. They were too easy with each other, too close. Were they gay? Or merely good friends? It was curious and worth watching.

This forced week in his parents' home felt like a punishment. He was almost finished with his degree, but he still had to pass exams at the end of the term, and missing class would make it more difficult for him to achieve the high grades he demanded of himself.

That was only the smallest part of the problem, though. He missed the chance to spend time with Cris. They did not share any classes because Cris was in a political science program. Most of their time was spent in cafés in Corte, in Michel's dormitory apartment, or in snatched moments at the cave behind the waterfall.

He did not know what would happen after they graduated. His parents expected him to return home, to live with them while he found a job and established his career. Cris had spoken vaguely of returning to his family on the northern coast of the island, to work, save money, help with his younger siblings and perhaps run for political office.

How could he explain to his parents if he wanted to move to a remote location like Cris's hometown? There would be no engineering jobs for him. Or how could he convince Cris to join him in the capital? He had been investigating jobs for his boyfriend in Ajaccio, without Cris's knowledge. He had neglected his own job hunt to look for something in government or politics so enticing it would force Cris to join him.

He couldn't imagine a future without Cris by his side. But could Cris see them moving apart? He had been too scared of the possibilities to raise the question strongly—all their conversations had been vague and general.

The mention of Niculaiu Aquaviva at dinner had unnerved him and reminded him how many obstacles must be overcome before he and Cris could be together. He knew his mother had treated Cris's youngest sister. Cris spoke highly of Agathe Perreau's professionalism and her care, but the little girl's death had been a hard blow for the family.

What if the bodyguards continued to dig into the family's secrets? He was certain his father knew nothing of his sexual orientation, though he thought his mother suspected, from casual comments she had made over the years.

His father had often said negative things about *pédérastes*, the French term for homosexuals. He had even said he felt homosexuals had to be mentally sick to experience their desires.

With time, perhaps, his father might accept that he had a gay son. But could he welcome to the fold as Michel's lover the son of Niculaiu Aquaviva, his primary antagonist? That would never happen.

He opened his laptop and connected to the house's Wi-Fi signal. There were a half-dozen new messages in his e-mail account, but only one mattered—the one from Cris.

Miss you already, he wrote. *Don't let your father get you down.* He wrote a few more lines and then closed with *Ti tengu caru*, Corsican for *I love you*.

Michel sat back against the pillows mounded on his bed and remembered the first time he had seen Cristoforu Aquaviva. It was early in the fall of his second year at the university. He lived in a dorm near the classroom buildings, and he'd spent most of his time in his room, in class, or in the library.

One day in October, his roommate had encouraged him to attend a football match between teams from the Corte campus and the one in Bastia. Cris was a forward on the Corte team, and Michel had been mesmerized by how handsome he was and how smoothly he moved on the field.

He had known he was gay for years by then. He'd fooled around with a few boys at his *lycée* in Ajaccio and had his first boyfriend there. But at the university he'd focused on his studies. He'd known there were other gay students there, but none of them appealed to him.

The handsome footballer, though, had excited him in a way no other boy had. His cocky grin, his bulging thighs, and the way dark hair bubbled up from the collar of his shirt made Michel's heart race and his dick swell.

His roommate—a Lothario who always had girls around—hadn't noticed Michel's reaction. They'd walked back to their dorm together, his roommate pleased that Michel had enjoyed himself at the game.

Michel became a regular fixture in the audience, sometimes even watching practices. By early December he knew all the players by name and position and had even become an expert on game statistics.

Still, he'd never spoken to any of the players beyond the one he knew from an engineering class. He thought he had kept his feelings a secret until one afternoon, just before the start of the Christmas holidays. He'd missed the last practice before the vacation because of an exam. That evening, he'd been on his way into the dining hall when Cris approached him.

* * *

"You weren't there to watch us today," Cris said. "I scored two goals."

Michel was startled. He'd never even spoken to Cris before—yet Cris had noticed he wasn't at the practice?

"I guess my not showing up was good luck for you, then," he said.

Cris smiled. His bottom teeth were perfect, but there was a small gap between the front ones on the top row. "Then I'd rather have the bad luck."

Michel felt his heart beat faster. Was this handsome guy flirting with him? Everything about Cris's posture said so—the open grin, the relaxed way he stood. He was good-looking and knew how people reacted to him.

"Are you going inside?" Cris asked, nodding toward the dining hall.

"Sure." They walked in together, Michel unsure of how to proceed. "I like the way you move," he said; then he blushed. Was that too much to say to another guy?

"I have some moves you haven't seen yet," Cris said, smiling slyly. "Maybe after dinner?"

Michel's heart skipped a couple of beats, and he glanced at Cris, but the other boy was already heading to the buffet line. They didn't speak again until they had loaded their trays and chosen a table.

"Where are you from?" Cris asked as they sat. "You have an interesting accent."

"Outside Paris. We moved to Ajaccio when I was twelve."

Cris nodded. "I thought you were from the continent. There's something different about you."

"In a good way, I hope," Michel said.

"A very good way." Cris moved his leg next to Michel's under the table, and that gentle pressure was enough to make Michel's dick spring to attention.

"How about you?" Michel asked, trying to keep his voice even. "Where are you from?"

"Cargése—a small town on the coast, west and a little south of here. I'm the oldest of five. Well, four now. My father is a fisherman and my mother makes art, stays home and takes care of us. I'm the first one in my family to go to college."

They kept talking all the way through the meal, and by the time they were eating their cheese, Michel was so horny his balls ached. He thought it was time he spoke up—Cris had tracked him down and expressed his interest. "I have some pictures I took of you playing," he said. "They're upstairs. Would you like to see them?"

"Do you have a roommate? I have two."

"Suite mates," Michel said. "The rooms in this building are all singles, with common living rooms and bathroom."

"Then I would very much like to come up to your room with you." Cris grinned wolfishly. He had slipped off his shoe, and his bare foot stroked Michel's leg. Cris slid farther down in the booth, and Michel was surprised to feel Cris's toes against his stiff dick. His mouth dropped open in surprise.

"If you like that, you'll like what I do upstairs even better."

When he stood up, Michel was embarrassed to see a wet spot at the front of his khaki slacks where his dick had leaked. "You didn't come, did you?" Cris whispered.

Michel hurriedly pulled the tails of his button-down shirt out so that they hung over the spot. "No, I'm saving that for you."

"Good boy," Cris said.

Michel was in a state of intense arousal as they walked across from the dining hall to the dormitory and then rode the elevator together. They stayed apart the whole time, but once they were inside Michel's single room, they came together with a passion, each of them slamming toward the other in a frenzy of withheld desire.

Cris was the aggressor, running his hands over Michel's body, forcing his tongue into Michel's mouth. Michel had never experienced such passion—the few boys he had kissed or touched had been as inexperienced and diffident as he was, unsure how far to go.

Cris seemed to have no inhibitions. He pulled his football shirt over his head and quickly unbuttoned Michel's shirt. He returned to kissing, beginning with Michel's lips, then moving to his chin, his throat, his neck. At the same time, his hands were busy opening Michel's jeans and pushing them down.

Within moments they were both naked. Cris pushed Michel onto his bed and began humping his leg, rubbing his stiff dick against Michel's smooth thigh. His head was held back like a wolf ready to bay at the moon.

Then he stopped and took Michel's dick in his mouth. Michel

had never been swallowed before—the only guy who had given him a blowjob had barely taken in the head of Michel's dick, using his hand to stimulate the shaft. But Cris took it all, pressing his nose against Michel's pubic hairs.

Then, like a jackrabbit, Cris was on to something else. He swung his body around on the bed so that his dick was at Michel's mouth, both of them lying sideways. He grasped the plump globes of Michel's ass and went down on him again.

Michel mimicked his movement, pulling Cris's dick toward his face. He had never sucked a dick before, but he figured it out from imitating what Cris was doing to him.

Sensations welled up inside him, more powerful than anything he had ever felt before, either in masturbation or in his experiments with other boys. Suddenly his dick exploded down Cris's throat.

Cris backed off, coughing. "Next time give me a little warning," he said, licking his lips.

"Sorry," Michel said.

"Hey, why did you stop? I won't come in your mouth if you don't want me to."

Michel began sucking Cris again. The other boy pushed his dick farther and farther into Michel's mouth until Michel was afraid he'd choke. "Here I come, baby," Cris said, pulling his dick out. He shot a spurt of come right onto Michel's cheek and laughed.

"That was great," Cris said, squirming around to be next to Michel, who wiped his cheek with the back of his hand, then sniffed and tasted the come. It was salty and tangy, like old cheese or pickles.

He liked it.

"Was this your first time?" Cris asked.

"No." Michel looked at the smile in Cris's eyes. "Well, the first time I sucked anybody, at least."

"You did fine. But you'll have to get a lot more practice before you're as good as I am."

"That's the kind of studying I won't mind doing," Michel said.

* * *

He could still remember every detail of that experience—the way they had made love a second time, taking longer, learning the ins and outs of each other's bodies. They had both cut short Christmas holidays with their families to return to Corte, and Cris had holed up in Michel's single room with him until the rest of the suite mates returned.

They were careful together. Cris did not want his teammates to know about his inclinations, and Michel worried that if he was too obvious, word would leak back to his father somehow.

Standing at his bedroom window, Michel yawned. It was late, and he'd had a long, stressful day. Classes in the morning, then this summons from his father to return home, and the pressure to pack up what he might need and then hurry back to Ajaccio. He stripped naked, tossed his dirty clothes into a pile on the floor, and flopped onto his bed.

He wondered what Cris was doing. He would have practiced with the team that afternoon, grabbed a quick dinner, then gone to his part-time job with the campus maintenance department. He'd have finished work an hour or so before, then headed back to his room to study for the next day.

His dick hardened once more at the thought of Cris. He stroked it idly with his right hand. The world was changing all around him—soon he would graduate, and so would Cris, and they would no longer have the smoke screen of the university to protect them. What would they do?

9 – SPLINTERS

Liam woke as the sun rose over the mountains, and slipped out of bed, careful not to wake Aidan. He donned a jockstrap, shorts, and a T-shirt that outlined his chest and the gold rings in his nipples, and opened one of the French doors, wincing at the squeak of the hinge. Aidan didn't react, and he stepped out onto the patio. It was cool outside, barely sixty degrees, but that was perfect workout weather for him.

He walked around the swimming pool to the flat lawn just beyond it, where he began his daily ritual of jumping jacks, push-ups, and sit-ups. By the time Aidan joined him, he had built up a fine sheen of sweat on his body, soaking through the T-shirt in patches and pooling under his arms.

Aidan's workout was much less strenuous, and they finished together. "How are you this morning?" Aidan asked as Liam sat up and began his post-workout stretches.

"Ready to get to work. You?"

Aidan stood, stuck his right leg out, and leaned forward on it. He still had to work on his form, Liam thought.

"Confused, I think. Maybe disoriented is more the word. First we move from Tunis to Nice. I've just started to get comfortable there, and suddenly we pick up and move here."

"You're going to have to get accustomed to moving around," Liam said. "But I thought you wanted us to move to Nice."

"I just want to be with you, Liam. You know that. I could have stayed in Tunis."

Liam leaned forward, touched his toes, then leaned backward. "Don't start that again. You hated Tunis. You were always complaining about the Islamists—what if they took over? What would happen to us? When Jean-Luc offered us the jobs, I thought that would solve all your problems."

Sometimes Aidan's worrying began to get irritating, he thought. He'd never be a good bodyguard if he couldn't put aside his personal troubles and focus on the clients.

Aidan turned from side to side. "I'll be all right," he said. "Just give me a chance to get acclimated."

"We'll have to split up, because Olivier and the doctor both insist on working today. I'll go with him, you with her. Are you okay with that?"

"Sure. And Michel?"

"He can tag along with his mother or his father. We can't let him stay by himself."

"He's not going to like that."

"Well, he'll have to suck it up," Liam said. "We have no idea when these nationalists, or terrorists, or whatever they are, will strike again. We'll have to keep a close eye on Michel—I don't think he's going to react well to confinement. He may try to sneak away."

They completed their cooldown routines and walked back through the French doors. Maria was already in the kitchen, and the aroma of frying bacon slid into their room like a cat burglar. They each took showers and dressed, and joined the family in the kitchen.

It was a cozier, less formal room than the dining room, painted a sunny yellow with glass-fronted cabinets of white wood. Aidan led the way, slipping into a straight-backed wooden chair next to Michel like he was already one of the family.

And like any family, the Perreaus were in the middle of an argument. "Why can't I just stay here?" Michel demanded of his father. "I don't need a babysitter."

"We have only two bodyguards," Olivier said as Liam sat down beside him. "You must come with your mother or with me. I would not leave myself if I did not have work I had to complete before Monday."

"You can help at the clinic," Agathe said. "We have boxes of old client files that must be shredded."

"I have homework," Michel said. "I'll go with Papa. At least he has Internet at his office I can use."

Michel scowled, and Liam worried about how he could keep an eye on the boy if he decided to wander away.

After breakfast, Liam used the long-handled inspection mirror to check under both cars. When he was satisfied no one had tampered with either vehicle, he joined Olivier in the late-model Mercedes for the trip down the winding mountain road and into downtown Ajaccio. Michel slumped in the backseat with his headphones on, listening to music.

"Please be honest with me," Olivier said as they passed the stone bulk of the Caserne Battesti, the headquarters of the gendarmerie on

Corsica. "How much danger do you feel my family is in?"

"I can't say for certain," Liam said. "I want to do more research on the FLNC and their spin-off groups this morning. And I have a friend at the American embassy in Tunis who is looking into things for me as well."

"Tunis?"

Liam nodded. "That's where Aidan and I were based before we joined the Agence de Securité and relocated to Nice."

Olivier navigated the narrow streets of Ajaccio with ease. Liam kept his eyes on the cars and people around them, though he doubted an attack would come in such a public place. Olivier's office was in an eight-story building a few blocks inland from the harbor, with a garage on the ground floor.

"What exactly do you do all day?" Liam asked as they pulled into the garage beneath the building.

"I plan and design mines for the best possible extraction of minerals," he said. "I consult with large companies who have specific problems with regard to mineral extraction. I have focused exclusively on my own silver mine for the last year, however. Most of my work is very tedious—calculations and computer simulations. My assistant helps with the most repetitive chores."

"You mentioned him yesterday," Liam said. "He knows everything about your operations?"

"As much as a young apprentice can," Olivier said as they walked through the garage to the elevator, Michel trailing behind them. "You will meet him and my secretary, Edith. George is only a few years older than Michel. He held an internship with me while he was in school, and his work was so good that I continued his employment."

The three of them rode up in the elevator. When they arrived on the fourth floor, Liam noted the position of the exit stairway as they walked down the hall to the Argentum office. Olivier introduced Liam to Edith, a Frenchwoman in her fifties, with the faded glamour of a woman who had once been very pretty. From behind her semicircular wood desk, telephone and computer in front of her, she shook Liam's hand and then gave Olivier several pink telephone memos.

There were three doorways behind Edith. Michel took his laptop and entered the one on the far right, which looked unoccupied. The one on the far left was the largest, with a floor-to-ceiling window that looked out at the harbor. A twentysomething guy with tanned skin and mouse-brown hair sat in the middle office behind a computer, and Olivier rapped lightly on the door frame and introduced Liam.

"George Phthalis, Liam McCullough," he said, stumbling as the French often did on the pronunciation of the last syllable. "Liam is here to make sure we are all safe until the deal is signed. You will help him with anything he needs, please."

"Of course." George rose to shake Liam's hand. He was, to Liam's eye, average in the extreme. About five-ten, a hundred fifty pounds. From his appearance and last name, he was probably Greek. His handshake was limp, and he kept his gaze down. Liam had the feeling George preferred to blend into the background.

George sat back at his desk as Olivier walked out. Liam turned to him and asked, "You're working on the silver mine?"

"On the output calculations." He turned his computer monitor so that Liam saw the complicated flow chart. He pointed to a series of bright red triangles in the midst of the chart. "There is a place here, where I believe we can improve the work flow. That is what I am doing now, trying different levels of input and time."

It meant nothing to Liam, but he smiled and thanked him. He went next door to Olivier's office and had the man write down the first and last names of his two employees, and then carried the paper with him into the third office, where Michel had already set up his laptop.

"I left the computer for you," Michel said, nodding at an older model PC on the second desk. "It connects to the Internet when you turn it on."

That was probably the friendliest thing Michel had said since he and Aidan had arrived, and Liam thanked him. He did not like doing research; Aidan was better at it than he was, for one thing, more attuned to the ins and outs of the Internet. He preferred physical action—patrolling, investigating, anything that played to his strengths.

But he needed to know more about the political situation in Corsica and how the different offshoots functioned in order to identify more clearly which one might be responsible for the threats against the Perreaus.

Liam turned the computer on, and once he could, he connected to his e-mail account and passed the two names on to his hacker friend Richard, a Brit who could find out anything about anybody. He also included the three Perreaus and their maid, Maria.

He glanced over at Michel. He assumed the boy was doing his schoolwork, though he could just as easily have been surfing the Internet for porn, playing video games, or any one of a hundred other things.

Liam began to look for information on the FLNC, the Fronte di Liberazione Naziunale Corsu, created in 1976. Following the lead of the IRA and the Basque separatist group Eta, the FLNC began bombing public infrastructure, banks, tourist facilities, military or police buildings, and other symbolic targets across Corsica with plastic explosives. They also decided to "bring the Corsican problem to the French" by carrying out bomb attacks on continental France and towns considered to represent the Corsican diaspora like Marseille, Nice, and Paris. Attacks on the French mainland ranged from machine-gunning gendarmes to setting off car bombs at the police headquarters and the law courts in Paris.

By the 1990s, after nearly ten thousand terrorist attacks and over a hundred deaths, the FLNC broke into splinter groups, which warred against each other. Though the groups had come together more in the recent past, it appeared that the group Niculaiu Aquaviva led had remained independent. Though the FLNC had claimed a number of bomb attacks in the past decade, including hotels and military barracks, it wasn't clear if those had been carried out by Aquaviva's faction or by others.

Liam's phone rang with an unidentified number. It had to be Louis Fleck, he thought. He stood up and walked out of the office. "Hello?" he said as he passed the receptionist.

"How are you and Aidan adjusting to Corsica?" Louis asked. "I'll bet he's fussing, isn't he? Where can I get the best croissants? What kind of wine will Liam want?"

Liam laughed as he stepped into the hallway. "We're staying with the clients at their house," Liam said. "That cuts down on a lot of the agitation. But he's feeling disoriented, he said this morning. Too much moving around."

"Hassan's the same way. Even on vacation, it takes him a day or two to get accustomed."

"You didn't call to chat about boyfriends and lovers, I hope," Liam said. "Did you find any information for me?"

"Still working," Louis said. "I have some deep background to send you. There are a couple of groups that might be responsible for your threats; I've identified them. Did you know there was a bombing last week? Four vacation homes under construction, on the grounds of a resort hotel on the coast?"

"I didn't."

"Watch your ass, McCullough. These people mean business."

"Thanks for the reminder." Liam hung up and looked down the hallway toward the exit stair. He wanted to get back to his research, but what if the door was locked at the ground level? Or led into a dead-end alley? If danger came to the office, how would they get away? He walked toward the door to check it out.

10 – Explosion

After he satisfied himself that the exit stair was usable, Liam returned to the office, where he went back to the e-mail account and checked for new messages. The report Louis had promised was there, and Liam spent the rest of the morning reading it and taking notes.

At noon, Olivier appeared in the office doorway. "Lunch?"

"Can you have something brought in?" Liam asked.

"No! I want to get out of here for a while," Michel said.

Liam had worked with enough young clients to recognize when he had to pick his battles. "Do you know anywhere close by?" he asked Olivier.

"A restaurant around the corner," Olivier said. "We can sit at a table in the back."

"Sounds good." Liam stood up, and Michel followed suit, hooking his earphones back in his ears.

They rode the elevator downstairs together; then Liam stepped outside first, scanning the area for any dangers. When he was confident the street was safe, he motioned Olivier and Michel to follow him.

The restaurant was only about a quarter full, and Olivier was able to get them a table in the back. Liam sat with his back to the wall, facing the door.

"You're really serious about this," Michel said.

"It's my job to be serious." He scanned the menu.

"It's just not what I expected from a…" He paused. "A homosexual."

Liam put the menu down and glared. "My private life does not enter into my work."

"How can it not, when you work with your boyfriend?" Michel demanded. "If it comes to protecting him or us, who will you save?"

"Aidan is your…" Olivier said, letting the sentence trail off.

"Aidan and I are partners in business as well as in our private life," Liam said. He was angry that this boy was challenging him, but kept his voice low and steady. "Our relationship strengthens our ability to carry out our duties. There will never be a reason for me to choose between protecting him and protecting a client, because we both will be focused on our clients."

Olivier looked like he had smelled something unpleasant. The waitress arrived, and Olivier ordered a whole sautéed fish for them to share, with a side of roasted potatoes. Liam noticed the body language of both father and son. Michel's arms were crossed and his head leaned forward—an aggressive posture. Olivier seemed to retreat back into his seat, refusing to meet Liam's glance.

"Is this the case with all the employees of your agency?" Olivier asked after a long pause and the delivery of crusty French bread and glasses of white wine.

"No." Liam was determined to short-circuit this topic as soon as possible. He and Aidan had worked for gay clients and straight clients. The gay clients often wanted to know their bodyguards were gay so they could be more comfortable around them. The straight clients usually never noticed or, if they did, didn't make a big deal.

That was fine with Liam. His sexual orientation was his business and Aidan's, and no one else's. He had spent years in the closet, first in high school, then in the military, under the Don't Ask, Don't Tell policy. After a daring—but ultimately stupid—rescue of a fellow SEAL, he had realized that as long as he kept hiding and devaluing himself, he was bound to do something that would get him killed.

He spoke with his commanding officer and accepted an honorable discharge. After the policy was rescinded, he had considered reenlisting, because he loved the military lifestyle. But he couldn't give up Aidan, or the love he had found.

Olivier still looked angry.

Liam reached for a piece of bread and a pat of butter. "If you want, you can call the Agence and ask for different operatives. There is a man in Ajaccio who can fill in for the short term until a new team can arrive."

He looked down at his food but, out of the corner of his eye, watched Michel. Was Aidan right, and the boy was gay himself? Was that why he'd twigged to the relationship between Aidan and Liam? Was he using this to challenge his father somehow?

"We will manage," Olivier said. "It is only for a week, after all."

Liam looked up. Michel had relaxed, and Liam thought only he noticed how the boy's hand shook as he lifted his wineglass.

The waitress brought the fish on a large majolica platter, and they all began to eat. Liam allowed himself a brief memory of his own father, an alcoholic who had challenged and threatened his son so much that Liam took refuge in bodybuilding and escaped to the Navy as soon as he graduated from high school.

He had left behind his mother and two younger sisters, but at seventeen all he cared about was protecting himself. He still felt guilty over that desertion—that he should have remained there to take care of the three of them until his father died or his mother grew enough confidence to kick him out.

An accident on the New Jersey Turnpike had taken care of things for Liam. Two years into his enlistment, while he was applying for SEAL training, his father drank himself into a stupor and then got on the highway, destination unknown. After driving only a couple of miles, he rammed his sedan under the back of a slowing tractor-trailer.

Liam returned home for the funeral, then went directly to the BUD/S course. Since then, he'd rarely gone home to New Jersey, though he tried to call his mother once a month to make sure she was all right and had enough money. He sometimes sent postcards to his sisters' children, though he hardly knew them, and cash on their birthdays. Fortunately Aidan kept track of those dates.

Michel began to cough, and Liam looked over at him. His face was reddening, and it looked like he was having difficulty breathing. Liam quickly rehearsed the Heimlich maneuver in his head, ready to jump into action, but the boy stuck his hand into his mouth and twisted it.

Olivier and Liam watched him intently. Finally he pulled his hand out, holding a thin fish bone. Michel took a long drink of water and wiped his mouth with the back of his hand.

"You all right?" Liam asked.

Michel nodded and began eating again, but the incident reminded Liam of the threats that were all around, even in the bland setting of a restaurant.

When Olivier and Michel had finished their meal, Liam led the return to the office, regretting the second glass of wine he had allowed Olivier to press on him. Did the man not understand the need for a bodyguard to remain sharp and alert? He'd have to be more stern the next time.

Back at the office, he found it hard to concentrate on the FLNC file. Occasionally he felt Michel watching him, but when he looked up the boy always lowered his gaze and pretended to be focused on his music.

Liam was relieved at three o'clock when Olivier announced they could go home. "I can finish what I need to there. And Agathe should be returning soon as well."

They took the elevator down to the garage. "Can't I stay in the city for a while?" Michel asked. "I'll get someone to drive me home, or I'll call you later to pick me up."

"I am not your chauffeur," Olivier said. "And you know I cannot allow you to remain in the city on your own." He used his remote to open the car and strode forward before Liam could stop him.

Liam put his hand on Michel's arm. "Let's get in the car," he said as Olivier slid behind the wheel and turned it on.

There was a loud boom, and a gush of smoke belched from underneath the sedan. Liam pushed Michel aside and dived for the car, taking in a long breath of fresh air and holding it. Olivier had his seat belt on, and he was bent forward, choking on black smoke.

Liam turned off the car and removed the key. He pulled out his folding knife and sliced through the seat belt, then dragged Olivier out. He put his arm around the older man and pulled him along. "Out of here," he said to Michel. "Right now!"

11 – Waiting Room

"I'm sorry we have nothing to keep you busy," Agathe said as she pulled her car into a parking space reserved for doctors, beside a blank wall of the clinic. "We have no Internet, and we have no extra rooms."

"Don't worry about me." Aidan held up the pages he had printed out the night before from Olivier's home computer, background research on the FLNC and the smaller groups that had split off from it. "I have a lot to read."

Agathe turned the car off, and Aidan asked, "Could you wait just a moment while I look around?"

"Of course."

He scanned the immediate area. The building sat at the sunbaked intersection of two major roads, just outside the city center. There was no one else in the parking lot and no one outside any of the neighboring buildings. He heard Liam's voice in his head. *If you were aiming for the target, where would you position yourself?*

It was nearly impossible to get a clear shot from a moving vehicle, especially in this case, as there was a short distance from the clinic to the parking lot. That meant a shooter would have to be in one of the neighboring buildings or on a roof.

The only likely spot was a store across the street, with what looked like a floor of apartments above. A couple of windows were open, and the light breeze blew white curtains out of one. Aidan looked carefully but saw no movement in any window.

"Tomorrow, if you come to work, I'd rather you parked in the patient area, if that's all right," he said. "As close to the building as you can."

She nodded.

"I'll get out first, and then I'll come around to your door," he said.

"Is all this necessary?"

"Just precautions, Doctor. I'm sure nothing will happen—but better to be safe."

He opened his door and stepped out. The air was cool, and the breeze felt good against his skin. He walked around to Agathe's door and waited while she got out, collecting her purse and medical bag. Then he escorted her to the clinic's glass front door and held it open for her.

"Thank you," she said, inclining her head slightly.

He let the door close behind her and walked around the perimeter of the property. It was a single-story concrete building, with only two means of entry or exit—the front door and a metal door at the rear.

He stood under a palm tree and watched the traffic flow by—a mix of cars, trucks, and scooters. Parents arrived at the clinic with children in tow. A woman shook a blanket out through one of the windows across the street.

He went inside, settled in a hard plastic chair in the corner, and observed the routine. Patients entered, checked in with the receptionist—a pretty young girl named Catterina—then sat in the waiting room until they were called. They returned through the same door from the examining rooms and checked out with Catterina, who printed a bill from her computer. Standard operating procedure for a doctor's office.

He opened the file of information he had found easily on the Internet; it wouldn't help pinpoint the source of the threats, but it would be good background.

It was difficult to concentrate, because there was no place for him to stay out of the way. He stood up and moved several times to accommodate sick children and worried parents, and walked around the exterior of the building twice more in between reading.

When he returned from his last walk before lunch, a twenty-something woman in a dirty sweatshirt and faded denim shorts stood at the check-in desk, arguing with Catterina in what sounded to Aidan like a bastardized form of Italian. That must be Corsu, he thought. The woman carried a small boy in her arms who whimpered like a sad kitten.

Catterina and the mother were about the same age, but there the resemblance stopped. The receptionist had fine features, smooth skin, and dark hair in carefully curled ringlets. The mother had darker skin, and her shaggy hair looked like it hadn't been cut or combed in a while.

The woman's voice got louder, and it seemed like she was demanding to see Dr. Perreau, but Catterina was resistant.

Aidan doubted a terrorist cell would send a young woman with a baby to carry out a deadly mission—but then, such things had been done before, especially in cultures that put little value on the life of a woman or a child.

He watched in surprise as the woman smacked Catterina on the cheek with her free hand. He jumped up and strode over to the desk. "What's the matter?" he asked Catterina, positioning himself between her and the woman.

She explained in French that the woman's little boy was sick, but that they were not an emergency facility. Patients must have appointments. The woman could take her child to the Misericorde hospital, where they would be able to help her.

The woman unleashed another torrent of Corsican, and the other people in the waiting room shifted uneasily. Aidan took the woman by the arm and said, "Come with me, Madame," in French.

She glared at him.

"She says she has no money for the bus to the hospital," a woman in the waiting room said. "It is only two euros."

He opened his wallet and pulled out a ten-euro note. "For the bus," he said.

The woman looked around, then grabbed the note from Aidan's hand and hurried outside, her baby pressed against her chest.

"Thank you, monsieur," Catterina said.

"It's nothing." Aidan sat back in his corner, and the chatter in the waiting room resumed.

Around twelve thirty, Catterina called him over to her desk. "Dr. Perreau usually orders lunch from the café two blocks down," she said. "She would like to know if you wish something too."

"Sure." She handed him a paper menu, and he ordered a *croque monsieur*, a ham and cheese sandwich, with French fries and an Orangina soda. When the deliveryman arrived, Aidan paid for his lunch, and Catterina paid for the food for the rest of the staff. The office closed for a half hour, but Agathe did not come out to the lobby. Aidan sat and ate as Catterina remained behind her desk and did the same.

The routine of patients began again. Aidan had read all his material and he was bored, but boredom was the bane of the bodyguard. Most protection assignments were like this, waiting around for the client to handle business and keeping an eye out for trouble.

Just after three, his cell phone rang. "There's been an incident," Liam said. "Get Dr. Perreau and come to Olivier's office. Immediately." He hung up.

"But, but, what…" Aidan sputtered, though the line was already dead.

He stood up and explained to Catterina that he needed to speak with Dr. Perreau immediately. "She is with a patient," she said.

"This is an emergency."

Before Catterina could call in to the doctor, she appeared in the doorway to the examining rooms, holding her cell phone. "Monsieur Greene," she said. "My husband… There was a bomb."

Aidan knew it was important that he remain calm. He saw that she had already ended the call. "You'll have to cancel Dr. Perreau's appointments for the rest of the day," he said to Catterina. He took the doctor by the arm. "Let's get your things."

She led him back to her office, where she collected her purse and her medical bag. She looked badly shaken. "Can you drive?" he asked.

"Yes. Olivier and Michel are all right, God be thanked. But I am frightened."

They went out the back door, though Aidan made Agathe wait behind him until he had scanned the area. They walked quickly to her car, and she drove them into the city center.

Aidan called Liam's cell. "We're on our way. Where should we meet you?"

"Pick up Olivier and Michel in front of Olivier's office. I'll stay here with the police until they're finished. I'll call you then."

Agathe pulled up in front of the entrance to the bank on the building's ground floor and called her husband. Aidan stepped out of the car and waited until Olivier and Michel were safe inside before sliding into the backseat next to Michel.

The elder Perreaus were engaged in a low-voiced conversation in the front seat. Aidan turned to Michel and asked, "What happened?"

"A bomb." He was still pale and shaken. "My father was angry with me. He went ahead, turned on the car. There was a loud noise, and black smoke began to come out from underneath."

"Was he hurt?"

Michel shook his head. "Liam pulled him out of the car quickly, and we ran away. I don't know what happened after that."

Aidan sat back. He would have to wait to speak to Liam to get all the details. But in the meantime, he was worried about his partner. Had he been hurt? Had the car exploded? He looked out the window as Agathe navigated the narrow streets. He kept checking the display on his phone to make sure Liam had not called, to verify that he had service, that the ringer was on.

When they pulled up in front of the Perreaus' home, Aidan asked them all to remain in the car until he could check the house. Before he got out, he scanned the area. Windows were open in the house across the street, but there was no one outside in the cul-de-sac.

"Maria will be here," Agathe said. She removed the keys from the ignition and handed the chain to Aidan. "The Fichet key opens the front door."

Aidan got out of the car and scanned the hills. No movement, nothing out of the ordinary. He walked up to the front door of the house and used the key to enter. "Maria?" he called.

She stepped out of the kitchen and into the living room. "Yes, monsieur?"

He verified that she had been there all day, and that no one had been to the house. He walked back outside and gave the all clear to the Perreaus, and they left the car and walked inside.

Michel went up to his room, Agathe to the kitchen, Olivier to his home office. Aidan walked around the perimeter of the property, looking for problems. He realized he and Agathe had gotten into her car without him checking underneath for explosives. Why hadn't

Liam told him what "the incident" was, so he could act appropriately?

He loved Liam, but sometimes his partner's terseness got in the way of normal behavior. Was Aidan enabling him, as he'd done with Blake back in Philadelphia? Was that his lot in life, to be bossed around by a series of alpha males? Was that what he wanted?

He sat at one of the wrought-iron chairs by the pool, in the shade of a striped umbrella. He knew he'd never be as good at their work as Liam was, because he didn't have the years of training Liam had, or the physical abilities. Was he fooling himself that he could handle the job? Maybe he'd be better off the way he'd been with Blake, managing the household and smoothing the rough edges of life.

But he did love the adrenaline rush that came with the close protection business—the feeling that he could help someone in trouble. Wasn't that just an extension of his caretaker personality, though? It was why he'd enjoyed teaching, the chance to have an effect on a student's life. He had loved working with the immigrant population in Philadelphia, helping families reunite, guiding job searches, sometimes mediating with government agencies.

Was he stuck being who he was, regardless of which man shared his bed?

And where the hell was Liam?

12 – DETECTIVE BONNET

Aidan was restless for the next hour, always thinking of something new to check, walking around inside and outside the house. He tried to stay out of the way of the Perreaus for fear they would have questions he couldn't answer.

When he heard the sound of a car pulling into the driveway, Aidan hurried to the front door. Liam emerged from the passenger side of a white Fiat, and Aidan realized he'd been holding his breath. The driver, a portly, middle-aged man, joined him as he walked to the front door.

"This is Detective Bonnet," Liam said as Aidan met them. "He has some questions for the Perreaus. Detective, this is my partner, Aidan Greene. He was with Dr. Perreau today."

Bonnet nodded, and Aidan led them into the house. While Liam took Bonnet to the living room, Aidan walked to Olivier's office at the rear of the house, between the kitchen and the guest bath. Olivier sat at his desk with his wife beside him, the two of them speaking in low tones.

"There's a police detective here," Aidan said.

"Very good," Olivier said. He stood. "He will want to speak to Michel as well, I presume." He turned to Agathe. *"Ma cherie?"*

She nodded, and went upstairs to get Michel as Aidan and Olivier walked to the living room. He was struck once again by how formal most of the house was—the sofa and chairs were all gilt and scrollwork, looking almost locked in place around an antique coffee table. Bonnet stood and introduced himself to Olivier, and then to Agathe and Michel as they joined the group.

There wasn't enough seating for everyone, so Liam and Aidan stood by the wall, allowing Olivier and Agathe to sit together on the sofa, with the detective and Michel across from them in the armchairs. Bonnet turned his attention first to Agathe.

"Dr. Perreau?" he asked. "Where were you this afternoon?"

"My wife had nothing to do with this incident!" Olivier insisted.

Aidan was surprised the detective did not isolate Agathe from her husband and son.

"Of course, monsieur," Bonnet said. "It is just a formality, you know."

"I was at my office," Agathe said, putting her hand on her husband's arm. "I saw patients all day. Monsieur Greene was with me."

Technically, Aidan thought, he wasn't with the doctor, though he doubted she could have snuck out the back door, driven to her husband's office, planted a bomb beneath his car, and then returned without notice. Since Liam had checked beneath the car that morning, logic indicated the bomb must have been placed once the car was in the office building's garage.

Bonnet verified everyone's movements. "Do you park in the same space each day?" he asked Olivier.

Perreau nodded his head. "There are reserved spaces for each tenant."

Aidan looked at Liam. Why hadn't he insisted Olivier park somewhere unexpected? That was one of the basic tenets of close protection work—avoid the routine.

Bonnet nodded and made a note. Then he turned to Michel. "You are a student at the university?" he asked.

"Yes."

"What are you studying?"

Michel crossed his arms over his chest. "Civil engineering."

"Hmm," Bonnet said. "Do you study explosives as part of that discipline?"

Olivier Perreau began to say something, but Liam raised his hand to silence him.

Michel looked sullen. "I study how to build things, not destroy them."

"Like the new *hypermarché* beyond the airport?" he asked, his bushy eyebrows raised.

Michel shrugged. "I suppose."

"I saw them begin to build that," Bonnet said. "But there was an old house on the property. Had to be knocked down. Someone had to know how to destroy it. And wasn't there another one, to be built in Porto? A group of students from the university protested that, didn't they? Were you one of them?"

"This is ridiculous," Olivier protested. "My son was with me and Monsieur McCullough at all times today."

Aidan winced at the mangled pronunciation of Liam's last name, then stole a glance at his partner. Had he really been with Michel at all times? Or might the boy have had a chance to slip away during the morning?

"Just covering all the possibilities," Bonnet said.

"What about this Aquaviva man?" Olivier demanded. "Have you spoken to him?"

"Do you have any evidence to connect him to this matter?"

"He has led protests against my mine!"

"That is true. But he is a respected man who also speaks to the legislature about the ecology of the ocean. We have no evidence that would connect him to this matter, and therefore no authority to question him at this time."

Olivier blustered for a while, but Bonnet remained stoic. When Olivier gave up, Bonnet began a long-winded explanation of what the police could and could not do in this situation. As he listened, Aidan kept glancing at Liam, who showed no emotion. He hated the Buddha-like silence his partner sometimes demonstrated, and as Bonnet blathered on, Aidan felt his irritability grow. By the time Bonnet handed out his business cards and promised to be back in touch, Aidan felt his righteous anger, at Liam and at the situation, bubbling up inside him.

Liam and Aidan escorted Bonnet back to his car. As he drove away, Aidan said, "You have to treat me as your partner, Liam. I can't be effective unless you do."

"I've heard your 'poor me' story too many times, Aidan. What's your problem now?"

He was surprised at the grit in his partner's voice, but

determined to continue. "My problem," he said, putting emphasis on the word, "is that you were too abrupt with me on the phone this afternoon. You didn't tell me Olivier's car had been bombed, and so I didn't think to check underneath Agathe's car before we got in. It was just luck that they didn't go after both cars at the same time. You're always telling me it's important that we communicate, but that's a two-way street."

Aidan caught himself. He didn't want to get Liam angry or keep on repeating old gripes—but if Liam insisted on treating him like an employee rather than a partner, then they were going to put themselves in danger. He watched Liam clench his jaw and narrow his eyes.

Aidan crossed his arms over his chest. This wasn't some small domestic matter he could yield on—where to eat dinner or what kind of toy Hayam could play with. He waited for Liam to think the situation through, then saw his partner relax.

Liam nodded. "You're right. See if you can get us something to drink from Maria, and I'll meet you out by the pool."

Aidan walked to the kitchen, his feelings jumbled. He had made his point and stood up for himself, and Liam had recognized that. And then Liam had pushed him right back to the role of domestic servant by asking him to get them something to drink.

Maria was somewhere else in the house, so Aidan retrieved the pitcher of lemonade from the refrigerator and poured two tall glasses. He had made this role for himself, after all. He was so determined to fit into Liam's life that he did anything he could to ingratiate himself.

How was that different from the way he'd been with Blake? He stood at the window and looked out at the Corsican hills. The view couldn't compare to the trees of Rittenhouse Square in Philadelphia. *But no matter what surrounded us, did our hearts remain the same?* And would his relationship with Liam end the same way things had with Blake?

But then, he'd never stood up to Blake in the way he did with Liam. Blake had never once considered him an equal, never sought his opinion on anything more important than the choice of a new sofa. Things were different with Liam. Aidan was sure of that.

He carried the lemonade outside and sat at the round table by the pool. On another day, he might have found the low hills protective, enjoyed the sunshine and the peace of the still water in the swimming pool. But now he couldn't help envisioning snipers in the hills or hiding behind the chestnut trees, and he couldn't relax.

Liam walked out the back door of the house and crossed the lawn. "I was abrupt with you on the phone because I was angry with myself," he said as he sat down. "Right then I didn't want to face the fact that the whole incident was my fault."

"It's not your fault. You didn't put the bomb under the car."

"I should have insisted he park in a different space to make it harder for someone to find his car. And I shouldn't have let him start the car before I checked. I had too much wine at lunch, and I let myself get distracted by the argument between him and Michel. If I'd been on my game, I'd have checked the car again before I let Perreau get in. I would have seen the device, and I could have disabled it or called the cops."

Though Aidan was sorry Liam was upset, he was secretly pleased that at least he wasn't the source of his partner's irritation. "We're not perfect, Liam. We're human."

"It still bugs me. I'm better than that. But I shouldn't have taken it out on you." He looked down at the table. "I knew if I told you the details right then, you'd have quizzed me, and I'd have to admit I screwed up."

"Liam. Even when you screw up—and you have in the past, and you will in the future—you're still a smart, strong, amazing man, and nothing is ever going to change that for me."

Liam smiled, and Aidan felt his heart thump and his dick stiffen. But he forced himself to concentrate on the situation. "So. Tell me exactly what happened."

Liam recounted the argument between father and son, the way Olivier had gone ahead and started the car, the noise, and the explosion of black smoke. "The police think that's all the bomb was designed to do," he said. "That it was a warning."

"Have you called Jean-Luc?"

Liam nodded. "As soon as I could. He wants us to sit tight and keep the Perreaus from going anywhere."

"Easier said than done. Both Olivier and Agathe sound dedicated to their work."

"Olivier's pretty shaken up," Liam said. "I think he'll cooperate."

"Good. I believe he if does, Agathe will too. Especially after what she said about her background, seeing what terrorists in Algeria did to her family."

Liam stood up. "I've been meaning to climb up that hill over there and do some recon. I'll see you at dinner."

Aidan's heart skipped a beat. "You don't want me to come with you?"

Liam smiled at him. "I need some time on my own. I know I can trust you to keep tabs on the clients for an hour."

"Sure." Aidan watched Liam stride across the lawn to the rocky hillside. He couldn't help admiring his partner's butt and how snugly his khaki slacks fit. But at the same time he recognized the sure, determined stride. Liam was translating his discomfort into action, and that's what Aidan had to do as well.

He walked around the house, forcing his mind away from thoughts of Liam and romantic discord. Liam wasn't Blake, and Aidan wasn't the same man he'd been when he lived in Philadelphia. He focused on the proximity of the neighboring houses, the vantage points a shooter might use, the places an assailant might hide. He took notes, then met Liam and the Perreaus for dinner.

Maria had prepared lasagna, which Olivier carved up at the table and distributed. The pasta was *al dente*, the layers of cheese between light and airy, the meat and mushrooms tangy. Aidan had always associated Italian food with big, happy families, with cozy restaurants with red-and-white-checked tablecloths and candles in old wine bottles. It was oddly discordant to eat such food in the glacial formality of the Perreau dining room.

No one spoke, and once Agathe brought out the cheese, Michel asked to be excused. Agathe nodded, and he retreated upstairs.

After the four of them picked at the cheese, Agathe returned the plate to the kitchen, and then she and Olivier went to their bedroom.

Liam pushed back his chair. "Let's take a walk around the house once more before dark."

"I took some notes earlier," Aidan said.

"Good. Show me what you saw. I think we'll have a day or two to respond to this incident before we see anything else. But it pays to be careful."

Aidan was warmed by a renewed sense of partnership with Liam as they walked around the property, discussing what Aidan had noted. As always, Liam's observations were deeper, more incisive, but he praised Aidan's insight. "Good catch," he said when Aidan pointed out a pro-nationalist bumper sticker on a car in a neighbor's driveway. "Have we researched the neighbors yet?"

"I can go online tonight," Aidan said.

"You're the guru when it comes to that stuff, but you let me know if I can help."

They finished their circuit and headed back to their room, Aidan suffused with a warm glow.

13 – Rendezvous

Michel curled on his bed, clutching his cell phone. He had made a nest for himself of all the pillows in the room, the ones he slept with and the ones his mother used to decorate the bed when he was away. "I need to see you," he said. "I'm so shaken up. Can't you come down here?"

"What about the men guarding your family?" Cris asked.

"I'll slip away. I can get out my bedroom window. I used to do it when I was a teenager. If you keep going past my house, the road curves uphill. There's a tumbled-down stone thing after the curve. You can pull your bike in there. A couple of meters ahead there's an opening in the woods, and the trail leads to a rock that overlooks my house. I'll climb up there and meet you."

"Michel. It's dangerous. What if your father finds out?"

"I don't care, Cris. I need you."

"All right. But it's going to take me an hour and a half to get down there. I'll call you when I get close to Ajaccio."

"I love you," Michel said.

"I love you too, my little cabbage. I'll see you soon."

Michel ended the call and sat on his bed. As a teenager, when he first figured out that he was attracted to other boys rather than girls, he had begun perfecting his skills at deceiving his parents. He had engineered this escape route from his house and often met friends at the top of the hill, either for fun or to get a ride down into the city.

As far as he knew, his parents had never suspected.

He was restless, eager to get out of this prison cell and see Cris. He hopped up and walked over to the window that looked out at the pool. He opened it and felt the fresh, cool air stream inside. The two bodyguards were nowhere in sight. Probably gone to bed early, like his parents.

He pulled his head back inside. He put on his headphones and tried to listen to music, but nothing interested him. He kept pacing around the room, waiting for Cris's call. When it came, he pounced on the phone.

"Where are you?" he asked.

"On the Boulevard Abbe Recco, about to come into the edge of the city."

"All right, I'll leave now and climb up the mountain. If you get lost, call me."

Michel ended the call, then stared at the phone in his hand. He wished he could keep Cris on the phone, keep talking to him until he felt his touch, but that was too dangerous. For Cris, who needed to focus on keeping his bike on the road, and for Michel, who had to be quiet to sneak away from the house.

He switched the phone to vibrate and slipped it into the pocket of his jeans. He walked back to the window and sat on the sill. He swung his left leg out so he was straddling the window and then, ducking his head, pushed his upper body outside. It was chilly, and the night was quiet except for the noise of a car climbing the Rue des Magnolias.

He pulled his right leg close to him and squeezed it out the window, then sat there for a moment, getting his bearings. His butt still rested inside the house, though the rest of him was outside.

Awkwardly, he shifted around so that he faced into the window, holding tight to the frame for support. He dangled his right foot down and felt for the top of the stone that sheathed the first floor. He secured a toehold and lowered himself down the wall. The irregular pattern of the rock provided enough purchase for his toes and fingers.

He felt no fear, only exhilaration, the way he had when he was sneaking around as a teenager. He touched every facet of the rock beneath his fingers, the smoothness of the mortar, the sharp facets of the individual stones. His hearing was magnified by the darkness; he heard an owl hoot and the breeze ruffling the fronds of the palm trees at the side of the house.

His room was directly above the kitchen, so there was little chance anyone would be able to see him from inside the house. When he was only a few feet from the ground, he released his hold on the stone and dropped to the grass, landing hard on his sneakered feet but without stumbling or falling. He remained still for a moment, listening to be sure he hadn't disturbed anyone inside. Two small white egrets pecked at the grass near the swimming pool.

He turned and crept across the lawn to the twisting path that led up the hillside. He climbed carefully, holding on to tree branches and avoiding letting loose any pebbles. A foot-long brown gecko scurried across the path ahead of him, and he jumped back. He knew there were snakes up there, and didn't want to meet any of them.

After about twenty meters, the path leveled out as it curved its way to the top of the hill. Through the trees he got occasional glimpses of the lights of Ajaccio far below. A large bird swooped over his head and landed on a high branch of a chestnut tree, making the leaves shake with an ominous whisper.

He heard the buzz of Cris's motorcycle on the road. He knew the sound of that engine almost as well as he knew his own breathing, the guttural roar and the occasional popping noise. It drowned out any other noises from the forest.

He reached the top and sat down on the hard stone, cold under his butt. He should have worn a jacket, he thought, rubbing his upper arms. He looked up at the sky and saw the faint blur of the Milky Way, and placed the cluster of three stars in Orion's belt.

He heard Cris's bike slow, then the engine die. He got up and stretched, then rubbed his butt where the cold from the stone had sunk in. As he walked toward the path, he heard Cris's boots tramping over underbrush. He fantasized about having sex with Cris right there, on that chilly hilltop, under the stars.

Then strong hands grabbed him from behind, one clasped over his mouth to keep him from calling out a warning to Cris. He struggled but could not free himself. Across from him, he saw Cris step out of the woods and into the clearing, and then a big shape came out of the woods behind him and grasped him too.

14 – True Feelings

"I want to know what's going on here," Liam demanded. He had heard movement outside the Perreau house, and when he saw Michel creeping away, he and Aidan had followed.

It was almost funny—the way the boy tried to be quiet but only succeeded in making enough noise to make it easy to follow him. Liam had years of experience in silent movement as a SEAL, and he had trained Aidan to be aware of his surroundings, to consciously place each step in a way that minimized or eliminated noise and traces of passage.

Michel had no such skill. He knocked past branches, stepped hard on stones, as if announcing his approach as he went. It helped too, that there was nearly a full moon, and it was easy to follow his progress as he climbed the hill, then to circle around and anticipate the meeting between him and his collaborator.

The two young men sat Indian-style on the ground, their hands tied in front of them. "This is outrageous!" Michel said. "Wait until my father hears how you have treated me."

"Why don't we start with introductions," Aidan said. He and Liam were both still dressed as they'd been during the day, though it was clear the evening cold was starting to bother Aidan from the way he rubbed his exposed lower arms. "Do you want to do the honors, Michel?"

Michel glared at him and said nothing.

"My name is Aidan, and this is my partner, Liam. We're bodyguards, hired to protect the Perreaus." He looked at the other young man, who appeared to be the same age as Michel. He was burly and hairy, not the kind of friend he expected the bookish Michel to have. "You are?" he asked.

"Don't say anything," Michel said.

"My name is Cris. Michel is my boyfriend."

Aidan nodded. "I thought so." He looked at Michel. "Why all the drama? Why not just tell one of us you needed to slip out? Liam told me that you challenged him at lunch, that you figured out we're gay. Chances are we'd be willing to accommodate you."

"How do I know I can trust you?" Michel said. "If my father finds out…"

"We're not telling your father anything he doesn't need to know." Aidan leaned down to untie Michel's hands.

"Wait, Aidan." Liam squatted down in front of Michel and Cris. "If we untie you, you're going to promise to behave, aren't you?"

"I don't take orders from you," Michel said.

"Michel…" Cris said.

"If you act up, you'll make things worse," Liam said. "I know what it's like to have to sneak around in order to meet up with another guy. And believe me, we don't want to interfere with your personal life. But we were hired to protect you, and we'll do that to the best of our ability."

"We don't want to make your job any more difficult," Cris said. Liam wasn't nearly as perceptive about relationships as Aidan was, but even he saw Cris was the alpha male. He was relaxed and in control, whereas Michel looked like a scared rabbit.

Liam undid Cris's hands. The ropes had been loose enough not to hurt, and an experienced agent could have slipped out of them in under a minute. Liam had counted on both boys being frightened enough that they would cooperate.

Cris stood up, and Liam undid Michel's hands. Cris reached down and helped his boyfriend to his feet. Michel still looked angry and ready to run, and Liam thought the safest thing to do was escort Cris back to his bike, then frog-march Michel back home.

"You guys probably want some privacy," Aidan said. "Liam and I will be over there, out of sight. But if either of you tries to run away, we'll be right on top of you."

"Michel just wants to talk," Cris said.

Liam frowned. Why did Aidan have to bollocks up every plan? There was no need for Michel and Cris to talk or do anything else. He took a deep breath and looked at the two boys. Michel reached out and took Cris's hand, and the Perreau boy visibly relaxed.

It galled him that Aidan's human intuitions were sometimes better than his own. Aidan had observed the relationship between Michel and Cris and figured out that the boyfriend could be useful in keeping control of Michel, that it would help them establish a connection with the younger Perreau and have some assurance that he'd cooperate during the coming week.

He nodded to Aidan, and the two of them walked out of the clearing, leaving the boys behind. After their argument that afternoon, Liam knew he owed Aidan an apology or compliment. "You're pretty sharp when it comes to people, you know that?" he asked. "You don't think they'll run?"

"I think they just wanted to see each other. Cris is the boss—and he'll keep Michel in line." Aidan smiled up at him. "Kind of like us."

"The question of who's the boss between us is still up for discussion," Liam said drily. "But about them. How can you tell?"

Liam was always curious about Aidan's ability to understand character and personality. As a SEAL, he had been forced to assume every opponent had one goal in mind—to triumph over his adversaries. Working in close protection and then living with Aidan had showed him there were many shades to behavior.

"Cris is more masculine," Aidan said. "I bet he can pass more easily for straight. From the way he moves, I'll bet he's an athlete too. This is a pretty conservative culture, so he's not out to his family or his friends. I'll bet you he's the one who got their relationship going—and only because Michel was more obviously gay."

"Speculation," Liam said. "But a reasonable interpretation of the facts."

They positioned themselves so that they saw the two young men through the trees—not closely, but clearly enough so that if one or both of them took off, they'd be able to follow.

"Michel is more freaked out about what happened today than he's willing to let on," Aidan continued. "I bet he convinced Cris to come down and look after him."

Liam considered that. "If I were Cris, I'd be worried about

Michel too. Wouldn't take much to convince me."

He knew in a way he was talking about himself, that if Aidan were in danger, he'd be right there. Despite Aidan's intuitive skills and growing abilities as a bodyguard, Liam still thought of himself as the senior partner—and he knew Aidan, despite his self-confidence, would have to agree.

Liam worried that someday they would come up against an adversary who could take advantage of Aidan's weaknesses. Despite what he had said to Olivier earlier, that both he and Aidan would focus on protecting the client, he wasn't sure he would make that choice if he had to.

"Look at the body language," Aidan whispered. "See how it's Cris who comforts Michel? He's in charge. He'll be on our side."

"If you say so," Liam said. It felt uncomfortably intimate, spying on the two young men when one of them was the client—or at least the client's son. But there was no getting around it. Michel had proved he couldn't be trusted, and this other boy, Cris, was an unknown quantity.

But as the young men kissed, Liam felt his body reacting, as if he was watching a porn video. Cris and Michel were both handsome, and the passion between them was not forced or faked. The rawness of their emotion and need was more erotic than if they'd been naked and fucking.

"Are you getting turned on?" Aidan whispered. His hand brushed over Liam's crotch, where his dick had stiffened and was pressing against his pants.

"Aidan." Liam brushed his partner's hand away.

"It's nothing to be embarrassed about," Aidan said. "It's a natural reaction."

"We're working. Michel is a client."

"I know."

Liam looked over at him. There was something in his tone of voice that said this was a topic they would continue, in private, and that thought excited Liam even more.

"They're certainly going at it," Liam said. In the moonlight it was easy to see the way Cris held Michel's head in his hands, the passion of their kisses, Michel's hands stroking his boyfriend's back and ass. "I wish they'd get it over with already."

Aidan laughed. "No you don't."

Cris gently pushed Michel away, and they sat beside each other, talking. Then Cris leaned in and kissed Michel. This kiss was different from the earlier one—it was quicker, with less passion but somehow more intensity.

Cris stood, then backed away from Michel. Aidan and Liam walked out to join them. "Au revoir, *mon petit chou*," Cris said, using the sweet French term for *little cabbage*.

Michel stood too and responded with something Liam didn't understand, perhaps in the Corsican language, and then Cris walked back the way he had come, to where he had left his motorcycle.

"Do you feel better?" Aidan asked Michel.

"My balls hurt," Michel said. "But Cris wouldn't do anything more than kiss me while you watched."

"Blue balls won't kill you," Liam said. "I used to go without sex for a year or more at a time."

The three of them walked back down the hillside path toward the Perreau home. Michel was noisy, but Liam resisted the urge to show him how to move more quietly. There was no use teaching the client how to escape them.

A pair of white egrets by the swimming pool took flight when they emerged from the woods. The still water glimmered in the moonlight. The only sounds were a truck climbing the main road, and the distant, throaty bark of a large dog.

They walked in through the back door, and Michel climbed the stairs to the second floor. Liam and Aidan returned to the guest room. It was after one o'clock, and Liam was tired.

When the door was closed behind them, Aidan said, "I'm kind of cold. Think you can warm me up?" He pulled his sweatshirt over his head, exposing his hairy chest and flat stomach.

"If you're cold, keep your clothes on," Liam said, though he couldn't look Aidan in the eye when he said it, or he'd have betrayed his true feelings.

"Oh really?" Aidan put his right hand on Liam's lower arm. The hand was cold, and Liam shivered slightly—though from more than the temperature.

Liam took the cold hand between his two warm ones, savoring the sensation. He leaned forward and kissed Aidan gently on the lips.

Aidan pulled back a bit, sticking his tongue out and wiggling it. Liam knew what he was asking, and stuck his out as well. The two of them dueled as their bodies moved closer together. Liam released his grip on Aidan's hand and pulled his partner to him. He inhaled Aidan's scent—the murkiness of the woods mixed with sweat and the faintest traces of lemon soap.

The tightness in his chest loosened, and he leaned down to kiss Aidan properly, lips together, tongues embedded within. When they both pulled back he stripped off his shirt and shucked his pants while Aidan removed his clothes as well. They were careful to be quiet as they slid down onto the bed. Liam went right for Aidan's dick, swallowing it as his partner lay on his back, timing his hip thrusts to match Liam's eager sucking. Aidan reached down to Liam's nipples and grabbed the two gold rings there, twisting them as Liam sucked.

Then Liam scrambled around so that his dick was at Aidan's mouth, and both of them sucked with a passion fueled not only by their love for each other but by what they had witnessed earlier. Liam's orgasm swirled in his gut, and he had to gasp for breath as it overtook him.

He didn't usually come first—he wanted to please Aidan and to remain in control. But that night he couldn't help himself, and he shot off into Aidan's mouth. He felt his partner gulp as he swallowed, and despite all the sensations going on around his dick, he forced himself back to sucking Aidan and a moment later was rewarded with his own mouthful of come.

Liam crawled back up next to Aidan, and the two of them fell asleep to the sound of the wind and the crickets and frogs outside their bedroom window.

15 – Love and Other Dangers

When Aidan woke the next morning, Liam was already outside in the chill dawn air, doing his workout. Aidan stretched comfortably, remembering the passion of the night before. He knew he ought to get up and join Liam outside, but it felt so good to stay in bed for a few more minutes, inhaling the scent Liam had left behind.

He dozed off again and woke to Liam standing beside the bed, running his fingers up and down Aidan's upper arm. "Wake up, sleepyhead," he said.

"Wow. I guess I was really tired," Aidan said, then yawned.

"Not surprising. You gave me a good workout last night."

Aidan sat up and watched Liam strip off his sweat-soaked T-shirt and shorts, then grab a towel and wrap it around his waist. His gold nipple rings glinted with droplets of sweat. The sight never failed to excite Aidan, even as he remembered the passion they had shared the night before. "I'm going to take a shower," Liam said.

Aidan watched his partner leave the room, focused on his broad shoulders, the sharp angle of his scapulae, the way his bulky chest tapered to a narrow waist. His dick stiffened under the covers. He lay there, lazily diddling himself, until Liam returned, stray droplets shimmering on his upper body and his well-formed, hairless calves.

Liam whipped the towel off and slapped it toward Aidan. "Get out of bed, you lazy jerk off. And I mean that literally."

Aidan laughed and hopped out of the bed, his stiff dick wagging in front of him. He tried to cuddle up to Liam, but his partner pushed him away. "We've got work to do, sex maniac." Aidan saw the humor in Liam's eyes, though. He wrapped a towel around his waist, but his dick pushed the fabric forward.

"I can't go out there like this," he said to Liam.

"Math problems," Liam said. "Women's vaginas. That fishy smell."

"Enough!" Aidan laughed and held up his hands in front of him, and felt his dick wilt.

By the time he finished his shower, Liam was already dressed, reading e-mails on his cell phone. "Got the reports on the maid, the secretary, and the assistant," he said as Aidan pulled a pair of boxers from a shelf inside the armoire.

"Anything interesting?"

"Maria has a husband and a six-year-old son. Husband is a gardener. They live in an apartment about a mile down the hill. No apparent financial problems, no unusual bank transfers, and no known association with any terrorist or nationalist groups."

Aidan pulled on the boxers and then a pair of khaki slacks. "How about the secretary? What's her name?"

"Edith Lavalle. Born in Grenoble, moved to Corsica twenty years ago with her husband, now deceased. With Olivier for five years, well-paid, no apparent resentments against him. Again, no red flags. I met her yesterday. Very innocuous."

Aidan took a polo shirt from a drawer and pulled it over his head. As he tucked it in, he said, "That leaves the assistant."

"George Phthalis. His parents are Greek, and he was born in Glyfada, outside Athens. They moved to Corsica a few years later, and he was raised in Ajaccio. Full scholarship to the university; Argentum is the only place he's ever worked. Lives with his parents, belonged to several groups as a student, but nothing unusual."

"So no good leads from any of the three of them," Aidan said. He walked over to the bedroom door. "Which leaves us back at the Perreaus."

They walked to the kitchen, where Maria was preparing breakfast. None of the three Perreaus had come down yet. They greeted her and sat at the kitchen table. Aidan felt strange, having a maid to wait on them, but he didn't want to cause a fuss.

"You would like eggs?" Maria asked.

"Thank you, Maria," Aidan said, and Liam nodded.

"You think Olivier will want to go to work again?" Aidan asked in English, speaking under the sizzling noises coming from Maria's frying pan.

"He has to contact the police and get his car back first," Liam said. "I'd rather he stayed home, but he was insistent that he had a lot of work to do."

The aroma of frying ham tickled Aidan's nostrils, and he realized how hungry he was. Maria's eggs were light and fluffy, the ham perfectly seared, accompanied by a platter of sliced ripe tomatoes.

As they were finishing, Olivier and Agathe came in. "Can you talk sense to my husband, please?" Agathe said. "He insists he must go to the office again. I have canceled my patients, so I will remain at home."

"You have an office here," Aidan said to Olivier. "Can't you ask Edith and George to come up here and work with you?"

Agathe turned to her husband. "It is a good idea, Olivier. It will be cramped but much safer for you."

"I don't need either of them," Olivier said. "It will be easier for George to remain at the office, and Edith must be there to handle the phones. But I must talk to the police. I will need my car back."

"We'll call Detective Bonnet after breakfast," Liam said.

Michel entered the kitchen, and Aidan and Liam stood up. "We'll speak again after you all finish eating," Liam said.

They walked back to their bedroom. "We should tell Olivier and Agathe that Michel slipped out last night," Liam said. "They need to know."

"They do not," Aidan said. "You told me how uncomfortable Olivier was when Michel outed you yesterday. Olivier will go ballistic if he hears that Michel is gay, and that will make things even more tense here."

"I wasn't going to out him," Liam said. "Just say he met a friend."

"I'm telling you, it's a bad idea. You've seen the way Michel is with his father—they'll get into an argument, and it'll escalate, and who knows what will happen."

"I want you to talk to Michel about this boyfriend, at least,"

Liam said. "See what you can find out about him. Make sure he's legitimate."

"You're such a worrywart," Aidan said. "But I'll talk to him after they finish breakfast."

"Good. I'm going to call the cops and see when we can pick up Olivier's car." He walked out, and Aidan turned to his laptop. He had an idea about how to find more information on the mysterious boyfriend.

He found the Web site for the University of Corsica Pascal Paoli. If he was right, Cris was an athlete, and there might be a photo of him. Sure enough, after filtering through a dozen pictures, he found a shot of the football team, and there to one side was Cris—with his last name, Aquaviva.

That was a start, though there was something familiar about that name. Aidan couldn't place it, but he began searching for more information, now that he had the boy's last name.

He wasn't the star of the team, but he had a solid record over the past two years. He was about to graduate in the spring with a degree in political science. He had a profile on a French-language social-networking site called Skyrock, but it appeared that it was just to share information and schedules with his teammates.

Liam walked back into the bedroom. "The police can't find anything on the bomb that would link it to anyone. Typical. But at least there was no damage to the car other than the seat belt I sliced through. I'm going to drive him down to the police station in Agathe's car and then follow him over to the dealership. We'll get the seat belt replaced and then come back up here."

"All right. I'll keep an eye on Michel."

"Richard's e-mail this morning also had some background on the Perreaus," Liam said. "I archived it after I read it."

That explained why Aidan hadn't seen the message when he checked earlier. He wanted to say something to Liam but held his tongue. It was a minor issue, after all. After Liam left, he went back to the e-mail account and checked the archived folder.

There was nothing new in Olivier's biography, though Aidan wondered where he had gotten the money to buy the mine. He e-mailed Richard to ask for more research on Perreau's finances. It was possible there was some financial motive behind these threats—an investor who wanted Perreau out of the picture, for example.

Agathe Lecolombier Perreau had been born in Algeria in 1962 and moved to Marseille as a child. She studied medicine at Paris Descartes University and married Olivier after completing her residency. She worked as a pediatrician until her son was born in 1992, took two years off, then joined the staff at a small clinic in a Paris suburb. A few months after the family moved to Corsica, she returned to work and had been at the same clinic in Ajaccio since then.

Michel had profiles on several social-networking sites but posted little there other than the occasional gripe about classes. He had been tagged in the photos of friends—a few times at football matches, and several times at parties. If Cris was in the same photo, he was never close to Michel.

Aidan looked up to see Michel standing in the doorway of the guest room. "How long have you two been…" Michel began, letting the question trail off.

Aidan closed the laptop and looked up. "We met about two years ago. I had been living in Philadelphia with a partner for eleven years. One day he came home and told me it was over, and he kicked me out."

He motioned Michel to come into the bedroom, and the boy sat down in a chair by the door. Aidan stretched out on the bed. "I wanted to get as far away from him as I could, so I went online and looked for teaching jobs. I thought I found one in Tunis."

"You are a teacher?"

Aidan nodded. "My background is in ESL—English as a Second Language. I flew to Tunis and discovered the job wasn't what I was expecting. I didn't know what to do—and then I met Liam."

"He was a teacher too?" Michel asked.

"No. He had been in the US military, and after he left, he wandered around for a while, until someone made a connection for him in Tunis, and he started working there as a bodyguard."

Aidan remembered the first time he'd seen Liam—showering naked in the courtyard at the back of a bar in Tunis where Aidan had sought shelter from someone who wanted to steal his wallet. The way he'd fallen in lust at first sight.

"By coincidence, I looked a lot like a man Liam had been hired to protect, and when that man was killed, Liam needed my help to take care of some things." It was too complicated to explain any more. "We fell in love and discovered we worked well together. I moved in with Liam in Tunis and began to help him."

"And your families? Do they know about you?"

"We're both older than you are, Michel. My parents are both dead—but yes, they knew I was gay before they died. They met my partner, Blake." He smiled. "I don't think either of them liked him very much, but they thought he would take care of me."

"And Liam?" Michel asked.

"His father died many years ago. His mother and his sisters live back in New Jersey—the part of the US where we both come from. He doesn't discuss his personal life with them."

"So he had to move far away before he could be gay?"

That was one way to look at it, Aidan thought. He had never met any member of Liam's family, only seen pictures of them on the Internet. As far as he knew, Liam had never mentioned his sexual orientation to his mother or his sisters, and they believed he was a single man living on his own.

"He was gay long before he left home," Aidan said gently. "And those were different times."

"You are not much older than I am," Michel said. "I am twenty. You are?"

"Thirty-five," Aidan said. "And Liam is thirty-six. But those years—things have changed so much." He looked up at the young man. "It's much easier to be open today than it was back then."

"In the US perhaps. But not here."

"Cris's family—they don't know about him?"

Michel shook his head. "We have been very careful. Not even our friends know about us." He slumped. "I want to be with him so much. But it's impossible."

"Nothing is impossible. What are you going to do when you finish your studies?"

"I want to move back here, to Ajaccio. There are several companies that hire engineering students from the university. I want Cris to come here too, but he says he will go back to his family on the north coast."

"Why?"

"His parents are poor. His father is a fisherman, his mother a housewife. He has two younger brothers and a sister, and they have made many sacrifices so he could accept his scholarship to university. He says he must go back there and help make sure his brothers and sister can succeed as he did."

"You don't have to live together to see each other. It will be difficult, but you can still meet." Aidan leaned back against the bed pillows. "I know it's hard to imagine, but there is not just one man in the world for any of us. I fell in love very easily when I was in college. I would meet a boy, and my hormones would take over. I'd go crazy if I couldn't be with him. And then, something would happen. He would cheat on me, or I would meet someone else, or we would just fall out of love with each other."

"How can you treat such things so lightly?" Michel asked.

Aidan shook his head. "I didn't treat them lightly at all. I thought my heart would break every time something ended. That I would never meet anyone else like him, that I would never love like that again." He shrugged. "And then another boy would smile at me, or I would meet someone at a club, and the whole cycle would start over again."

"I don't want to be like that." Michel crossed his arms over his chest. "I want to love Cris for the rest of my life."

"And perhaps you will," Aidan said. "Back in Philadelphia, I know some couples who have been together since college—men who are in their sixties now. But you need to remember that if it doesn't happen, it's not the end of the world."

"It will be for me," Michel said. He stood up and walked out.

16 – Polite Conversations

Liam would have preferred to drive Olivier down to the police station Wednesday morning to retrieve his car, but Perreau wanted to drive himself. Liam had to settle for the passenger seat.

"What do you think I should do?" Olivier asked as he drove down the winding road toward the Caserne Battesti.

Liam looked left and then right. "Giving in to terrorists is always a bad idea," he said. "But if you can postpone your deal? That's a possibility. Make it look like you're giving in. Remove the immediate threat and give the police some time to find out who's behind these incidents."

Olivier sighed. "I will speak to my contact at Outremer this morning. I cannot risk any harm to my family. Who knows what these animals will do next?"

At least the man was beginning to see reason, Liam thought. There was only so much he and Aidan could do, after all. With three principals, two offices and a home, there was too much ground to cover to be effective against all threats, and he couldn't count on the other Agence operative for much. The car bomb the day before had demonstrated just how vulnerable the Perreaus were.

Detective Bonnet was unavailable; a uniformed officer produced the keys to Perreau's car and led them to the yard, then opened the gate so Perreau could drive it out. As Liam followed Olivier to the car dealership in Agathe's car, he called Louis Fleck. "Come up with anything more for me?"

"Good morning to you, too, Liam. I see Aidan still has not civilized you to the point where you can carry on polite conversations."

"Aidan and I have better things to do with our time together than work on civilizing me," Liam said, but he knew Louis was right. He had to put more effort into being nice to people, Aidan most of all.

"Yes, Hassan speculates on that all the time," Louis said. "I think he has a bit of a crush on you. But then who doesn't?"

Liam let that remark go without saying anything. "Things are heating up here." He described the car bombing. "Can you see if that MO matches any known groups?"

"I'll see. And I found some more information on the man you asked about—Aquaviva. I'll e-mail it to you. So far he's been nothing more than a garden-variety nationalist—a local fisherman with a way with words who has roused his neighbors to various actions. But it's possible he is getting more active. His family lives near this mine, and he's been complaining that new activity there will pollute the waters where he fishes."

"Thanks, Louis. Anything else?"

"Just a rumor right now—a group of students from the university who have been protesting any kind of development. A sort of Green Party, if you will. I have someone looking for more information on them."

Liam was about to say good-bye and hang up, but then

remembered his manners. "I appreciate your help. Say hi to Hassan from me and Aidan, all right?"

"Very good, Liam. You're learning. Talk to you later."

Liam pulled Agathe's car up in front of the dealership. While Olivier made arrangements to have his sedan checked carefully and have the sliced seat belt replaced, Liam considered his conversation with Louis. What did he mean about Hassan having a bit of a crush on him? And saying "who doesn't" in that way that implied perhaps he did too?

He had never considered himself handsome. As a kid, everyone said he looked like his father, which Liam did not appreciate. His father's name was William too, though everyone called him Bill. Liam had been called Billy—a diminutive he didn't care for, but one he'd stuck with all through his service in the military.

When he left the SEALs behind, he changed his name, using the last bit of his original one. His passport and official documents still read William Joseph McCullough—his maternal grandfather's name the only thing that kept him from being a junior. He had taken his confirmation name, Augustine, from the patron saint of brewers, because he thought that show of faith would cause the saint to cure his father's alcoholism.

Hadn't worked. That was the start of his loss of faith in Catholicism, helped along by the church's disdain for homosexuals as he realized the nature of his own desires.

Girls began getting interested in him when he reached puberty. He spent a lot of time in the gym, and he assumed for a long time that it was his muscles that attracted them rather than his face. He had resisted their advances until he was seventeen, citing his Catholic faith that kept him a virgin.

But just before shipping out to the Navy, he'd given in to the ministrations of a neighborhood girl. He'd been so horny back then that just another person's touch was enough to get him hard, and he'd performed with her—well enough, he guessed, from her reaction. For the next few years he'd tried to ignore the urges he had for other men, pretending they were just a phase. He'd had sex with a few more women—prostitutes and military groupies—but none of them had been able to make him believe he was straight.

He was twenty-one before he had sex with another man—a hurried blowjob in a bar men's room. It was quick and cheap and without emotional attachment—but it reinforced that he was irrevocably gay.

Once he acknowledged that fact, he was able to start noticing the way other men—gay men—looked at him. He still believed they were interested only in his body. It wasn't until he was in his mid-twenties that he was able to look at himself objectively and realize that he was, in fact, handsome—not a movie star or a model, but that his square jaw, deep-set green eyes, and blondish brown hair combined with his tall, athletic body to present an attractive package.

He'd taken his looks for granted for years, acknowledging that when he wanted sex, there would be a guy there to provide it. It was only when he met Aidan and fell in love for the first time that he began to see that someone could care for him because of what was underneath the handsome facade.

Olivier walked out of the car dealership and over to Agathe's car. "It will be a few hours," he said. "May we go to my office?"

Liam hesitated. But there was no reason to drive all the way back up to the house, only to return downtown. "If you wish," he said.

Olivier directed him through the city, and Liam paid more attention to the roads now that he was driving. Ajaccio hugged the shore of the bay, and most of the streets curved around the hills or along the waterfront. The five- and six-story stone and stucco buildings were painted in pastel colors, or faded by the sun's rays. Tables at a sidewalk café were shaded by umbrellas advertising the local beer, Pietra.

The streets were crowded with cars, vans, trucks, and motor scooters. Pedestrians strolled along the sidewalks, shaded by narrow awnings. When the street veered close to the water, he saw dozens of rowboats, sailboats, and powerboats at anchor in a multitude of bright primary colors. As the road curved, he spied the citadel in the distance, with its stone walls at the water's edge, and the newer high-rise buildings on the bluff.

They parked in the office building's garage once again, though in a different spot, and Liam accompanied Olivier up to the office. Edith was surprised to see them. "Just stopping by for a few hours," Olivier said.

Olivier retreated into his office, and Liam stopped in the doorway to George's office. The young man looked up.

"You heard what happened yesterday?" Liam asked him in

French.

George nodded. "Terrible. The boss is okay, though?"

"Yes. You have any ideas about who could be behind these threats?"

"No, not at all." George looked down at his computer keyboard.

Liam stepped into the office and sat down across from him. "Anything you tell me will be in confidence, George."

George said nothing. Liam thought back to the report he had read on the young engineer. "You belonged to a couple of student groups when you were at the university," Liam said.

George looked up in alarm. Bingo, Liam thought.

"I have done nothing," George said.

"I believe you," Liam said. "You have too much at stake to risk losing your job here. But I wonder if you might have said something to someone…"

George's body sagged. "I did not mean to betray any confidences." He looked at Liam. "When Monsieur Perreau finds out what I have done, he will fire me. I know."

"Let's not jump ahead. What did you do?"

George fidgeted with his computer keyboard. Liam wished Aidan were here; he had more patience with this kind of slow interrogation. "You spoke to someone about the silver mine," Liam said. "To someone from the university?"

George nodded. "I was so proud to work here. I believe in what Monsieur Perreau wants to do. To reopen the mine, to bring prosperity to Corsica. I was with friends one Saturday night, at a café up in Corte."

"I don't blame you," Liam said. "It sounds like the mine will be successful, if Monsieur Perreau can complete his deal. But your friends—they disagreed?"

"Not all," George said. "Just one. Vanina."

Liam noted the name. "Is she still in school?"

"Yes. She is in Michel's class, and she will graduate this year."

"Another engineer?"

"No, she is in the faculty of political science."

"Vanina," Liam said. "That's a pretty name. Is she Corsican?"

"Yes. She is very passionate about the land. I am afraid she may have told others in a group she belongs to. That they may have made the threats."

Liam drew a pad of paper over to him and ripped off a page, then picked up a pen. "Her full name?" he asked.

"You won't tell her I told you, will you?" he asked.

"I can't promise anything, George. But if she's connected to these terrorists…"

"Vanina Andreadi." He spelled it for Liam.

"The group?"

"Students for a Green Corsica," he said. "At first they were just environmentalists. Vanina used to ask me questions about engineering and building construction. Then the group invited a man to come and speak, the father of one of the other students. He convinced them to become more radical."

"Do you remember his name?" Liam asked.

"Aquaviva," George said. "Niculaiu Aquaviva. He is a fisherman by trade, but I believe now he manages to agitate for political causes."

That was the name Olivier Perreau had mentioned, which Louis Fleck had verified. "Is that a common name here in Corsica?" Liam asked. "Aquaviva?"

George shrugged. "I only know two by that name," he said. "A guy in Vanina's class, Cris, and his father."

"Cris?" he asked. "Michel's…" He almost said *boyfriend* but caught himself. "Friend?"

George cocked his head. "I don't think Michel knows him. Michel is in engineering, and Cris is in poli-sci like Vanina. And besides, Cris is a footballer. Not a guy Michel would know."

Liam stood up. "Thank you, George. You've been very helpful. I hope for your sake that Vanina has nothing to do with this."

And for Michel's sake, that Cris is just as blameless, he thought to himself.

17 – No Picnic

Liam went next door to the bland, undecorated office he had used the day before. He closed the door and turned on the computer, and while it booted up, he called Aidan. "We picked the car up from the police and dropped it at the dealer's to have the seat belt fixed and get everything else checked. We're at the office now, where I had a very interesting conversation with George."

"The assistant?"

"Yup. Guess what Michel's boyfriend's last name is."

"Oh, I already know that. I found it on the college Web site. It's Aquaviva."

"And you didn't think to mention that to me?"

"Don't raise your voice to me, Liam. I just found it this morning, and I didn't get a chance to tell you before you left. Why is it important?"

Liam took a deep breath. He hadn't realized he sounded angry. "Sorry. But his father is the man Perreau told us about the first night. The fisherman making trouble for him."

"Holy shit," Aidan said. "Michel is dating the son of his father's sworn enemy. It's like a Shakespeare plot."

"Let's hope things work out better for our star-crossed lovers than they did for Romeo and Juliet," Liam said. He turned behind him and closed the venetian blinds on the window to reduce the glare on the computer screen. "How's everything at the house?"

"Quiet. You didn't out Michel, did you?"

"Almost. But I caught myself. George told me he had been talking about the silver mine with a girl he knew from the university, and that it turned out she's involved with the group that Cris's father leads."

"Ouch," Aidan said. "That can't be good."

"We don't know yet that Cris's father is behind the threats and the bombing. But you're right; it's not looking good for our young lovers."

"You have the girl's name?"

Liam looked over at the computer, which had completed its startup cycle. "Yup. Vanina Andreadi. I'll e-mail Richard and see what he can find on her and on the group."

"We should talk to her," Aidan said. "Do you think Cris knows her?"

"Probably. He's in the same course she is, and if she knows his father…"

"I'll talk to Michel," Aidan said. "Maybe he knows her too."

"George didn't think so. In any case, wait until I get there. We'll do it together."

"All right. Be careful, sweetheart. We have no idea how fast these guys are going to accelerate."

"Will do. You too. Love you."

"Love you too. Bye."

Liam logged into their e-mail account and sent a request to Richard in England. He tried to do some searching himself, but the results he found came up in French, and his command of the language wasn't strong enough to catch nuances. The automatic translation to English was miserable. He copied the links and pasted them into an e-mail to Aidan.

He had just clicked Send on the message when he heard a tentative tap on the closed door. He got up and opened it to George. "Sorry, had to make a call," he said. "Did you think of anything else?"

George nodded.

Liam suppressed a sigh at the thought of another drawn-out series of questions and answers, and stepped back into the office, sitting behind the desk once again. He motioned George to the square metal chair across from him.

"A picnic," George said as he sat down.

"You and Vanina?" Liam asked.

"Yes. I wanted to show her the mine and how pretty the area around it is."

Liam picked up his pen. "When was this?"

George pressed his lips together and thought. "In January. Just before school began again after the Christmas holidays."

Liam added that information to his notes. "Does Vanina know where this office is?"

"Yes, she has visited here before." He looked at Liam. "But she could not have hurt Monsieur Perreau's car. She is not violent!"

"Maybe not. But she could be hanging around with violent people."

George sat there moping, and Liam wanted to send him back to his own office. But he tried to think about what Aidan would do in that situation. Even when he knew what he wanted to ask, he stumbled for the right word. "Vanina, *est-elle ta petite amie?*" he asked. Considering that French was the language of love, he found it somewhat inadequate when it came to the nuances of relationships. *Petite amie* literally meant "little female friend," which reminded him of being five or six and getting an extra present at Sharon Sullivan's birthday party because her mother said he was Sharon's "little boyfriend."

He ran through the other terms he knew. *Copine?* It could mean girlfriend, but just as easily a female friend.

George shifted uneasily in his chair. Maybe he had unfortunate connections to the term too. "We do not…"

Liam nodded. "I understand." George wanted to have sex with Vanina, but she wasn't interested. Then he caught himself. Jesus, he was starting to think like Aidan, as if everything revolved around sex. But from the look in George's eyes, it appeared Liam was on the mark.

"If we wanted to talk to Vanina, how could we find her?" he asked.

"She is a waitress at a café in Corte," he said. "*L'Auberge des Etudiants*. On the Cours Paoli in the center of town. She works each evening from six until ten."

Olivier appeared in the doorway, looking first at George, then at Liam. George hopped up from the chair. "I must return to work," he said, and he hurried past Olivier.

"My car is ready," Olivier said.

Liam turned off the computer and grabbed his notes. "Then let's go." In the elevator, he asked, "Were you able to speak with your contacts at Outremer?"

"It is not an easy process," he said. "I have begun the conversation. They are worried, of course. No one wants anyone to be hurt. But it will take time. Decisions must be made at the highest levels."

"I hope they decide quickly," Liam said.

Olivier hesitated, then asked, "You had questions for George?"

Liam realized, living with the Perreaus and speaking to them every day, that his French was not as bad as he'd thought—though sometimes the language still failed him. He wanted to say something innocuous about following up an idea, but couldn't find the words that would keep George out of trouble and at the same time allay any of Olivier's fears. So he just said, "Nothing much."

Olivier drove Agathe's car back to the dealership, and then Liam slid behind the wheel. As he waited for Olivier to retrieve his car, he considered the relationship between Michel and Cris. Could Cris be a pawn, being used by his father?

Liam hated dealing with touchy-feely issues. Until he met Aidan, sex had been a transaction to him. His few sexual encounters with girls and women had been something that was expected of him but not rewarding of itself. His first groping experiences with other men had been wild moments of unbridled passion followed by guilt and anxiety. When he finally pushed aside his Catholic upbringing, he'd looked at sex as adventure and fun.

It was only when he fell in love with Aidan that he allowed emotion to return to sex. Sometimes he felt like he'd fallen through a trap door, that opening his heart that way had exposed him to an almost unbelievable possibility of pain. He remembered what he had said to Perreau when confronted, that his first duty was to protect the client, not his partner. But could he do that? When faced with the choice between Aidan and one of the Perreaus, which would he choose?

Olivier walked out of the dealership dangling his keys in his hand and waved them at Liam. Liam waved back and watched as the man retrieved his car. Traffic was heavy on the Cours Grandval, and it took a few minutes for enough space to open up for both cars to turn. At least Perreau was savvy enough to wait, Liam thought.

As they climbed the Chemin de Loretto, past cypress trees and square stone homes, Liam returned to the question of Michel and Cris. It was Aidan's opinion that Cris had made the first move, because Michel was more obviously gay. But suppose there had been more to it than that—what if Cris had been directed to cultivate Michel's friendship?

He followed Olivier into the cul-de-sac and parked Agathe's car beside him. "Thank you," Olivier said when they were both walking toward the front door.

"Don't feel you have to thank me until this is all over," Liam said.

Olivier nodded. The front door opened, and Aidan stepped out. He nodded hello to Olivier and asked Liam, "Want to take a look around with me?"

"Sure."

Olivier went inside, and they walked around to the back of the house.

"Discover anything new?" Aidan asked.

"Other than that I'm starting to think like you?"

Aidan cocked his head. "Really?"

Liam described his second encounter with George Phthalis. "I was ready to move on when I thought about what you'd do in that situation. And it came to me right away—George and Vanina were dating. Or, as it happens, George wants to date Vanina but she's not interested."

"Which explains why he was trying to impress her with information about his job and the trip out to the mine for a picnic," Aidan said.

They sat beside the pool. A light breeze rippled the blue-green water and kept the chemical dispenser bobbing. "Uh-huh. And then, as I was waiting for Olivier at the dealership, I thought of something else."

"What's that?"

"What if Cris's father knows he's gay, and he sent Cris deliberately to seduce Michel, to get close to Olivier Perreau?"

Aidan leaned back in his chair. "That's awfully Machiavellian, Liam."

"It may be. But what's playing on your emotional radar? Does it make sense to you?"

"When I look at the two of them, I see puppy love," Aidan said. "They both seem to be crushing on each other. I don't see any ulterior motive going on, from either of them." He shrugged. "Cris could be acting, sure. But knowing the culture, I doubt his father is using him that way. Maybe if Cris was a girl. And maybe if there was no sex involved. But I think the chances are much greater that if Cris's father knew he was gay, he'd kick him out of the house."

"Could Cris be doing this on his own? You know, maybe a way to get in his father's good graces?" Liam asked. He thought of his own father. What might he have done if he'd thought there was a chance of gaining his father's love? He doubted he'd have gone very far; his own moral code was strong, and his father wasn't the type of man to inspire affection.

Aidan frowned. "That's a better possibility. But I'd have to know more about both of them to even begin to speculate." He leaned across and took Liam's hand. "But honestly, sweetheart? I think Cris really loves Michel."

Liam squeezed his hand and then released it, and they stood up and started to walk again. It was late afternoon, and the sun had begun to sink beyond the hills, bringing a chill to the air. A hawk soared on a thermal high above them.

After a moment, Liam said, "As long as we're speculating. Do you think other men are attracted to me?"

"Cris and Michel?" Aidan asked.

Liam shook his head. "Hassan. And maybe Louis too."

Aidan laughed. "Liam, you're gorgeous. Of course men are attracted to you."

"I've just never…"

"Liam. Listen to me. You have the kind of looks men swoon over in ads and porn magazines. Very masculine face, with the faintest traces of wear and tear—something guys who are into real men find very attractive. You have the physique of a bodybuilder without the creepy excess. You're smart and kind, and you have a sort of inner altar-boy vibe—that you have a strong moral core as well as the beautiful exterior."

"You just believe that because you love me."

They crossed the lawn in the direction of the hillside. "Obviously Louis must have said something when you spoke to him. What exactly did he say?"

Liam tried to remember the exact words. "Something like 'Hassan has a bit of a crush on you. But then who doesn't?'"

Aidan laughed again. "That's not news, Liam. You mean you never noticed the way Hassan looks at you?"

Liam was horrified. "What do you mean?"

"Not like you're a piece of meat, Liam. But like you're…I don't know, Prince Charming or something. Which of course you are, to me."

"You're exaggerating." Liam looked at Aidan. "But you can continue."

Aidan shook his head. "If you really knew how wonderful you

were, you'd be dangerous. I'll keep the rest of my opinions to myself." He leaned over and whispered, "However, when we're alone, I might be persuaded to go into further detail."

Liam laughed. "I'll hold you to that." They reached the trees at the back of the Perreau property, out of sight of the house, and he pulled Aidan close and kissed him. "Consider that a down payment," he said.

18 – L'Auberge

Aidan's lips tingled where Liam had kissed him. They walked around the woods for a few minutes, checking out the views back to the house, and then returned the way they had come, across the lawn and around the pool. As they approached the house, Olivier stepped out the back door. "My wife's close friend has invited us for dinner," he said. "She would like to go, but their home is small and it would be awkward to bring additional guests."

"Would Michel go with you?" Liam asked.

Olivier nodded. "They have a son a few years younger, just ready to attend university. He and Michel are friends."

Aidan leaned over to whisper to Liam. "If we can get Paul Dubois to keep an eye on the Perreaus tonight, we can go up to Corte together and talk to Vanina."

"Good idea," Liam said. He turned to Olivier. "Aidan and I would like to do some research, but we don't want to leave your family unprotected. The Agence has a contact here in Corsica. Let me call him and see if I can arrange to have him escort you to dinner and remain outside the house until you're finished, then bring you back home."

He picked up his cell phone and walked over to the swimming pool. "I hope Liam can get this guy to help us," Aidan said to Olivier. "It would be good for you and your family to have a nice evening, away from your troubles."

"Yes, that is what I hope." They stood there awkwardly, neither speaking, until Liam returned.

"A man named Paul Dubois will be here at six o'clock," he said. "He'll remain with you until we return."

"That is excellent," Olivier said. "I will tell Agathe."

They followed Olivier inside, where they found Agathe in the kitchen with Maria. "Thank you for allowing us these arrangements," she said.

"We'd like to go up to Corte," Liam said. "To speak to someone. It's all right if we take your car up there?"

"Certainly," Agathe said. "But it is not a quick trip. You will need at least one hour and a half in each direction."

Aidan and Liam returned to their room. "I'll check for e-mail," Liam said. "You want to pack up whatever you think we might need?"

"Sure." Aidan pulled out a day pack and began loading it with a pair of long-range binoculars, two small flashlights, a notepad and pen, a map of the island, and a microcassette recorder. At a few minutes before six, they heard a car pull into the driveway, Aidan picked up the pack, and they walked out of the bedroom and into the hall.

Liam stepped out the front door, and Aidan watched from the window as a man emerged from the battered Fiat. Dubois had salt-and-pepper hair and black eyeglasses with round frames that gave him an owlish appearance. After a few minutes' conversation, Liam and Dubois came inside, and Liam introduced Dubois to him.

Aidan was always intrigued to meet other operatives. He had read a lot of Hammett and Chandler in his twenties, and his image of the private eye had come from that. He was surprised that Dubois appeared so mild-mannered—not the hard-drinking, two-fisted, careworn guy of fiction.

Agathe and Olivier came downstairs then, and Liam carried out further introductions. When they were finished, Olivier called back upstairs. "Michel, we are ready to leave. Now!"

Michel clumped down the stairs, and they all walked outside. As Olivier locked the house, Agathe asked, "Do you know the way to Corte?"

"I think so," Liam said. "Just follow the N193, right?"

"Correct."

Liam used the long-handled mirror to check under both cars. "Necessary?" Dubois whispered to Aidan.

"There was an incident yesterday. Just a smoke bomb, but we have to be very careful."

Dubois nodded. Liam finished his inspections and gave the all-clear.

Michel pulled Aidan aside as they walked to the cars. "You're not going to Corte to talk to Cris, are you?" he demanded.

"No. A girl named Vanina Andreadi," Aidan said. "Do you know her?"

Michel looked confused. "Just casually. She's been in some classes with me. Why are you talking to her?"

"Just for background," Aidan said. He held the back door of

Olivier's sedan open for Michel, who tried to protest. Aidan gave him a gentle shove on the shoulder to move him into the car. "See you later."

Liam joined him by Agathe's car, and they watched Dubois follow Olivier in the Fiat, out to the Rue des Magnolias and then farther up the hill. "You know where we're going?" Aidan asked.

"I can get us to Corte. After that we'll have to look for the restaurant."

Aidan slipped into the passenger seat, laying the day pack on the floor but keeping the map handy, just in case.

The N193 to Corte ran through the hilly, forested heart of the island. Evening fell as they entered the national park, and Aidan thought it was eerie driving along the curving, unlit roads, passing only the occasional car or motorcycle.

"What do you think this girl's role is?" Aidan asked. "Michel said he barely knows her."

"No idea yet. But she's a connection, certainly. She's in the same program with Michel, and she's involved with this group somehow, these Students for a Green Corsica. She knows George Phthalis, and she's been to Olivier's office and to the mine." Liam looked over at him. "Don't start spinning your stories yet. She may be totally irrelevant to what we're looking for."

Aidan snorted and looked out the window as lights appeared ahead, welcoming after the darkness of the woods. The old capital city, Corte nestled at the meeting of two enormous gorges, the Restonica and the Tavignano. On their way into the city, they drove through the Campus Grimaldi, past parking lots, playing fields and high-rise dormitories, all lit with tall mercury-vapor streetlights. Aidan felt oddly at home in a college environment, though he had not taught full-time for years. He wondered if he would ever lose the feeling that he was a teacher at heart, just playing at being a bodyguard in order to please Liam.

Mountains loomed in the distance, lit only by a few tiny moving pinpricks, the headlights of cars or trucks. "It's a shame we couldn't come up here in daylight," Aidan said, looking wistfully at the landscape. "I'm sure it's beautiful."

"We're not sightseeing, Aidan."

Aidan crossed his arms over his chest. "Just saying."

They crossed a bridge over the Restonica River, then kept left onto the Avenue Jean Nicoli. The narrow streets in the center of town were lined with small shops and student hangouts. The sidewalks were crowded with jeans-clad students toting backpacks. Some of the stucco walls were spattered with nationalist graffiti, often a realistic image of a man with a bandanna tied around his forehead, and the slogan *Corsica Nazione*.

As the streets steepened, Aidan realized that close-up, Corte was a grungy place, with litter in the streets and cracks in the sidewalk. Many of the old-fashioned streetlights were out. Liam had to navigate carefully to the Cours Paoli, then turn up a steep side street and maneuver Agathe's small car into a minuscule parking space.

Aidan stepped out of the car, inhaling the cool, refreshing mountain air. He breathed deeply and looked around. He had spent his college years at Penn, in the middle of West Philadelphia, and the city encroached on its edges—a few blocks from campus, the streets had been rough and downtrodden. One year he had traveled to Penn State for a long New Year's Eve weekend. State College was nestled in a valley much like Corte was, and Aidan had the same sense of entering a world ruled by the young.

Penn State dominated its environment, and Corte was the same way. Every store window catered to a student population, from the clothes on sale to the ads for computers and used textbooks. The town fathers appeared to have given up on policing the trash and graffiti.

Aidan followed Liam back down the steep hill, avoiding a motorbike that veered very close to them. The Auberge des Etudiants was a few blocks away on the Cours Paoli. When they stepped inside, Aidan felt as if he'd walked into a cave. The stucco ceiling was low and curved, with torch-like lights mounted into niches along the walls. The female staff wore broad blue skirts with white blouses, the long sleeves pushed up to the elbows.

The restaurant was only half-full, mostly young students clustered around large tables. "We'd like a table with Vanina," Aidan told the hostess. "We've been told she's the best."

"The prettiest, perhaps," the hostess said somewhat sourly. "Follow me."

Aidan shared a glance with Liam, who raised his eyebrow.

They sat at a table for two along the wall and perused the heavy, leather-covered menu. The dishes were a mix of French and Italian, focused on the native wild boar, veal, and lamb.

After a few minutes, Aidan looked around. "I'll bet that's Vanina," he said, nodding to a slim but buxom waitress lounging against the wall across from them, talking to a table of young male students. She had lustrous black hair pulled back from her face and cascading in ringlets down her back.

Her white blouse seemed to be cut lower than those of the other waitresses, to show off her ample cleavage. Aidan caught her eye and beckoned to her with his index finger.

She said something that made the boys laugh, and then ambled over to Liam and Aidan. "Bonsoir, Vanina," Aidan said.

She looked at him. "Do I know you?"

He shook his head. "But we've heard a lot about you. We'll start with a bottle of Vermentino, and the *prisutu* appetizer." He looked at Liam and said, "Smoked ham."

Liam nodded and smiled at Vanina. She appeared confused at their familiarity.

"We'll both have the *agneau corse*, the roasted lamb," Aidan said. He closed the menu and handed it to her. "Thank you."

She took the menus and walked away, still looking uncertain.

"Think we'll get what we ordered?" Liam asked. "Doesn't look like her elevator goes all the way to the top."

"I think we caught her off balance," Aidan said. "Though I have the feeling she doesn't care much about waitressing."

She returned a few minutes later with a bottle of the white Corsican wine and two glasses. She had trouble with the bottle opener, so Liam said, "Let me."

While Liam opened the wine, Aidan asked, "You study political science?"

She nodded. "How do you know who I am?"

"We have some mutual friends who are very interested in the future of this beautiful island and in what Students for a Green Corsica can accomplish," Aidan said.

Liam popped the cork and handed the wine bottle to Vanina, who poured a glass for each of them.

"We'd like to talk to you if you ever get a break," Aidan said.

She looked around. "I talk when I want."

"How do you feel Students for a Green Corsica can best make a difference?"

It was as if a different person had stepped into Vanina's body. "We must take a stand against outside interferences," she said, becoming animated for the first time. "Keep the land pristine for generations to come. Refuse to agree to new construction that will make us a clone of Ibiza or St. Tropez. Deny the despoliation of the land."

Aidan nodded. "Those are worthy goals. But can a group of students accomplish any of that?"

"With the help of those who care about Corsica," she said. "Men like Nic Aquaviva, who are not afraid to say what needs to be said."

The male students from the other table called for Vanina, and she turned away from Aidan and Liam.

"The hostess was right," Liam said as he lifted his wineglass.

"Vanina's not a very good waitress."

"Just because she didn't pour a little wine in your glass for you to sample?" Aidan asked. He tasted the wine. "It's fine, anyway."

"It's her whole attitude," Liam said. "The way she only came alive when you asked about her activism."

"Well, we know she likes Cris's father," Aidan said.

Vanina returned a few minutes later with the smoked ham appetizer. It was cool, as if it had been sitting out on the counter waiting for her to pick it up.

She drifted away before Aidan could ask her anything more. She dropped off their roasted lamb platters, still warm, but immediately turned back to the student table. By the time Aidan and Liam were finished, though, the students had left, and they appeared to be Vanina's only customers.

"How do you think Nic Aquaviva can make a difference?" Aidan asked as she slouched back to their table to pick up the dirty dishes.

"He is an amazing man. He is an example of how Corsica tries to ruin its best men and women. He has a great intellect, but he could not go to university and was forced to work as a fisherman."

"At least he's not afraid to get his hands dirty," Aidan said. "In many ways, I suppose."

Vanina looked confused but said, "He is willing to take action for his principles. Whether that is in protest or in something stronger. Only time will tell what will be required."

They ordered cappuccino and chestnut-flour beignets for dessert, and Vanina floated away.

"I can see a connection," Liam said. "George tells Vanina about the mine, and then she passes the information on to Aquaviva."

"I agree. I doubt it would take much prompting from Vanina to get George to spill whatever details she wants."

"She's a student, so she must know how to use a computer and have access to a printer at the university," Liam said. "She could have prepared the threats for Aquaviva."

"If he's a fisherman, he must have some level of mechanical skill," Aidan said. "To keep his boat's engine going, for example. He could know how to put together a simple bomb like the one under Olivier's car."

"I agree," Liam said as Vanina returned, awkwardly balancing a tray of coffee cups and beignets.

Aidan watched her approach the table, the tray bouncing up and down, the espresso cups sliding. Could she deliver everything without a disaster? She managed somehow. The last thing she dropped on the table was the check. "I have to leave soon," she said. "Can you pay now?"

Liam again raised an eyebrow to Aidan, but he opened his wallet and pulled out a credit card. "We don't take those," she said. "Cash only."

Aidan could tell Liam was struggling to maintain his temper. "No problem," he said, pulling euros out of his wallet and dropping them on the table for Vanina to retrieve.

When she was gone, Aidan said, "This is why European restaurants should take tips. Otherwise the servers have no incentive to do a good job."

"I think Vanina has very specific incentives," Liam said. "And I'm willing to bet Cris's father has something to do with those."

19 – Laurenzia

Michel found it hard to focus at dinner. His parents seemed able to put aside the threats they had received, and they chatted and laughed with their friends. But he couldn't help thinking about the threats and how they might impact any chances he had of a future with Cris.

Though he hadn't admitted it was a fantasy, Michel had been thinking there was a chance he and Cris could live together in Ajaccio. They would both get jobs in the capital and present themselves to their families as college friends who had chosen to share an apartment.

But that could never come to pass if Cris's father was behind the threats. Neither set of parents would agree. And suppose Michel's father had Nic Aquaviva arrested and sent to jail? Cris might never want to see Michel again.

He moped through dinner, ignoring all conversation, and was relieved when they left for home. His father immediately went into his office, but his mother asked him to remain in the living room with her. "Sit down," she said, pointing to the easy chair. "I know this whole business has been very upsetting for you, but you are almost an adult now, and you must accept the situation. You cannot go on as you did tonight. You were very rude."

"I want to go back to college," Michel said defiantly.

"That may not be possible. I think you should be prepared for us to return to Paris. This mine project may prove too dangerous. I am trying to convince your father to sell the whole thing to Outremer and go back to work for them."

Michel was horrified. Go back to Paris? Leave Cris in Corsica? That was even worse than anything he'd anticipated. "I don't want to go back there. My life is here."

"There are engineering jobs in Paris. If you need additional credentials, you can always go to a university there." She smiled. "Remember how happy you were in Paris?"

"I was a child," Michel said, crossing his arms over his chest. How could his mother compare the two experiences? And how could she be so blasé when their world was falling apart around them?

"I don't want to talk about this," he said, and he ran up to his room, taking the stairs two at a time. All he could think about was the desire to call Cris, to talk to him about everything. The awful way he felt all the time when he was away from Cris, and the horrible idea that his parents might force him to move to Paris. And then there was Vanina Andreadi. He hardly knew the girl, but Cris did. She was always hanging around the football team. And she knew Cris's father too.

He curled up under the covers and dialed Cris. "The bodyguards went up to Corte tonight," he said when Cris answered.

"They didn't talk to me," Cris said.

"No, they said they were going to that girl Vanina. The one who saw us in the boat the last time we went to the waterfall. She knows your father, remember? We saw her talking to him that day."

"She's just a pretty airhead," Cris said. "I talked to her after that. She didn't even mention seeing us."

"She's involved with that group, isn't she? Students for a Green Corsica? Are the bodyguards making connections between her and that group and your father?"

"I've told you over and over. My father would not make threats or commit violence. He is a good and honorable man."

"But he hates my family."

It took a while for Cris to answer. "I don't think we should see each other for a while. Until all this is ended."

"No!" Michel cried. "You can't leave me."

"I'm not leaving you, my little cabbage. I'm just saying…"

Michel began to cry. "I'll die without you."

"Oh Michel," Cris said. "Don't be so dramatic. You won't die. Now I have to meet my study group at the library to prepare for our government final. I'll call you after I finish." He hung up, and Michel sat there staring at the phone.

When he looked up, Aidan was standing in the doorway of his room. "I heard the last part of your conversation," he said.

Michel could not stop crying.

"May I come in?" Aidan asked.

Michel nodded. "My life is over. Cris is breaking up with me, and my family will have to move back to France."

Aidan sat down on the bed next to Michel. "Did Cris say he wanted to break up?"

"He said he didn't want to see me for a while."

"That's not exactly the same thing," Aidan said. He put his arm around Michel's shoulders, and Michel leaned into him, still sniffling. "This is a difficult time for both of you. I think Cris is wise to suggest that you hold back a little."

"But what if he doesn't come back to me?"

"You'll feel like your heart has broken and there's no reason to go on living," Aidan said. "But after some time, the pain will be less, and then less again. And then you will meet someone else…"

"There is no one else for me but Cris."

"Trust me, I've felt exactly as you do now. Have I told you about the man I lived with in Philadelphia? Blake?"

"A little."

"When he kicked me out, I felt like my world was ending. All I wanted to do was run away. And I had spent eleven years with him."

"How did you get over him?"

"I met Liam. And I started to see Blake differently."

Michel straightened up. "There is something you don't know," he said.

"Really? What's that?"

"Cris's father hates my family."

"You've said that before. He's angry about the mine."

"No, there's more. He thinks my mother is responsible for his daughter's death."

Aidan released his hold on Michel's shoulder and turned to face him. "Really? How?"

"Laurenzia had a tumor that was pressing against her lungs and making it difficult for her to breathe. My mother is the one who diagnosed her and recommended she go to a hospital in France. She didn't believe there was anyone in Corsica who could do the surgery."

Aidan withdrew a tissue from his pocket and handed it to Michel. "That's so sad. Did they take her to France?"

Michel blew his nose. He still felt that achy, empty space in his stomach. "They have no money, and it took a long time for the arrangements to be made. While they waited, the little girl died. Cris's father thinks there must have been something my mother could have done to save her."

Michel looked at Aidan. "Cris's father doesn't understand that she did the best she could. Because she is the one who identified what was wrong with Laurenzia but didn't save her, he blames her. And that has made him even more angry about the mine."

"Why?" Aidan asked.

"I think that maybe in his head, he has mixed the two things up—Laurenzia's death and the reopening of the mine. He believes that we are evil people, and that we have to be stopped before we can cause more damage."

"This is not good," Aidan said.

"What if Cris knows his father has made these threats, but he hasn't wanted to tell me?" Michel asked. It was almost too horrible to contemplate, but that would explain his boyfriend's actions. "That's why he doesn't want to see me."

Aidan put his arm around Michel's shoulders again. "Let's give

Cris some time. I know it's tough, but sometimes the things that matter most to us are the ones that take the most sacrifice to achieve."

What more could he sacrifice, Michel thought, now that he had given up his heart?

20 – STUPID IN LOVE

Liam was checking e-mail when Aidan walked into the bedroom. "I just spoke to Michel, and it turns out that Nic Aquaviva has a grudge against Agathe Perreau for his daughter's death." He explained what Michel had told him.

"It gives him an even stronger motive," Liam said. "We have to call Bonnet and have Michel speak to him."

"Hold off for a little while," Aidan said. "I'd hate to break up Michel and Cris. And we don't want to send the police off in the wrong direction. It's a connection, but I'm not sure it's a motive."

"I'm going to take a walk outside, and then I want to talk to Michel myself," Liam said. "Just to make sure he's all right and that he's not going to try something stupid."

"Such as?" Aidan asked.

"Such as sneaking out to meet Cris again. If he's worried the boy is breaking up with him, I wouldn't be surprised if he tried to run up to Corte to see him."

"All right. I'll be here when you get back."

Liam walked outside, his mind a jumble of thoughts and memories. Visiting the college town had made him think about education—which was one of the biggest differences between him and Aidan. He had gone into the military straight out of high school, and though he'd taken classes and gotten his associate's degree while he was in the Navy he'd never had the real college experience. He had given up on studying toward his bachelor's when he joined the SEALs; his job was too hard and too irregular to allow him to focus on studying.

Aidan had not only an Ivy League college degree, but a master's on top of it. Sometimes Liam felt like the dumb one in the partnership, the one who had to use brawn instead of brains. He knew Aidan would never say that—but that was because he was so sweet.

Could he go back to college at his age? There were plenty of online programs. At least he could get a bachelor's degree in something—maybe criminal justice, maybe business. Just to have some backup in place when he was too old to run around after bad guys.

A cracking noise brought him back to the present. He paused in the shadow of the house, listening carefully. When the sound repeated, he identified it—just wind through the trees on the hillside. When he was satisfied there was no human out there, he continued his walk, now thinking about what Vanina had said. Every indicator pointed at Nic Aquaviva as being behind the threats to the Perreaus, and now they had an idea of how he might have had the computer-printed pages generated.

If Cris's father was responsible for the threats, that would destroy the relationship between Michel and Cris. But they were young, and they'd find other lovers in the future. Look at him and Aidan—they hadn't hooked up until they were both in their thirties. Sometimes it paid to wait until you became the person you were destined to be before finding your true love.

He walked back into the house and got Aidan. They climbed the stairs to the second floor, and Liam rapped on Michel's closed door. "Michel? It's Aidan and Liam. We'd like to talk to you."

There was no response.

Had the boy already run off? Liam wondered. Yes, he could be that stupid. He was in love after all. He held up a finger to Aidan, who appeared ready to knock again. He touched the doorknob, and it turned easily.

He pushed the door open, expecting to find the bedroom empty and the window open, a breeze blowing the curtains inward. But instead he saw Michel sitting on his bed, head down to his knees, earphones in his ears.

"Michel," Liam said, and the boy looked up. He pulled the earphones off.

"Sorry, but you didn't answer when we knocked," Aidan said. He walked over and sat on the bed next to the boy. "How are you holding up?"

"I am very sad," Michel said.

Liam was glad Aidan was there. His partner sat with the boy, comforting him in a low voice. "So you understand," Aidan said, "why we have to wait before we do anything."

Michel nodded. "Do you think he will come back to me?"

Not if you keep crying, Liam thought, but he didn't say anything.

"I don't know," Aidan said. "But I've seen the way Cris looks at you, and the way he treats you. He cares about you a lot. You need to have faith in that and hold on."

"You're not going to sneak away again, are you?" Liam asked. "Because you know we'd catch you."

"Cris is studying for his exams," Michel said. "Which I should be doing too. No, we won't see each other. At least not for a few days."

Aidan patted him on the back. "That's a good idea. You're both upset and worried. This will all pass over; you'll see."

Liam agreed that it would pass—though he had a feeling the situation would not play out to Michel's satisfaction. As they walked back downstairs, he said to Aidan, "You have so much more patience than I do. I admire that."

"Really?" Aidan turned to look at him. "I've seen the way you can slow yourself down when you have to wait for something. It's remarkable. I can't do that."

"What I mean is that you have more patience with people," Liam said. "You're right; I don't mind shutting down and going into waiting mode. But dealing with crybabies—that's a whole different skill."

Aidan stepped ahead to open the door to the guest room. "He's not a crybaby, Liam. His whole world is falling apart. It's natural for him to be upset."

"Hardly his whole world," Liam said, following him inside. "I've seen kids way younger than he is watch their houses burn, see their whole families slaughtered. Kids in refugee camps with big eyes and empty bellies. His problems are nothing compared to that."

"But they're his problems. Yes, he's been spoiled. But haven't you ever had your heart broken?"

Liam thought about it. What did that mean, to have your heart broken? Had his been broken when his father got drunk and beat him? When men he had bonded with in the heat of battle were suddenly vaporized by IEDs?

He knew what Aidan was really saying, though. "I never loved anyone before you. And you're still with me."

"Oh, Liam," Aidan said. He stepped up to Liam and kissed the side of his cheek. "Somehow that's even sadder."

"Just stay with me, all right?" Liam said. He reached out and took Aidan in his arms. "I don't ever want to feel what Michel's feeling."

"All I can promise you is that I'll do my best," Aidan said.

Their mouths connected, and Liam inhaled Aidan's breath, which tasted like wine and sugar, coffee and the spiciness of the roasted lamb. As their bodies pressed together, he felt an ache in his chest, unconnected to the sexual desire he usually felt with Aidan. What would happen if they broke up? If Aidan died? Could he pull some reserve from his guts and carry on? He'd have to, of course. Years as a SEAL had trained him to never quit, never give up. But the thought of having to go on alone, after he'd finally opened himself up to someone else? That would be damned hard.

"About that down payment you made earlier," Aidan said, his hands moving slowly down Liam's back toward his waist.

"Oh, that," Liam said, remembering the kiss they had shared earlier that evening at the base of the hill.

"Yes, that," Aidan said.

Liam pulled his polo shirt over his head. He caught a glimpse of himself in the mirror, his broad chest, narrow waist, bulging pecs, his nipple rings. He did have a great body.

He turned back to his partner, who had already shucked his shirt, shoes, and slacks, and stood there in only a pair of boxers printed with tropical fish, his stiff dick pressing forward against the fabric.

"You're a goofball," he said to Aidan, pulling him close.

"Me? Why?"

"Those boxer shorts."

"Just because you like plain vanilla doesn't mean I always do," Aidan said. He reached over and slid his hands behind the waistband of Liam's slacks, over his butt cheeks.

"Would you rather have chocolate?" Liam asked.

"Been there, done that," Aidan said. "Long ago, of course. Even before Blake."

"Seriously? You've had sex with a black guy?" Liam pulled back.

"Sure. You haven't?"

Liam shook his head. "Closest I came to that was Abdullah."

Abdullah was a queeny young Tunisian who hung out at the Bar Mamounia—the bar across the courtyard from their house in Tunis. Aidan didn't like Abdullah, and the feeling was mutual. Liam had fooled around with Abdullah a few times before meeting Aidan, and Abdullah had made it abundantly clear he was up anytime for another session. Liam had to admit it had been a relief to leave Abdullah behind in Tunis, shacked up in the little house behind the Bar Mamounia with his ex-soldier boyfriend.

Aidan began kissing his way down Liam's chest, undoing Liam's belt as he did. Liam remembered how different sex with Abdullah had been—the slim Tunisian's supple skin, the firm globes of his mocha-tinged ass. He realized his dick had stiffened.

Was that because of Aidan's ministrations? Or because of the memory of sex with Abdullah?

He groaned as Aidan shoved his pants down, and his dick pronged back. He wore only a jockstrap under his slacks; he liked the ease and freedom it provided, while protecting his valuable assets.

Aidan went down on his knees and began licking Liam's dick up and down through the cotton fabric of the jockstrap.

Aidan got such a sexual thrill over Liam's underwear. Liam didn't get it. Underwear was something to be shucked as soon as possible so you could get to the sex. That's the way it had always been with men before Aidan.

Sometimes he regretted the fact that he hadn't had much experience before settling down with Aidan. He hadn't been a virgin, of course, but being in the military for so long had restricted his chances and choices. He'd been careful only to hook up on leave, and anonymously. After his discharge, he'd lived with his mother in New Jersey for a while, further limiting his opportunities, then moved to Tunis.

The new openness that came with his life with Aidan showed him how much he had missed. Sexy young guys who were always horny and could come multiple times in one session. Older men full of tricks and techniques. Slim, hairless guys and beefy bears covered in hair. Redheads, blonds, and brunets. Skin colors from the blue-black of Africans to the mocha of South Asians to the pale white of Scandinavians.

But he'd given up on all that variety when he committed to Aidan. Or had he? He'd never broached the idea of bringing anyone else into their bedroom, and neither had Aidan. Nor had either of them ever considered an open relationship, giving either the chance for sexual exploration.

What if Louis or Hassan had proposed group sex—or a swap? Would Aidan have gone along with it?

"You're very excited tonight," Aidan said, looking up from Liam's crotch. "You don't often get this hard."

Aidan peeled the jockstrap down, and Liam's dick jumped forward, the head pushing beyond its protective cowl. Yeah, it was very hard, he thought. His balls had tightened and pulled up close to the base, like they knew something good was coming.

Liam pushed all thoughts of other men out of his head. He dropped the jock and stepped out of it, and then took Aidan's hand and led him to the bed. He knew just the way his partner liked things, and there was comfort in that. No performance anxiety.

He pushed Aidan lightly down to the bed and then climbed on top of him, resting his body against his partner's so they touched in a hundred places. He leaned down and they kissed, and then began to rub his body against Aidan's. He could feel the roll of his nipple rings against Aidan's chest.

Did he feel guilty about imagining other men? He worked to make sure Aidan was pleased—he knew that one of his partner's favorite turn-ons was when he had to struggle for breath against his approaching orgasm, from the pressure of Liam's body against his, having his mouth occupied with kissing.

He felt Aidan's pulse quickening beneath him, and that drove him forward. He pressed and rubbed, and the bed began to shake. He knew he ought to stop before he attracted attention from anyone in the house, but he couldn't help himself. He was driven forward by his own needs and the desire to please Aidan.

"I want you in me," Aidan said, lightly pushing him away. "The lube is in the green bag in the armoire."

Liam didn't want to stop to change positions. But it was what Aidan wanted, and that's what mattered. He pulled back, his dick uncomfortably stiff and leaking precome. The only light in the room was the bedside lamp, which cast a comforting glow as he opened the door of the armoire and looked for the green bag.

Liam had to bend forward to reach the bag, at the back of the cabinet, and his ass pointed back at Aidan on the bed.

"I will never get tired of looking at your ass," Aidan said. "It's a work of art."

Liam grabbed the bottle of lube and stood up, his dick banging against his abdomen. "You are such a horndog," he said, but he smiled. All those hours working out were worth the effort if his body pleased Aidan this much.

Aidan leaned back against the pillows and raised his legs. Liam knelt on the bed beside him and squirted some lube in his hand, then began stroking the area around Aidan's hole and the sensitive spot behind his balls. Aidan groaned with pleasure and lust and said, "You're teasing me."

"I'm just getting you ready," Liam said. "No howling tonight, all right? There are straight people in the house."

"I'll be quiet," Aidan said. "Just please, Liam, fuck me."

"At your service," Liam said, and he positioned his dick at Aidan's puckered hole. He grabbed Aidan's thighs and pushed, and Aidan's intake of breath told him he had hit his target.

The only man who had ever fucked him was Aidan, who was circumcised, and Liam wondered if it would feel differently to have a man in him who wasn't. When he fucked Aidan, did that extra bit of foreskin make a difference?

Aidan took a couple of deep breaths, and Liam thrust forward as his partner winced. "All right?" Liam asked.

"Better than all right," Aidan said.

Liam prided himself on his control, his ability to move slowly in and out of Aidan's ass, prolonging the pleasure for both of them, but that night he couldn't hold back. His body took on a rhythm of its own, his forward thrusts matching Aidan's as his balls slapped against Aidan's skin.

He reached around and grasped Aidan's dick and began stroking it. Aidan's body tensed beneath him, and Aidan said, "Oh, oh, oh," his voice low and husky. Then he gulped and inhaled sharply, and

Liam felt the warm spurt of semen against his hand. That was enough to push him over the edge. His body shook with the power of his orgasm.

He stayed inside Aidan as long as he could, his dick softening, looking Aidan in the eyes, feeling all that lust and longing welling up inside him. He finally pulled out and slumped beside Aidan, his partner nestling against him.

The morning would bring a resumption of their problems. Whoever was behind the threats would not give up. The Perreaus would remain in danger, and it would be up to Liam and Aidan to keep them safe. Liam tried to think about plans for the next day, but he was asleep before he could formulate any coherent thoughts.

21 – Unexpected Visitor

Liam woke early Thursday morning, his body uncomfortably sticky, and he cleaned up in the bathroom before going outside to exercise. By the time he had finished working out and showering, he found Aidan already in the kitchen with Maria, the two of them gossiping in French like a pair of hens. Liam swallowed his immediate irritation, reminding himself he and his partner had different skills that complemented each other. Who knew what interesting information the maid might be able to impart.

They stopped speaking as soon as Liam walked in, and he couldn't help feeling like he had been the subject of the conversation, foolish as that seemed. He smiled, though, and took his seat at the table. Maria had bought a fresh boule at the market, and he sensed Aidan's hand in that.

The Perreaus joined them soon after. Olivier had some paperwork to complete, which he could do from his home office. Agathe was going to relax in the living room and enjoy her day off. Michel would be in his room, studying for his upcoming exams. Liam left Aidan in the spare bedroom to check e-mail and took a long, slow walk around the house and grounds, becoming increasingly irritated that he couldn't find anything suspicious.

When he returned to the house, it seemed like every room was occupied. He was usually able to still himself, watch and wait, but having nothing to focus on made him restless. After lunch, he pulled

Aidan aside. "Come take a walk with me," he said.

"What's wrong with you, Liam?" Aidan asked when they were out of hearing. "You've been as nervous as a rabbit all morning."

"I've got a bad feeling. Everything's too quiet."

"You said yesterday that the nationalists or terrorists or whoever would give us a day or two to react to the car bomb."

"I know. But there wasn't any note with the bomb or any follow-up. Why not?"

"I don't know, Liam. Maybe they figure we already know what they want."

Liam shook his head. "These people aren't subtle."

Aidan was about to say something else, but Liam noticed movement at the base of the hill, and he put his hand on Aidan's arm to stop him. He said in a soft voice, "We may have an intruder. There's cover over there behind the pool chairs. Be ready to run on my motion."

He pivoted slowly on his right foot, shielding Aidan with his body. He felt as tense as a bowstring, and he regretted not carrying his gun with him.

Then Cris Aquaviva leaned out from behind a tree.

Liam looked toward him and focused on keeping his voice even. "There a reason why you didn't come to the front door?"

"I don't want Michel to know I'm here. May I talk with you?"

Aidan started forward, but Liam held a hand out. "Careful, Aidan, We don't know that he's alone."

"I am by myself," Cris said. "But if I step out, Michel may see me."

"The clearing," Aidan said. "If Cris climbs up there, we can see him."

Liam nodded. "Go back to the place where we met you last night. We'll follow."

Cris faded back into the trees. Liam gave him a minute to move away, and then approached the woods carefully, all his senses on alert. Why had the boy returned? Was he an advance guard for his father, or his father's group?

He scanned the narrow path, looking from left to right, up to down. A drab brown bird jumped from one branch to another, and something slithered in the underbrush. But it appeared Cris was alone.

Liam motioned Aidan to follow. He climbed quietly through the woods, looking around and above. The tall chestnut trees stretched high, their canopies framing brief bits of blue sky. When he came to the clearing, he saw Cris standing in the center.

He motioned Aidan to stay under cover. "What's this about?" he asked as he stepped out of the woods.

"I need to talk to you," Cris said. "About my father."

Aidan stepped out beside Liam. He never followed instructions, Liam thought.

"Your last name is Aquaviva," Aidan said. "There's a terrorist leader by that name. He's your father, isn't he?"

Cris shook his head. "My father is not a terrorist. But he is very opposed to Michel's father and his plan to reopen the mine."

"Let's sit down," Liam said. He motioned Cris to join them in a patch of shade. "I want to hear about a group called Students for a Green Corsica."

Cris looked surprised. "It's just a club of university students. Why do you want to know about them?"

"Do you know a girl named Vanina Andreadi?"

"Sure. She belongs to the group, and she's in some of my classes. Another political science student."

"How about your father?" Liam asked. "Is he a member of this group too?"

Cris looked down at the ground. "No, but he came to talk a couple of times. Many of the members agree with his ideas."

Aidan leaned back on his hands. "Let's step back for a second. Why don't you tell us about your father? What kind of man is he?"

Liam looked over at him. He never liked it when Aidan took control of an interrogation, but he recognized that his partner had the people skills he sometimes lacked.

A light breeze rattled the dead leaves on the ground. "He's a good man, you must understand that," Cris said.

Liam looked at him and felt Cris really believed that. If you'd asked Liam about his dad when he was Cris's age, he'd have said quite the opposite. A son can be his father's worst critic or most fervent defender, he thought. It was clear which camp Cris fell into.

"I grew up in a small town called Cargése, on the north coast," Cris said, leaning forward. "My father fishes those waters, like his father and his grandfather before him. He wanted something better for me, so he pushed me to stay in school and to play football so that I could get a scholarship to the university. I owe him everything."

"How did he turn into an activist?" Aidan asked.

"It was a few years ago. One spring, a farmer used pesticide on his land, and right after he applied it, there were terrible rains. The poison ran down into the sea and killed all the fish."

He wrinkled his nose. "I was a boy then, and the other boys of the town and I helped our fathers clear the dead fish from the beach and bury them. My father was very angry, especially because there was no punishment for the farmer who caused so much damage. It took many years for the waters to be healthy again and for the fish to return. He had to spend much more time on the ocean, travel much farther, in order to catch enough. It was very difficult."

He looked down at the ground. "He even believes the sickness of the fish is what caused my little sister to become ill, to have trouble with breathing. Michel's mother, she said this was not true, that the problem was with Laurenzia from when she was born."

"How angry was he?" Aidan asked gently.

"Oh no, not in the way you are thinking," Cris said, looking up at them. "He would never hurt someone or cause damage. He began to go to Ajaccio sometimes to talk to politicians. He organized the people to complain when bad things happen."

"Why is he opposed to the mine Michel's father wants to reopen?"

"He's worried there will be runoff from the mine that would pollute the ocean water off the coast, where he and other men fish. If the fish die, he has no way to support our family. And maybe chemicals will kill other children like my sister."

Liam unhooked his legs and stretched them out ahead of him. "I understand that," he said. "Any man would care about providing for his family. But there is a step beyond caring to causing harm to others."

"He would not," Cris said, shaking his head. "I know my father."

"You know Michel's father has received some threatening letters," Aidan said. "Do you think your father sent them?"

"I don't know. But I am worried."

"Does your father have a computer?" Aidan asked.

Cris shook his head. "He only graduated from the *école élémentaire* in the village at eleven before he had to join his father in the fishing boats. He could not go to the Collège Camille Borossi in Vico, where I went, and he does not type." He looked at them. "These letters, they were prepared on a computer?"

Liam shifted his legs again. When he was a SEAL, he could have stayed in position for hours. Was he getting old, only halfway through his thirties? "Do you think someone could have written them for him?" he asked.

"I don't know. He has a group of men and women who follow him, as well as some of the students. One of them may know computers."

"Can you find out?" Liam asked. "Don't ask your father directly. Can you get us a list of the people who belong to his group?"

"You are asking me to spy on my father!"

"You're the one who came to us," Liam said. "You must be worried. I can either pass this information to the police, or…"

"No! No police. He has already had some problems."

"Then you have to help us," Aidan said, leaning forward. "If your father couldn't use a computer, then he couldn't have sent the threats Monsieur Perreau has received. You will be helping him by pointing the police toward someone who can write such threats—and protecting Michel and his family at the same time."

Aidan reached into his pocket and pulled out a business card, which he handed to Cris. "Here's our e-mail address—we use the same one. And both our cell numbers, in case you need to reach either of us."

Cris took the card, looking miserable. "There is an old Corsican saying my grandmother used to repeat. If you walk under the waterfall, don't complain if you get wet." He smiled ruefully. "There is a cave Michel and I have been to several times, behind a waterfall near the marina in Cargése. We have been playing there, forgetting my grandmother's wise words." He stood up. "I will find out what I can."

Liam stood and watched Cris walk back through the woods, then listened for the sound of his motorcycle starting up. He shook out his arms and legs.

"That ground is hard," he said to Aidan, who had turned on his side.

"You don't have any padding. Your ass is all muscle."

"Both our asses need to get back down to the Perreaus," Liam said. He extended a hand to Aidan, who grasped it. Liam pulled Aidan up. "Ooof! Are you gaining weight?"

"All muscle," Aidan said.

Liam looked at him appraisingly. Aidan had become more muscular since they met; he had lost the padding around his stomach that good living back in the States had given him, and been developing his biceps and his calves.

As the sound of the motorcycle faded, they walked toward the path down the hillside. "What do you think?" Aidan asked.

"I think poor Cris is in a very tough place. Betray his father or allow his boyfriend to remain in danger."

Aidan raised his hand toward the crown of a tree, palm sideways. "'O Romeo, Romeo! wherefore art thou, Romeo? Deny thy father and refuse thy name.'"

Liam said, "You're insane, you know that?"

Aidan shook his head. "Just quoting. We've already talked about having our own *Romeo and Juliet* going on here." He began to declaim:

"Two households, both alike in dignity

In fair Verona, where we lay our scene,

From ancient grudge break to new mutiny,

Where civil blood makes civil hands unclean.

From forth the fatal loins of these two foes

A pair of star-cross'd lovers take their life;

Whose misadventured piteous overthrows

Do with their death bury their parents' strife."

Liam was once again shaking his head. "Don't tell me you use that stuff in your classroom."

"Pay attention, Liam. Shakespeare has lots of lessons to teach us, even today. What we have here is two young lovers whose affection is counter to the rivalry between their fathers."

"Yeah, but look how things ended for Romeo and Juliet. They both died."

Aidan nodded and continued his quote. "'For never was a story of more woe than this of Juliet and her Romeo.'"

"Or in this case, Romeo and Julio," Liam said. "Seems like it's up to us to make sure they don't both end up dead by the conclusion of this play."

"My thoughts exactly," Aidan said as they entered the woods and began descending the narrow dirt path down to the Perreaus' house. "But how do we do that?"

"There's the rub," Liam said. "Isn't that a Shakespeare quote?"

"Different play," Aidan said. "*Hamlet*. But I'm impressed."

Liam smiled slyly. "You should be."

22 – The Lobsters Will Wait

As he left the mountain clearing after his meeting with the two bodyguards, Cris knew he should return to Corte; he had a class that afternoon. But it was more important that he go home to Cargése and confront his father. He had to know for sure that he wasn't involved in these threats against Michel's father.

It was a glorious day to be on a motorbike, riding on the curving roads through the tree-lined hills toward his home. Despite the seriousness of his mission, he felt free, untethered by his regular schedule, responsible only to traffic signs and speed limits—and even then he exceeded when he could.

After about forty-five minutes, he reached Masorchia, where the D81 finally turned to the coast and began to parallel it. Puffy white clouds dotted the light blue sky, and to his left the sunlight sparkled on the ocean. He stopped in Tiuccia and bought a sandwich and an Orangina from a little store, then pulled the bike off the road at a beach a few miles farther up and sat overlooking the ocean to eat.

His father was out there somewhere on his boat. The legal period for the red spiny lobster had just begun, and Nic tried to take full advantage. He had a crew of local men who helped with the nets during the spring and summer season. As well, he caught whatever he could of local fish: anchovy, sea spider, squid, and monkfish, which he sold to restaurants and hotels in the area.

Nic would be surprised to see his oldest son at the dock, perhaps even angry that Cris had skipped college for the day. But what Cris had to say couldn't wait. His whole future centered on this one conversation. He felt queasy, and worried that he shouldn't have eaten the sandwich.

He looked up at the sky. Long before he owned a watch, he had learned to tell time from the position of the sun, out on the fishing boat with his father. It was after three o'clock by then, and his father would probably be at the dock by four. He stood up, stretched, and got back on his bike.

He entered the town where he had grown up, passing small coral-roofed houses of white stucco. He waved to the grandmother of a school friend as he passed, then followed the road left into the center of town.

When his father was a boy, fishing boats moored off the beach, to the south of the village, and in the winter the boats had to be hauled onto the beach with a windlass. Then in the 1970s, a marina was built to accommodate over two hundred boats, protected by a jetty, with a number of slips reserved for the local fishermen.

He paused at the cliff above the harbor and scanned the sea ahead of him, looking for his father's boat. He spotted *L'Ange de la Mer* just outside the breakwater, preparing for its approach, and he turned the bike down the road to the water's edge. He reached the marina as the boat was docking in its usual spot along the apron, and he was there to accept the bow line from his father's old friend, Uncle Andre, as his father maneuvered the boat into position.

It was noisy, men shouting, engines roaring, sailboat lines

clanking. Uncle Andre was a short, burly man with a ready smile and fading green tattoos up and down his arms. He had a tightly banded rat tail of white hair that stuck out the back of his ball cap. Since he was a small boy, this skinny ponytail had fascinated Cris—he wanted to sneak up behind Uncle Andre and tug on it, and he and his brothers had dared each other to do so. None had ever had the courage, though.

Nic waved a greeting to his eldest son and then began working the winch to lift the nets onto the dock.

Cris helped his father, Uncle Andre, and the other man, whom he didn't know, unload and sort the cargo. Despite the cool breeze off the ocean, it was messy, backbreaking work, and by the time they were finished, Cris stank of fish and sweat. There were still the deliveries to be made; he strapped several packages of fish and lobster to the back of his bike and took off for the north side of town, and it wasn't until an hour later that he was at his family's house on the rue du General Gambetta, showered and changed and sitting at the dinner table with his parents, his brothers, and sister.

"What brings you home, Cristo?" his mother asked. "You are *en vacances?*" She was a slim woman who had broadened a bit with each child, with dark, frizzy hair and dimpled cheeks.

He shook his head. "I need to speak to Papa. After dinner."

"Nothing wrong at school, I hope?" she asked. "You will still graduate?"

"Yes, Maman. I will still graduate."

She smiled and passed the platter of lobster to him. "Our first college graduate," she said. "How proud the whole village will be!"

Cris smiled back but didn't say anything. He wondered how proud the village would be once his news spread.

His brothers and sister pestered him for stories about college, but he didn't have the heart to oblige them. Leo was two years younger, a graduate of the lycée in Vico, working at the Club Med on the outskirts of Cargése and hoping to get a promotion soon. Jean-Paul was about to go on to the university, and Elodia, the baby, was only sixteen and already a beauty. Finally his father had to tell them to be quiet.

Though he was very nervous, Cris struggled to eat, knowing it would upset his mother if he didn't.

Finally, after what seemed like hours but was surely much less, the meal was over. "Come, Cristo," his father said. "You have been like an ant dancing around honey all evening. Take a walk with me and tell me what you have come home to say."

He followed his father outside. The air had gotten chilly, and he was glad he had put on a long-sleeved shirt. "So," his father said as they walked in the center of the narrow street, in the direction of the port. "It is not about football, because your season is finished. And you told your mother you would still graduate, so it is not about academics."

"Neither of those," Cris said.

"Your health?"

"I'm fine, Papa." Cris's stomach churned, and he felt like he might throw up. "I have a friend at school, Papa. Michel."

"Yes?"

"Michel Perreau."

His father stopped and cocked his head. "The son of the doctor?"

Cris nodded.

"You are worried that I resent her, because of what happened to Laurenzia?" He put his arm around Cris's shoulder. "She is a good woman, Dr. Perreau. She did what she could. It was not her fault that your sister died." He began walking again, and Cris hurried to follow him.

"It's not her," Cris said. "Her husband."

"Who is that?"

"His name is Olivier Perreau. He owns the mine in Ménasina."

"Oh. I never made the connection. That one, he is not so good."

"Papa, you wouldn't… I know you. I know you are a good man…"

"I wouldn't what? Stop talking in riddles, *jeune homme*. Tell me what's the matter."

It was like a dam burst inside Cris. "There have been threats against Michel's family—letters, a car bomb; they think it's you, because of Students for a Green Corsica, because you spoke to them, because you're against the mine. I told them it couldn't be, that you would never do such a thing, that you couldn't…"

His father held up his hand. "Now you must slow down. Tell me this again, but slowly."

Cris repeated the story as he had heard it, taking his time. When he finished, he said, "I told Michel again and again that you could not be responsible. But the bodyguards, they say it cannot be a coincidence, that you are against the mine, and that Dr. Perreau treated Laurenzia. I had to come and tell you and make sure."

"I am glad you did. Tomorrow, you and I will go to visit your friend and his father and explain to him that I have no involvement in this."

"Oh, Papa! You'll do that? But what about your fishing?"

"The lobsters will wait for me."

23 – Uncomfortable Territory

Liam felt better after their meeting with Cris Aquaviva. He believed the boy, which made him more hopeful that the two young lovers would not be torn apart. But on the other hand, if Nic Aquaviva was not behind the threats, then who was?

Late in the afternoon, Olivier met them in the living room and asked, "I have finished most of what I need to do before Monday. Would it be all right if Agathe and I took a swim? As long as we are at home, it seems a waste not to use the pool."

Given the way Cris Aquaviva was able to so easily sneak up on the house, Liam wasn't comfortable with the idea of the Perreaus outside, but he didn't want them to feel like prisoners in their home, because that would only make them jittery. "When you're ready, let us know," Liam said. "We'll check out the area, and we'll stay out there with you."

A half hour later, he and Aidan were sitting at the wrought-iron table as Olivier dived into the deep end of the pool and began to swim. Olivier had a fit body for a man of his age, though Liam hoped Aidan would swat him if he tried to wear such a skimpy bikini when he reached his fifties.

Olivier was a strong swimmer; he swam a dozen laps before his wife appeared. Agathe wore a one-piece hot-pink bathing suit that accented her narrow hips. She stepped into the pool from the shallow end and paddled around with Olivier for a half hour. They talked and laughed together like young lovers.

Liam hoped he and Aidan would always be that close. He could tell from the way Agathe looked at Olivier that she was still in love with her husband, and he appeared to feel the same way about her.

Olivier helped his wife climb out of the pool, then brought her a big towel to drape around her shoulders. The two of them relaxed on the lounge chairs in the sun, Agathe with a broad-brimmed sun hat shading her face. Michel came outside in baggy bathing trunks after his parents had finished their swim, but did not go into the water. He moved a chair to the far end of the pool and settled down to read a textbook.

"Do you want to swim?" Aidan asked. "I brought suits for both of us."

Liam shook his head. "We're working, not playing."

"I thought we were supposed to blend in with clients. Not make them feel like they're being watched."

"It would be different if we were in a less vulnerable space," Liam said. "Look up there on the hill."

He nodded upward, and Aidan followed his gaze. "No one there," Aidan said.

"Now. But someone could creep out of the underbrush and sight a rifle on either of the clients. If we're splashing around in the pool, how could we prevent that?"

"We can't prevent it no matter where we are," Aidan said. "The best we could do is warn the clients and get them out of the line of fire."

Liam smiled. "Good point. And I believe you've just proved my point too."

"I hate it when you're always right," Aidan grumbled.

"Get used to it, sweetheart." Liam laughed as Aidan feigned a punch at him.

Around four thirty, Olivier picked up his cell phone. After a brief conversation, he ended the call and looked up.

"I have closed the office tomorrow," he said. "Edith and George may have a day off, and whatever I need to finish I can do myself."

They heard the sound of a car pulling into the driveway, and Liam stood up. He motioned everyone to remain where they were, and walked quickly around the corner of the house. "It's the police," he called back.

He walked to the driveway and waited for the portly detective to climb out of his sedan. "Good afternoon, Detective Bonnet," he said. "The Perreaus are in the back, at the pool. Would you care to join them there?"

Bonnet nodded and lumbered behind him. Olivier and Agathe had covered themselves in towels and stood to greet him.

The detective bowed slightly.

"Do you have news about the bomb?" Olivier asked as they sat around the table.

"We are continuing our inquiries," Bonnet said. "The materials used in the construction of the car bomb were very common ones.

We were unable to retrieve any fingerprints or other evidence."

"Then how do you continue your inquiries?" Liam asked. "If you have no leads?"

"We have our sources," Bonnet said. "We are questioning known terrorists and our network of informants."

Which meant they had nothing, Liam thought. Bonnet left soon after, and Agathe and Olivier went inside to dress for dinner. Michel remained in his chair, his headphones on, reading his textbook as the sun began to sink and the air cooled. Liam's cell phone buzzed in his pocket, and when he pulled it out, he saw the number had been blocked. "This is probably Louis," he said to Aidan. "You stay here with Michel. I'll be back when I finish."

Aidan frowned. Liam knew his partner liked to be part of every conversation, but sadly for him, not everything was his business. He turned away from Aidan and walked toward the hillside as he answered. "Good evening, Louis. How are you?"

"Very good, Liam. Your manners are improving. I am well, and I have some interesting news."

"Really? Have you discovered something I can use about these nationalists?"

"Oh, sorry. No. I haven't been able to dig up anything. My news is more of a personal nature."

Liam felt his heart give a little flip. The last time he and Louis had spoken, the conversation had strayed into uncomfortable territory. "Yes?"

"I've been asked to make a transfer," Louis said. "In the past,

I've resisted relocation because Hassan's life and business are here in Tunis, and the State Department wasn't very generous when it came to moving same-sex partners around. But those policies are changing, and Hassan's firm has been developing contacts on the Côte d'Azur."

He paused, though Liam had a feeling he knew where the conversation was going.

"Hassan's firm is opening an office in Nice. Most diplomatic business is conducted out of the Consul General's office in Marseille," Louis said. "But there's enough activity in the area to merit a position for someone like me at the consular office in Nice."

"Aidan will be very happy if you guys move near us," Liam said. "Me too, of course."

"Nothing is confirmed yet," Louis said. "But the wheels are in motion."

"Keep us in the loop," Liam said. "Good luck."

"Thanks. And I'll keep an ear to the ground for anything about Corsica, and if I hear anything you should know, I'll be on the horn."

Liam ended the call but didn't return to Aidan immediately. Was there anything more to this potential move? Anything perhaps connected to the hints Louis had dropped in their last conversation?

He shook his head. He had developed a suspicious mind through all those years as a SEAL and then in the personal protection business. Louis and Hassan were their good friends, nothing more. Aidan would be happy to hear that they'd be moving to Nice.

He returned to the patio and collected Aidan and Michel, and they went inside to dinner. The mood was tense, as if each one of them, in his or her own way, was waiting for the next incident.

Maria delivered a platter of roast chicken to the table and retreated to the kitchen. "Why must we always have chicken?" Olivier grumbled, helping himself to a few slices. "Why not steak sometime?"

"If you want steak, all you have to do is ask," Agathe said as she took the platter from him.

"No one ever asks me what I want," Michel said.

"Because you are a child," Olivier said. "When you pay the bills, you can decide what to serve at dinner."

"I can't even decide where I live," Michel said.

"You are fortunate not to be living in Africa," Agathe said. "If your father had found a mine in Ghana or the Gabon…"

"If that had happened, you would be treating the sick children there," Olivier said. He nodded toward his son. "And you would be studying at the University of the Jungle if you had to."

"You wait. I will graduate soon, and then I can go wherever I want. Even out into the countryside of the island. Up to the north coast, for example."

"What, and work in my mine?" his father asked. "There are no jobs there beyond cleaning toilets for tourists. That's why I don't understand why those people are not welcoming me. There will be construction work first, then jobs for skilled operators. Even the low-level jobs will pay better than farming or fishing."

"The Corsicans have farmed and fished for generations," Michel said. "It is in their blood. Would you have them give up what their ancestors have done?"

"You are a stupid boy," Olivier said. "Be quiet and eat your dinner."

Michel stood up so fast he knocked his chair over. "I don't have any appetite," he said, and he stalked toward the stairs.

Olivier opened his mouth, but Agathe put her hand on his arm. "Let him go," she said in a low voice. "We are all under stress."

Olivier glared at her, but he said nothing more, and they finished the meal in silence. Agathe stood to clear the dishes and asked, "Cheese, anyone?"

They all declined. "Can I help you clean up?" Aidan asked.

"Thank you, no," she said. "I find it very calming."

Aidan and Liam walked to their room. "It's not your responsibility to help clean up after dinner," Liam grumbled when they were behind closed doors. "You're a bodyguard, not a maid."

"And you're just as grouchy as Olivier," Aidan said. "What crawled up your butt?"

Liam sighed. "I hate waiting around like this."

"But most of what we do is wait around. It's a good day when nothing happens."

"Yeah, but on most jobs, there's only a perceived threat. A celebrity who wants a buffer from his fans. A rich person who needs protection from the off chance that there might be a threat. In this case we have a real antagonist out there somewhere. We don't know who it is or what resources he has, or where he'll strike next. It's like knowing there's a cobra in the underbrush, constantly worrying you won't be able to react quick enough when you hear that rattle."

"Now who's being the drama queen?" Aidan asked, flopping down on the bed. "I know you. There must be more bothering you than just that."

Liam leaned against the chest of drawers. "I spoke to Louis today. It looks like he and Hassan might be moving to Nice."

"Really? Why?"

"He's been offered a transfer to the consulate there. And Hassan's firm is opening an office in Nice too. So it works out for both of them."

Aidan looked up at him. "And why does that bother you?"

"It doesn't."

"Liam."

Liam crossed his arms over his chest. It did bother him, and he didn't understand why. Was it just that casual comment Louis had made?

"Before you met me, you didn't even know Louis was gay, did you?" Aidan asked.

"He was a professional contact. I never asked about his personal life."

"And you couldn't tell."

"No, Aidan, I couldn't. We've had this conversation before. I don't have the finely tuned gaydar you have. Never had it, and don't plan on developing it."

"So you never had sex with him," Aidan said. "Did you want to?"

Liam shifted uncomfortably against the chest of drawers, aware that his dick was stiffening beneath his pants, and equally aware that Aidan could tell. "I didn't think of him that way."

"Come over here," Aidan said, patting the bed next to him.

"I'll stay here for now."

Aidan laughed. "You are such a straight arrow sometimes, Liam McCullough. You don't have to be embarrassed about your desires. As long as you're honest with me. Do you want to fuck Louis? Or Hassan? Or both of them?"

"You know I hate to talk about this kind of thing, Aidan."

"Yes, I do, sweetheart. But I also know that not talking about things is the kiss of death for a relationship. When people let things fester because they're afraid. And if there's one thing I know about you, it's that you're no coward."

Liam had always considered himself pretty fearless. In the end, it was the reason he had left the SEALs; he felt that the source of his fearlessness was a lack of self-respect, because he couldn't confront his sexual desires. And here he was, falling into the same trap again. He took a deep breath. "I don't know, Aidan. I don't have words to express how much I love you, and sex with you is more satisfying than I ever imagined sex could be. But when I think about other guys sometimes—not just Louis or Hassan—or I don't know, threesomes or foursomes or whatever—I get hard. It fucks with my mind."

Aidan laughed, which was not the reaction Liam was expecting at all. "You're a guy, Liam. There's nothing wrong with getting turned on by some sexual stimulus. I just want you to be honest with me. If you ever want to experiment, talk to me. That's all I ask."

Liam was frankly astonished. He had known Aidan to be possessive and jealous. "You wouldn't care?"

"Of course I would. I'm an only child. I don't share easily. But I know you don't have as much sexual experience as I do, and if you get it into your head that you don't want to die without sucking a black dick or doing a threesome with identical twins, then I'd rather know about it and maybe even be part of it than have you lie to me and sneak around behind my back."

Something about the way Aidan spoke made Liam's dick wilt. "You can be really crude, you know that?"

"It is what it is. Sex between two people can be an experience or a transaction. Or it can be an expression of love. What you and I do? That's love. You want to experiment with something else? That doesn't change what we have."

Liam walked over and sat down on the bed next to Aidan. "You're pretty amazing."

Aidan leaned over and kissed him. "You're pretty amazing yourself. Now come to bed. We've got clients to protect, and we both need our sleep. We don't know what tomorrow will bring."

24 – A Good Man

Friday morning, Liam woke early and exercised by the pool in the cool dawn. It was a great change from Tunis, where the summer heat had already begun. He worked up a good sweat and felt his muscles respond to pressure. Perhaps he wasn't getting old after all—at least not yet.

He showered and dressed and joined Olivier and Aidan at the breakfast table. "My wife sleeps in," Olivier said. "She has few chances to do so. My son, being a college student, has altogether too many such opportunities."

Aidan passed a platter of scrambled eggs and fried potatoes, and Liam helped himself.

"I assume we will remain here, hostages of a sort, until Monday," Olivier said. "I received an e-mail this morning from my contact at Outremer. Our agreement is scheduled for discussion at a board meeting in Paris on Monday morning. I asked to have it postponed, but I was told such a thing was not possible, that the agenda is set long in advance. Since the outstanding issues have been resolved and I have already signed my pages, it would be evidence of bad faith if I hesitate now."

He lifted his coffee cup to his lips and sipped, then continued. "I believe the board will affirm the agreement. If that happens, do you believe whoever opposes me will concede defeat, and that will be the end of our troubles?"

Liam put down his silverware and looked at the client. "My honest opinion is that your situation will not be resolved until you or the police identify who is behind the threats, and remove or neutralize that person or group."

Olivier nodded. "That is what I believe, also. But at least as of Monday, I will have the resources of Outremer to support me."

Agathe joined them, and they ate in an uneasy silence. When they finished, Olivier returned to his home office and Agathe went back upstairs.

"Let's take a walk," Liam said. Outside, the temperature had risen a few degrees, but the air was still cool and morning fresh. "I'm worried. The police have no leads, and with the Monday deadline approaching, it's likely there is going to be an acceleration. We need to be totally on our game for the next three days."

"But what about after that?" Aidan asked. "You said yourself, the problems won't stop until the police find whoever is behind the threats and stop them."

"After that is another problem," Liam said. "Maybe our problem, maybe not. Right now we need to focus on keeping everyone safe until then."

Their cell phones beeped in quick succession, an indication of new e-mail. "Richard," Liam said. He opened the message and read, as Aidan did the same.

Olivier Perreau's finances were as expected; he had everything he owned tied up in the mine. He had borrowed against his retirement account, taken a large mortgage against the home in

Ajaccio, and maxed out his credit cards.

"Umm, Liam?" Aidan asked, looking up.

"Yes?"

"Where do you think he's getting the money to pay the Agence for us?"

"For a change, the client finances aren't our problem. The Agence pays us, and they collect from the client." That was one good thing about no longer working on his own, Liam thought, though he felt bad for Olivier and his family. He knew how hard it was to live on the razor's edge of financial ruin. He had been there a few times himself, when work was slow or clients were unable to pay.

There was a second attachment, about Vanina Andreadi. The information there was scanty, however. She had been born in Ajaccio in 1993, the daughter of Pierre and Marguerite Andreadi. Marguerite died of cancer in 2000, and Pierre was killed in an automobile accident in Ajaccio six years later. She had been adopted by Pierre's brother Alberto and his wife, and graduated from the Lycée Laetitia Bonaparte before enrolling at the university. Her name appeared on several college websites but never more than just in a list or a photo caption.

Liam closed his phone. "Looks like an ordinary college student. Though I'm sure there's more to her somewhere." He heard a car pull up in the driveway, and they walked around the corner of the house, assuming it was Bonnet again. But the vehicle was a dented, rusty pickup, and he saw Cris Aquaviva hop down from the passenger seat. The driver appeared to be an older version of him.

"Since that's Cris, that's probably his father with him," Liam said. "You go say hello, and I'll get Olivier."

As Aidan walked forward, Liam backtracked to the rear door. He went inside and knocked on the door of Olivier's office. "Monsieur Perreau, you have visitors," he said.

"More police?" Olivier asked.

"I think it's Niculaiu Aquaviva and his son."

Olivier looked up from his desk. "That man? Why has he come to my home?"

"The only way you'll know is to speak with him."

Olivier pushed his chair back and stood, and they heard the sound of the front door opening and Aidan ushering the two visitors inside. In the entryway, they all came face-to-face.

"Monsieur Perreau?" Nic Aquaviva asked. "May we come in?"

"I'll get the doctor and Michel," Aidan said, crossing to the stairway.

"Why are you here?" Olivier asked. "It's not enough that you send threatening messages? Now you come to my house?"

"Hold on, Monsieur Perreau," Liam said, stepping between the two men. "You heard what the police said. They don't believe Monsieur Aquaviva has any connection to the threats you've received. So let's hear what he has to say."

Agathe descended the staircase, followed by Michel. "Monsieur Aquaviva," she said. "Good morning."

Michel stared, his mouth open in astonishment.

Liam ushered everyone to the living room. Agathe motioned to the sofa, and Cris and his father sat down side by side. She moved one of the formal armchairs close to the other and sat down, tugging her husband's arm so that he sat in the chair beside her. She nodded to Michel, who crossed the room to lean against the wall.

Aidan and Liam remained in the doorway. Liam noticed Cris flash a look to Michel that seemed to say *don't do anything*. Michel still looked shocked to see his boyfriend in his parents' living room, accompanied by his father's archenemy.

Liam looked around the room, which had a rigid formality that seemed to mirror the discomfort of all the parties there. The chairs were straight-backed and didn't allow for relaxation, and neither Cris nor his father reclined against the horsehair sofa. Even the artwork on the walls—a series of black-and-white etchings of classical scenes—was cold and uninviting.

He focused on Nic Aquaviva. He was a stocky man, with the same build as his son, the same black hair and eyes like cured olives. He looked like he had been quite handsome as a young man, though the years of hard outdoor work had taken their toll on him.

"I am very sorry for everything that has happened to you," Aquaviva said, breaking the silence. "But you must understand that I had nothing to do with anything." He looked at Agathe. "It is true, Doctor, that I was angry with you about Laurenzia." He took a deep breath and wiped a tear away from his eye with a knuckle. "She was my baby girl, and I loved her dearly. When she died…"

"You and your family have my greatest sympathy," Agathe said softly. "I only wish I could have done more to help her."

Nic nodded. "I have come to understand that. If we had known of your abilities and come to you earlier, perhaps then…but what is past, is past. My little one waits in heaven for me."

He looked at Olivier. "My son tells me that he is a friend of your son's, and that you believe I am responsible for threats against you, your family, and your business. I have come here to tell you I am not."

Olivier looked at Michel. "You know this boy?"

Liam saw Aidan look at Michel, as if to say, *Have some balls.*

"Yes, Papa," he said. "We are close friends."

"How can you do this to me? When you know how I feel about this man? How could you even contemplate a friendship with his son?"

Michel said nothing, just stared at the carpet.

Nic Aquaviva came to his rescue. "I do not agree with your plans to reopen the mine, monsieur. I have no college background, no science to understand. All I know is the sea, and the way chemicals in the water have harmed the fish and the lobsters. If you can convince me that what you plan to do will not endanger them, or my family's livelihood, I will bear you no ill will. And I assure you I have had no part in any threats against you, your family, or your business. I am but a fisherman who cares for the ocean and its creatures. And my son."

"I asked my father to come here," Cris said. "To make sure there was no doubt between our two families. To reassure you that he has done nothing to you, and that he intends no harm."

Olivier shook his head. "You are liars. Both of you. I want you to leave my house." He pointed to the door. "Right now." He turned to Michel. "And I do not want to hear that you have ever spoken to this boy or his father again."

"Papa!" Michel pleaded.

"Now!" Olivier thundered.

Agathe put her hand on Olivier's arm again, but he shook it off.

"We should return to Cargése," Aquaviva said. "We apologize for disturbing you." He stood and led his son to the door. Cris looked back just once at Michel, but neither of them said anything. Liam was reminded of the story of Lot's wife leaving Sodom, one of the many Biblical tales that had been beaten into his head in Sunday school. How she had been warned not to look back as her husband led her away from the evil town that had been her home, which God was about to destroy, and for that last, longing glance she had been turned to a pillar of salt. He hoped for a better outcome for Cris.

Olivier followed them to the front door and closed it hard behind them. "How long have you and this boy been friends?" he demanded of Michel.

"A few months. But his father is a good man. He can't be responsible for any of the things that have happened."

Olivier shook his head. "You are a child. So naïve."

"I am not a child!" Michel said. "And you have no right to choose my friends." He dashed out of the room and up the stairs, two at a time, his feet pounding against the treads. They heard his bedroom door slam.

Olivier turned to Liam. "Did you invite this man to my home?"

Liam shook his head. "Never spoke to him. But it says something that he was willing to come here, don't you think? That maybe he has nothing to do with the threats."

"I cannot believe that." He crossed his arms over his chest and glared.

"Sometimes the truth is the hardest thing to believe," Aidan said quietly.

Olivier stalked out of the room, and Liam noticed how much his posture matched his son's. Both of them angry and frustrated, stuck in the middle of problems too awkward and confusing to be managed.

Agathe sighed deeply. "Do you believe Monsieur Aquaviva?" she asked.

"The police have said they have no evidence against him," Liam said.

"It didn't seem like he came here to clear his name, so much as to reassure you and your husband," Aidan said. "And to help his son."

"I wondered about that," Agathe said. "Why would his son's friendship with Michel mean so much to him?"

Liam looked at Aidan, who said, "I think he's just a good father, madame."

"Perhaps."

The clock ticked loudly in the silence, and Aidan looked across at it. Not even ten, and already a busy morning. Who knew what the rest of the day would bring?

Agathe went back upstairs, and Aidan and Liam returned to their room. "You think he was earnest," Liam said. "Aquaviva."

"I do. I wonder if Cris told him what the relationship was between him and Michel."

Liam sat on the bed. "Do you think that matters?"

Aidan sat beside him and leaned back against the headboard. "I agonized for a year before coming out to my parents," he said. "An advisor at Penn told me I should wait until I graduated in case they decided to stop supporting me. A guy I dated for a while told me not to worry, that they already knew. Everybody had an opinion, and I was so confused."

"What did you do?"

"I got hold of this skinny paperback about how to come out to people. I read it cover to cover, then a second time. There were all these strategies—pick a neutral place, prepare what you wanted to say, and so on. I waited until I was ready to go back to college for my junior year, and my parents took me out to dinner to say good-bye."

Aidan pulled his knees up and wrapped his arms around them. "I waited until dessert, even though my stomach was so knotted up I could barely eat. And then I spit it out."

Liam put his arm around Aidan's shoulders and pulled him close. "What did they say?"

"Sort of a mix of everything I'd been told. My mother asked if it was something they'd done; my father asked if it was just a phase. Of course I said no to both. And then our desserts were delivered, and we ate. We went home, I went back to Penn the next day, and that was the last time we ever discussed it."

"Did you ever bring a boyfriend home?"

"Not to stay. Sometimes when they'd come in to Philadelphia to take me out to dinner or something, I'd bring a friend. But no PDA. And then I went to Europe and I'd write them letters and mention other guys occasionally. By the time I came back to the States and met Blake, and then introduced them to him, it was already an established fact."

"I can't imagine having that conversation with my parents," Liam said. "I don't think I ever went out to dinner with just the two of them, without my sisters along. And even then, it was usually some cheap local dive where you wouldn't want to have a personal conversation because all the neighbors would hear about it."

"Everybody's experience is different," Aidan said. "Cris may not have said anything to his father, but Nic might have figured it out already. Cris is pretty straight acting, but if he hasn't had girlfriends… And then, if Nic was looking, he'd have seen the eye contact between the two boys."

"You think?"

"I do." Aidan sat up, releasing Liam's hold over his shoulders. "I think Agathe saw it, even if no one else did."

Liam stood up. "I need to move around. Want to come for a walk with me?"

Aidan shook his head. "I'm going to stay here and read for a while." He picked up the mystery novel he'd been reading. Liam couldn't understand his appetite for deadly fiction when their lives were in danger.

Liam was restless, and he'd have rather had Aidan join him for a walk, even a run. Just something to get him moving. Instead he walked out to the pool and sat cross-legged on the warm grass. He closed his eyes and began to take measured breaths.

He stayed out there for an hour in a meditative state. By the time he stood up and stretched, he felt better. As he entered the house through the back door, he heard the phone ring, and Olivier answer it in his office.

Liam stopped at the doorway and watched as Olivier spoke for a moment; then his face darkened. Liam could only hear his side of the conversation, mostly a series of yeses, until his face paled and he said, "No. It is not possible."

He listened again, then said, "I will be there as soon as possible. But it is a drive of at least an hour."

He ended the call and looked at Liam. "There has been an explosion at the mine. They have retrieved a body, and they believe it is George."

25 – Les Spécialistes

Liam realized Agathe had come downstairs and was standing behind him. "My God, he's dead? George?" she asked.

Olivier nodded. "A motor scooter with his registration is at the mine, and a body which matches his description has been retrieved. The police are concerned he may have been trying to place the bomb and it exploded before he could leave."

"*Le pauvre petit*," Agathe said, shaking her head. "I cannot believe he would be involved in such things."

Michel had come downstairs too and looked as pale as his father. Liam wondered at that. Did he have a connection to George, perhaps through Vanina or Cris? They had all been at school together—Cris and Vanina in political science, George and Michel in engineering.

"I must leave immediately," Olivier said. "The police require me to come out to the mine and examine the situation. And I must know what kind of damage has been done, and then report back to Outremer if anything will affect our arrangements."

"I'll go with you," Liam said. "Aidan will stay here with Michel and Dr. Perreau. We must be very careful."

They left a few minutes later. When they were in the car, Liam asked, "It will take an hour to reach the mine?"

"If the roads are clear. There are many mountains, steep passages, and curves. Great potential for accidents."

"Do you believe George was responsible for the threats you

received?"

"I hate to think so. But he knew everything about the deal with Outremer. And he knew where we lived, and where Agathe worked."

"He had access to a computer and printer," Liam said. "To prepare the threats. And he has an engineering degree, so he had the skill to put together the car bomb."

Olivier looked over at him. "You think that while we were at lunch…"

Liam shrugged. "It's possible. He knew you were not going to back down, and he knew your car and where you parked."

"I had begun to think of him as another son," Olivier said quietly. "I hoped that once our deal was signed with Outremer and production began at the mine, I could pass more responsibility to him."

"Did he ever give you any indication that he disapproved of your techniques?"

Olivier shook his head. "He was very enthusiastic about the possibilities. He understood the importance of the project to Corsica, and to me and my family. I am still finding it very hard to understand his motivations. He must have been seduced by this man Aquaviva."

He pounded on the steering wheel. "That's it. Aquaviva recruited poor George to his cause and convinced him to make the threats and place the bombs. Of course the fisherman must have an alibi for everything—it would all be structured to place the blame on George. He just didn't count on George fumbling the bomb and getting killed in the explosion."

Olivier slowed behind a big truck, waiting impatiently for the opportunity to pass. "You don't know that yet," Liam said. "In the meantime, take it easy. If we get there a few minutes later, the police will still be there."

"I know," Olivier said. He gripped the steering wheel. "But I will not be able to accept what has happened until I see for myself."

"Did the police give you any idea of the damage?"

"No, just that there had been an explosion, and that George was dead. Is the mine still usable? How much work will be required to repair it? I need to know."

"I understand. But it won't do you any good if you have an accident on the way there."

Olivier relaxed his grip on the steering wheel and leaned back against the seat. The truck eventually turned off, and he was able to accelerate again. The road curved, and they found themselves following the coastline. The Mediterranean sparkled in the early afternoon sunshine. A tracing of cirrus clouds hovered on the horizon, and the fields to the right shimmered with new growth.

They passed a tiny village, a half-dozen run-down houses with a scrawny dog barking. Just afterward, a sign indicated the town of Ménasina was a kilometer away, and Olivier turned onto a narrow side road. A small wooden sign that hung on a chain-link fence read ARGENTUM, SA. The gate to the fence hung open, and ahead of them they saw the flashing blue lights of the police cars.

"Is this gate usually locked?" Liam asked as Olivier slipped his car through.

"Yes. But George often came out here on his own, so he had a key to the lock."

Olivier pulled up behind the last police car, and they got out. A young flic in a neatly pressed white uniform shirt with black epaulets approached them. He had close-cropped hair and the serious attitude of a young officer at his first crime scene. His navy slacks and black shoes were pristine. Olivier introduced himself and Liam.

"Come this way, please." The flic led them past the welter of police vehicles blocking the entrance to the mine, including an ambulance with the back doors open and a stretcher inside, with a body covered by a sheet. Liam pitied whoever would have to identify George's body—or what was left of it.

The mine access was tucked into the side of a sparsely wooded hillside, like the entrance to a bear's cave. Looking around, Liam couldn't see much reason to preserve the area. The hillside was covered with sun-parched dirt, interrupted only by a scattering of low shrubbery, perhaps the maquis Agathe had mentioned when she described the island.

Liam sniffed the air. If the maquis was supposed to have a pleasant scent, he couldn't distinguish it. Just the smell of gasoline and the lingering smoke from the explosion, and faint traces of seawater on the incoming breeze.

Was this barren landscape the result of the previous mining? Was this what Nic Aquaviva was worried would happen to more of the area? The only positive feature was the proximity to the coast. He couldn't imagine this area as a resort. Too drab. Even the narrow stream that meandered through the site was strewn with rocks.

The police detective in charge was named Bruno Desjardins. He was surprisingly young—about Liam's age, mid-thirties, with a shaved head and a military bearing. There were several chevrons on his black epaulets.

Once again, Olivier introduced himself and Liam. "Can you tell us what happened?" Olivier asked.

Desjardins consulted his notes. "At 13:40, we received a complaint from a Monsieur Chevalier. He heard an explosion from this area."

"He owns the farm over there," Olivier said, pointing in the direction the stream flowed. "He wishes to sell me some of his property once the mine is operational, so he has been watching my progress closely."

Desjardins continued. "An officer was dispatched, who noted that the gate was open and that there was smoke coming out of the mine. He approached the mine and noted the motorcycle there." He nodded toward the red bike propped on its kickstand. "He called out and received no answer. So he requested an ambulance and further backup. He attempted to enter the mine, but there was too much smoke."

Liam looked around. There was little smoke left in the air. So if there'd been a fire, it must have been a small one.

"I arrived on the site at 14:05 along with a hazmat team," Desjardins said. "They penetrated the interior of the mine and discovered the body of a Caucasian male in his early twenties. From the position of his body and the injuries he suffered, we believe he was in close proximity to the bomb when it went off. It is possible he was working with the timing mechanism. We found pieces of a crude device in the area."

He looked down at his notes. "The hazmat team found smoldering embers of several wooden support beams. They believe that much of the smoke came from a mix of gunpowder and lead residue from the interior of the mine."

"When may I enter the mine and survey the damage?" Olivier asked.

"Come with me, monsieur. We will see how much progress *les spécialistes* have made."

Liam tried to follow, but Desjardins said, "For now, just Monsieur Perreau, if you please."

Liam nodded. He missed Faisal Qasim, his contact with the Tunisian national police. Whenever anything happened back in Tunis that required a police presence, he had called Faisal and been allowed to participate in the investigation. That was clearly not going to happen here.

He began to wander around, looking for any evidence that might indicate what had happened there. Under a scrawny chestnut tree near the mine entrance, he noticed a scrap of paper and recognized the logo on it. It was a wrapper from a Cornetto ice cream cone, and the residue of ice cream on it was fresh. That was odd. Why would George bring an ice cream cone with him when he was planning a bombing?

And how did he get the materials there, when he had only a scooter? There was no indication of a carrier for his bike. Had he worn a backpack? If so, where was it? And wouldn't it be too dangerous to carry live explosives close to your body on a motorbike? That didn't sound like something a trained engineer would do.

He followed the stream a few hundred feet until he came up to the edge of the property, where a chain-link fence separated Perreau's land from his neighbor's. He saw that the stream continued to snake through the countryside in the direction of the ocean.

"I will harness the flow of this river," Olivier said, coming up to him. "To provide water for the process of separating the silver from the lead ore. That is one of the problems these people have—they fear the lead will flow through the river and down to the sea, polluting the landscape and the Mediterranean."

"And it won't?" Liam asked.

Olivier shook his head. "I have designed a sophisticated process to remove the lead from the water before it returns to the streambed, to smelt it into bars for sale."

"Interesting. But right now I'd like to know what you saw inside the mine."

"It is as the detective said. There was an explosion a few hundred feet inside. Fortunately there was not much damage to the mine structure; I believe it can be repaired fairly quickly." He shook his head. "Poor George. I will never understand his motives."

They walked back toward the mine entrance, and Liam spotted

Desjardins. "May I show you something?" he asked the detective.

Desjardins inclined his head slightly, and Liam led him to where he had seen the scrap of paper. "I didn't touch it, but it appears recent."

As Desjardins called over one of the crime scene technicians, Liam asked, "Were there any other signs of a picnic here?"

"A picnic?" Desjardins asked.

"George told me that some time ago he brought a girl here for a picnic. I wondered if he had done the same thing today."

The *spécialiste* arrived and bagged the wrapper, adding a tag to indicate where and when it had been found.

"We found no evidence of a picnic or of another person here," Desjardins said. He looked over to the motorbike.

"Any signs that another vehicle was here this afternoon?"

Desjardins frowned. "I am afraid that any such evidence may have been contaminated by the presence of police vehicles."

Olivier looked at Liam. "You don't believe George was alone?" he asked.

"I don't know," Liam said. "I'm just speculating."

"It is a point I will investigate," Desjardins said. "Do you know the name of the girl who accompanied Monsieur Phthalis previously?"

"Vanina Andreadi. She's a student at the university and works at a café in Corte called L'Auberge des Etudiants."

"Is that why you went to Corte on Wednesday night?" Olivier asked. "To speak with this girl?"

Liam nodded. "She's involved with that student group you mentioned, Students for a Green Corsica." He looked at Desjardins. "They've made some protests in the past and demonstrated against the mine's reopening."

Desjardins made a note.

"Be sure to speak with Aquaviva," Olivier said. "The fisherman. I'm sure he was behind all this."

"Niculaiu Aquaviva?" Desjardins asked.

"Yes, I've been trying to convince the flics in Ajaccio that he is behind all the threats I've received, but they won't listen."

"Do you know Aquaviva?" Liam asked Desjardins.

The detective nodded. "He has come to our attention for acts of civil disobedience. Nothing of this nature, but…" He shrugged. "I will speak with him and with the girl."

"Someone will talk to George's parents?" Olivier asked. "They will be devastated."

"I will be speaking with them shortly," Desjardins said. "When the spécialistes are finished, we will seal the property. You will not be able to use it until we have released it."

Olivier nodded. "I understand. I had not planned to begin operations here for some time anyway."

They left Desjardins and walked back to Olivier's car. "I feel very bad for George's parents," Olivier said. "They were so proud of him." He looked at Liam. "Agathe and I would be destroyed if anything happened to Michel. You must protect us all."

"I will," Liam said.

26 – FULL OF DRAMA

Liam was quiet on the drive back from the mine, trying to understand what might have happened that afternoon. He was troubled by the ice cream wrapper; that implied to him that George had arranged another picnic at the mine site, most likely with Vanina. But why was there no other evidence of their meal?

Fortunately Olivier was lost in his own thoughts and did not disturb Liam's meditations. When they pulled into the driveway, Agathe appeared at the front door, and the next hour was consumed with a recitation of all that had happened that day.

After they were finished, Liam pulled Aidan aside. "How's Michel doing?"

"Not well. He's been calling and texting Cris all day and not getting a response. I've tried to reason with him. Maybe Cris is in class or working, or just doesn't have his phone. But he's not listening to me."

"Where is he now?"

"His room."

"Let's go up and talk to him."

Aidan shook his head. "Leave him alone for now, Liam. Remember what it was like when we were in Bizerte?"

The summer before, they had spent six weeks at a summer academy for international students studying English on Tunisia's Mediterranean coast. The teenagers had been full of drama, even before one of them had been kidnapped.

"Not an experience I'd like to recreate," Liam said. "But we can wait until after dinner."

Maria had left the family a cold platter, and Liam and Aidan joined the three Perreaus at the dining room table. No one spoke beyond the usual platitudes of the meal, and Liam felt tension radiating from each member of the family.

They skipped the cheese course once again. Michel volunteered to clear the table, and his parents went upstairs to their bedroom. Aidan and Liam waited until Michel had finished loading the dishwasher; then Liam asked, "Would you like to take a walk outside with us?"

The boy nodded, and the three of them walked out the rear door and into the cool evening. A sprinkling of stars was spread across the sky, and a three-quarter moon hung low over the horizon. "Have you heard from Cris yet?" Aidan asked as they walked past the pool.

Michel shook his head. "I texted him again."

Aidan put his hand on Michel's shoulder. "You have to give him some space. This is a very difficult time for everyone. And if you keep chasing after him, that will only make him feel more closed in."

"But I love him!" Michel burst into tears, and Aidan put his arm around the boy's shoulders. Michel leaned against him and cried.

Liam looked over at Liam and mouthed, *Better you than me.* Aidan only smiled.

"Would you like to see how we work, as bodyguards?" Aidan asked after Michel's sobs had subsided to sniffles.

Michel shrugged.

Aidan said, "Liam, why don't you tell him?"

Liam glared at his partner but picked up the lead. "We take a walk out here a couple of times a day to check for any threats. See up there on the hill?" He pointed. "Somebody could set up a machine gun aimed at the house or the driveway. A sniper could hide in the underbrush. The average soldier can throw a grenade forty meters, and the casualty-producing radius is another fifteen meters, so we make sure that distance from the house is clear."

"Liam!" Aidan said, and Liam looked over at Michel, whose eyes were wide with shock.

"You think we're in that much danger?" Michel asked.

"Makes a missed call from your boyfriend less of a big deal, huh?" Liam asked.

Aidan released Michel and punched Liam in the arm. "Not helping!" he said.

"Sure it is," Liam said. He turned to the boy. "Now, Michel, which is more important? Getting through the next couple of days with your family safe, or getting a text from your boyfriend with hearts and smiley faces?"

Michel looked down at the ground.

"Let's keep walking," Aidan said.

They passed around the side of the house and along the semicircular driveway to the dead-end street off the Rue des Magnolias. A brown hare darted beneath the cover of a pine tree, and somewhere in the canopy above a bird sang. Then, as if in answer,

Michel's phone chirped.

He eagerly pulled it from his pants pocket. "It's a text, from Cris!" he said. Then he began to cry again.

Liam looked at Aidan, who gently took the phone from Michel and read it. "Cris says he went fishing with his father today," Aidan said, peering at the phone under the glare of an exterior light from the next-door neighbor's house. "He needs to take a break and think about his life."

He took a deep breath and looked up at Liam. "He's not going to come out to his father, and he knows Michel won't either."

"How can I live without him?" Michel looked up, his face tearstained, and Liam was glad he hadn't confronted his sexuality until long after his hormone-laden youth had passed.

"Let's go inside," Aidan said. "I have some pills you can take."

He took Michel by the arm and led him toward the house. Liam went to their bedroom and checked for e-mail and any news reports on the bombing. Aidan returned as he was finishing. "What kind of pills did you have for him?" Liam asked.

"Sleeping pills," Aidan said.

"Since when do you take sleeping pills?"

Aidan sat down on the bed. "I had trouble falling asleep at first in Nice. New bed, strange surroundings. Victoire recommended a doctor who prescribed some pills. You didn't know?"

"I never noticed."

"Some observer you are." Aidan reached to the bedside table and picked up his paperback again. "I'm going to read for a while before going to sleep."

"Observe this," Liam said. "I'm going outside." He stalked out of the bedroom and through the house, back out to the patio. The lights were out on the second floor, so he stripped off his shirt, pants, and shorts, leaving him only in his jockstrap in the cold night air. Goose pimples rose on his arms and legs as he began a set of push-ups, then sit-ups. By the time he had moved on to jumping jacks, he had warmed up.

He repeated his entire morning routine, and by the time he finished, he had shaken off his anger and the impatience once more. When he returned to their room, the lights were out and he thought Aidan was already asleep. He took a quick shower, and when he returned to the bedroom, Aidan was no longer under the covers. He was sitting up in the darkness.

"Liam, we need to talk," he said.

27 – A Belief in Fish

Aidan was tired. Physically worn down from the stress of being on guard all the time. And tired of the drama between him and Liam.

"Talk about what?" Liam asked as he unwrapped the towel from around his waist sat on the bed beside Aidan.

"You need an attitude adjustment," Aidan said, turning to face him. "You are putting this whole house on edge, and you're not acting like a professional."

"You're going to lecture me about professionalism?"

"You bet your sexy ass I am." He held up one finger. "You were pretty harsh with Michel. His heart is breaking."

"And people are trying to kill him and his family. Like I asked him, which is more important?"

"It's not an either-or question. You could use a lighter hand sometimes."

"And you could focus on the bigger picture."

"There's my second point. I'm your partner, and even though I'm not some big bodybuilder with wicked military skills, I do contribute, and I deserve to be treated more like an equal."

"Aidan."

"Don't Aidan me." Aidan launched himself on top of Liam in a move they had practiced many times, and landed with his legs on either side of Liam's waist. His hands pressed Liam's shoulders to the bed. "I'm going to show you who's the real boss around here."

His dick was stiff and wagged in front of him. Beneath him he saw Liam stiffening as well, the head of his dick pushing beyond the foreskin.

"Oh yeah?" Liam asked. He grabbed Aidan's dick and squeezed.

"You bastard," Aidan said as the pain ratcheted from his dick throughout his nervous system. Then he leaned down and kissed Liam hard on the mouth.

Liam released his grip as they kissed. Aidan didn't often take the dominant role when they made love; he was happy to lie back and let Liam have his way, knowing the result would be amazing. But tonight he was in the mood for something different.

He lowered his body and pressed his dick against Liam's. It was a small source of pride that his was a fraction longer than his partner's, though no thicker. *Liam may have the big muscles, but I have size where it counts.*

He clenched his ass muscles so that his dick slid alongside Liam's, both of them lubed by precome. They kissed again, and then Aidan said, "Turn over on your stomach."

He released his grip on Liam's shoulders and sat back. Beneath him, Liam squirmed around until the globes of his ass faced up. He spread his arms above his head.

Aidan leaned down and rubbed his stubbled cheek against Liam's ass. He felt his partner shiver beneath him. Then he sat back and slapped Liam, hard, against his right butt cheek.

"Ow!" Liam said, his voice muffled by the pillow.

"You've been a bad boy," Aidan said. "You need to be

spanked." He slapped the other cheek.

Liam yelped again.

"Suck it up, sailor," Aidan said. "You're lucky I don't have a cat-o'-nine-tails here."

He spanked Liam again and again, until Liam's butt glowed pink in the darkness. Then he spit on his dick and, with no preparation, slammed it into Liam's ass.

Liam grunted into the pillow and squirmed, but he took all Aidan had to give. Aidan had to admit it thrilled him to take charge for once, to be the dom and make tough, muscular Liam into his love slave.

He leaned forward, pressing against Liam's tender ass, and felt his partner shiver beneath him. He began to pump into Liam, slamming forward until the pressure on his dick was too great and he surrendered himself to orgasm.

Breathing hard, he rolled off his partner. Liam turned to face him. "I won't be able to sit for a week," he complained, but he smiled, and Aidan recognized the lust in his eyes.

"Did you come?" he demanded.

Liam nodded sheepishly, and Aidan sighed. "Wait here."

He wrapped Liam's damp towel around his waist and padded next door to the bathroom. "Why do I always get stuck cleaning up?" he grumbled as he rinsed his groin and then soaked a washcloth.

Back in the bedroom, Liam had switched to Aidan's side of the bed. "I used your T-shirt to clean your come out of my ass," he said and smiled wickedly. "Good night." He rolled over and was asleep before Aidan had finished cleaning the stain from the bedspread.

* * *

When Aidan awoke the next morning, Liam was out at the pool performing his exercises. Aidan cleaned up what he could, then showered and dressed and went out to the kitchen to join Maria.

Olivier arrived a few minutes later. "I still cannot believe George betrayed me," he said, sitting down at the kitchen table across from them. "I gave him so much."

"We won't know for certain that George was at fault until after the police complete their investigations," Aidan said.

Olivier poured himself a glass of orange juice. "What if he had other associates?" he asked. "Suppose there are still threats to come against us?"

Agathe entered the kitchen. "I have tried to convince my husband we should return to Paris, at least for a short time. But he insists on remaining here."

"I cannot simply walk away from everything here," Olivier said.

"But at what cost?" She turned to Aidan. "Please, monsieur, try to convince my husband that we must leave this place immediately if we are to remain safe."

Aidan hated to interfere in an argument between husband and wife, even when he had strong opinions for or against something. So all he said was, "For right now, we're here to protect you. You don't have to make any quick decisions."

Liam joined them, fresh from his shower, his brownish-blond

hair plastered down. Aidan noted that he slid carefully into his chair at the kitchen table.

Aidan kept looking at Liam out of the corner of his eye as they ate breakfast. He and his partner didn't argue often, and it seemed like they were at odds more than usual on this assignment. Was it because Aidan was getting increasingly comfortable as a bodyguard, more willing to express his own opinions? Did that mean they would argue more and more as time passed, to the point where they could no longer work together, when sex wouldn't be enough to make things better between them?

He was determined not to make the same mistakes he'd made with Blake, keeping his emotions bottled up, sacrificing his own thoughts and desires in an effort to make his partner happy. That approach hadn't worked. He'd thought things were better with Liam, that they were more of a partnership.

Maybe it was just the stress of the assignment. When they were back in Nice, working shorter-term jobs, living in their own apartment, things would be better. Or at least he hoped they would.

They were almost finished eating when Michel arrived, clearly in a dark depression over the idea that his relationship with Cris was ending. He wanted nothing more than coffee for breakfast, but his mother insisted he eat. "Have some fruit, at least," she said. "And a croissant. Maria brought them from the bakery in Ajaccio this morning."

"I don't want a croissant, fresh or stale."

"I know, you are upset about your studies, mon petit," she said.

"But you will be able to finish, even if we return to Paris."

Michel grabbed his coffee cup. "I'm not going back to Paris," he said and stalked out of the kitchen. Aidan looked down at the table, and he saw Liam do the same thing.

Bodyguards were often inserted into peoples' lives at moments of high stress, and both of them knew they had to try to remain as objective and as removed from the conflict as they could. The price of familiarity was often a loss of vigilance, and that could be deadly.

"That's a car outside," Liam said, standing. He looked out the window and said, "It's the two police detectives, Bonnet from Ajaccio and Desjardins from Ménasina."

He answered the door as Olivier, Agathe, and Aidan went into the living room.

"I am pleased to see the police are finally taking my threats seriously," Olivier said when they were all seated.

"We have always taken this matter seriously," Bonnet said. Though he was the older of the two, it was clear to Aidan from the way the two flics interacted that Desjardins was the more aggressive investigator. "It is simply that we had no evidence."

Olivier addressed Desjardins. "And you have now?"

"With Detective Bonnet's assistance, I have pieced together the history of these incidents," the bald detective said. "I have interviewed many people and investigated motives and alibis."

"Aquaviva?" Olivier asked.

Aidan noticed Michel tensed when hearing the name. Was he thinking of Cris? Or of his father?

"After consulting with Detective Bonnet, I sought out Niculaiu Aquaviva yesterday," Desjardins said. "His wife indicated he and his eldest son were out on his fishing boat and would return to the harbor at Cargése."

Aidan made a note of that. It confirmed Cris's text that the reason why he hadn't returned Michel's calls and messsages was that he had been on the boat with his father during the day. But he didn't feel the need to provide that information to the police. He'd already seen how angry Olivier got at the notion that his son had been in contact with Cris.

"I left an officer there who was able to intercept Monsieur Aquaviva and his son as they returned," Bonnet continued. "They were brought to my station, and I interviewed both of them at great length. Along with another man, they were on the boat, *L'Ange de la Mer*, from early in the morning until late in the evening, and the quantity of fish and lobster they returned with supports that alibi."

"Fish!" Olivier said. "You believe fish?"

"It is not that I believe the fish, monsieur," Desjardins said gently. "I have fishermen in my family and have spent some time in those pursuits myself. I know how much one boat may bring in from a day's work."

As Olivier began to interrupt, Desjardins held up his hand. "Yes, I am aware it might have been possible for Aquaviva to depart Cargése in his fishing boat, then meet up with another man in a boat who could take him to shore, leaving his son and his crewman to catch sufficient fish and lobster. He could then be taken to shore, driven to the mine, where he could detonate the bomb and remove all traces that he had been there. This unknown accomplice would then drive him back to the ocean and transport him back to a rendezvous with the fishing boat so he could return with the catch. But that would require a great deal of initiative and planning, and I do not see that in Monsieur Aquaviva."

"You know the man?" Liam asked.

"As I mentioned yesterday, I have become acquainted with him in the course of my work," Desjardins said. "He has organized numerous demonstrations and protests, both in Ménasina and in Ajaccio. I do not remove him from my list of suspects, but I have significant doubts—because of his alibi, and because we were unable to find any physical evidence to tie him to the crime scene."

"What about that ice cream wrapper?" Liam asked. "Any fingerprints on it?"

Desjardins nodded. "The only fingerprints belonged to the victim. I spoke at length with his parents yesterday, and they confirmed his intention to visit the mine. His mother indicated that she believed he had plans to meet with someone there for a picnic—but she had no idea which of his many college friends that might be."

He opened a manila folder. "At your suggestion I spoke with Mademoiselle Vanina Andreadi yesterday evening at the university in Corte. She was unable to provide an alibi; she said she had worked Thursday night at her part-time waitress job and remained in bed for most of the day Friday."

He looked up. "Typical student behavior. She admits to knowing

Monsieur Phthalis but insisted she had not seen him since his graduation from the university."

"That's not right," Liam said. "George told me himself that he had taken Vanina up to the mine for a picnic."

"When?" Desjardins asked.

"Some time shortly before the new term began, in January. So if she says no, then she's lying."

"Unfortunately, monsieur, we cannot question the dead man on this point. I believe this is a pretty, spoiled girl. Not the kind to blow up a car or a mine."

From the look on his face, Aidan could tell Liam disagreed but that he wasn't going to argue with the detective.

"What will you do now?" Olivier asked.

"We must continue making inquiries," Desjardins said. "To investigate how the bomb was constructed and where Monsieur Phthalis might have acquired the materials."

"So you believe he was the bomber?" Liam asked.

"That is our conclusion at present," Bonnet said.

Desjardins stood, and Bonnet followed. "We will keep you apprised of our progress," the younger detective said. "Now, we must go to the lab in Ajaccio for analysis of the bomb materials."

"You cannot leave us unprotected," Olivier said. "What if these animals, whoever they are, attack our home next?"

"We believe the person responsible for these assaults is dead, monsieur. And besides, you have your own security," Bonnet said. "The police could do no better than these gentlemen."

Olivier argued, but Bonnet refused to do anything more, and finally the two detectives sketched short bows and walked to the door. Olivier followed them, once again slamming the door.

"Do you agree with them?" he demanded of Liam. "I do not. I still cannot believe George would act alone in this. That I could have been so wrong about him."

"I'm afraid there's nothing we can do," Liam said. "Aidan and I are your bodyguards, not investigators. We leave that to the police."

"If you don't believe George was the one who has been threatening us, then why don't we fly to Paris today?" Agathe asked her husband. "You can be in the office with Outremer on Monday when they sign the agreement. And we will all be safe."

"Do you know how expensive it will be to get last-minute plane tickets?" Olivier asked.

"Probably cheaper than paying for us," Aidan said.

Olivier shook his head. "No. I am not a coward to run away. We have our protection. We will stay here. We will not leave the house until after I hear on Monday that Outremer has validated the contract. And then we will have their full resources behind us."

"Olivier…" Agathe began.

"No. It is decided."

"We'll stay with you until Monday," Aidan said. "And then you and Outremer and the Agence can discuss how you want to proceed."

"Good," Olivier said. He stalked back to his office. Agathe, who did not look happy, went upstairs, and Liam and Aidan returned to their own room.

"I don't buy it," Liam said when they were behind closed doors. "I keep thinking about that ice cream wrapper. There was no reason for George to take an ice cream cone with him on his way to blow up a mine."

"Maybe he was hungry," Aidan said, sitting on the bed. "On his way to the mine, he stopped in Ménasina and bought himself a Cornetto. Remember, Liam, he was barely more than a kid himself."

Liam shook his head. "You can't really believe that. He couldn't have eaten it on his motorbike. If he did buy it in Ménasina, he would have eaten it there. It would have melted by the time he got to the mine if he didn't."

"So what are you saying?"

"I'm saying that there was someone else at the mine with him. Someone who brought a cooler with lunch and ice cream. And who brought the bomb."

"Who would that be? Vanina? The pretty airhead?"

"Not so dumb as she'd like you to think," Liam said.

"What do you want to do? You told Olivier yourself, we're bodyguards, not investigators."

"So I'll eat some of my words. I want to go back up to Corte and talk to Vanina again. See if we can get her to admit to going out to the mine with George."

Liam didn't often change his mind. And when he did, Aidan paid attention. "Call Paul Dubois then. See if he can look after the Perreaus for a while. And we'll do some investigating."

28 – Like a Princess

Liam stepped outside to call Dubois, and Aidan began to pull together a bag of gear to take with them: a map of Corsica, a miniature tape recorder, their digital camera. Liam came back into the room and said, "Good news. Dubois just finished a case, and he's free to come out here right away. Let's talk to Perreau and make sure it's all right with him."

They walked down the hall to Olivier's office. He was staring at a set of drawings and chewing on the end of a cheap black pen. "You have some news?" he asked as he looked up at them.

"A request," Liam said. "We'd like to go back up to Corte and talk to that girl again, Vanina. I keep thinking she was involved in all this. We've got Paul Dubois—the man who followed you to dinner the other night—to come over and keep an eye on things. If that's all right with you, then we'd like to borrow your wife's car again for the trip."

"Certainly. You think this girl might have worked with George?"

"I think she might have been at the mine with George yesterday," Liam said. "That's what we want to find out."

"But the police have already spoken with her."

"I don't think the police asked her the right questions," Liam said.

"If you think it will help," Olivier said. "And you trust this other man."

"We do," Liam said.

They returned to their room, and Aidan asked, "Are we taking our guns?"

"I think so. We have no idea what we'll find. Maybe just an innocent, dim waitress. But maybe something more."

"How are we going to find her?" Aidan asked. "Do we know she works on Saturday? It'll barely be noon when we get up there. The restaurant may not even be open."

Liam pursed his lips. "Ideas?"

"Michel. Or Cris. One of them may know her schedule or how to find her."

They walked down the hall to Michel's room. He was sitting on his bed cross-legged, with his headphones on, a fat textbook spread open on his lap. Aidan banged hard on the open door, and Michel looked up.

"You said you know Vanina a little," Aidan said. "Do you know where she lives?"

Michel peeled off the headphones and shook his head. "But there's a girl in my course who knows her. What do you want with Vanina?"

"We want to talk to her about George," Aidan said. "Can you call the girl who knows her? Find out where she lives, or where we could find her today."

"Sure." Michel grabbed his cell phone from the table by his bed and punched some buttons. "Bonjour, Dominique," he said. And then the French was too rapid for Aidan to follow closely, though he caught a few key words and the name Vanina repeated a few times.

Michel grabbed a piece of lined notebook paper and began writing, repeating "*ah, oui,*" several times. Then he hung up and turned back to them. "She doesn't live in a dormitory. She shares an apartment in town with another girl. Here's the address. You should talk to Dominique first, though. Her address is right below Vanina's."

"Why?" Liam asked.

Michel shrugged. "Because I don't know her, and Dominique does. Maybe she can tell you something." He hesitated, then asked, "Do you think she…"

"We don't know anything yet," Aidan said. "But we hope to figure it out."

They went downstairs as Dubois arrived. Liam left Aidan to brief him and retrieved the duffle bag with their gear from the bedroom.

When he returned, Dubois asked, "How long will you be?"

"It's an hour each way," Liam said. "It's what, ten thirty now? We should be back by two at the latest."

"*Ça va,*" Dubois said. "I'll be here. And I have your numbers if anything arises."

Liam shouldered the duffle and led the way out to Agathe's car. He retrieved the long-handled mirror from the bag and checked under the car, just to be safe. There was nothing unusual.

He couldn't help but note that trip up through the interior of the island was much prettier in the daylight. Tall chestnut trees towered by the roadside, and every so often they'd round a curve and find a vista of mountains and farms spread out before them. The road was lined with trees as straight and slim as toothpicks, towering above ferns and low bushes. Tiny blue butterflies darted alongside them as they passed.

Dominique lived in a dormitory called Cité Grossetti—a solid block of white against the blue sky and gray hills. They parked outside and walked into the bland lobby, decorated mostly with posters advertising various campus events. The carpeting was worn and frayed, and the few lounge chairs were scarred with tears and stains. A young female student at the front desk said she would have to get Dominique's permission before allowing them into the building. She picked up the handset for a multiline phone and pressed four buttons.

Liam's French was good enough to understand the clerk's part of the conversation. "Dominique, it's Elise. There are two Americans here to see you. Very cute!"

She listened, then turned to them. "She says she doesn't want to talk to you."

Liam started to protest, but Aidan took his arm and said, "No problem. We'll go."

Once they were outside, Liam said, "What's up? We could have gotten past her."

"And we will. When I lived in a dorm, people used to prop open at least one door to avoid having to check in and out. I'm betting these kids are no different."

"A big bet," Liam grumbled as they walked around to the side of the building. "We still need to know her room number."

"I have an idea about that too. The number the girl called was one three two two. Since there aren't thirteen floors here, that puts her in room three twenty-two, on the third floor. That's usually the way those phones work."

"The things you learn in college," Liam said, shaking his head.

They rounded the corner of the building and walked up to a fire door. Liam saw that it wasn't completely closed, and sure enough, someone had slid a matchbook into the lock mechanism.

"Score one for the college boy," Liam said, opening the door into a stairwell with one of the light timers so common in French buildings. He pressed the button and the light came on. They climbed to the first floor and were halfway to the second when the light went out.

"Cheap Frenchmen," Liam muttered. At the second landing he pressed the button again, and the light stayed on until they had reached the third and pushed open the fire door to the hallway.

The walls were painted an industrial shade of pale green, and the linoleum floor was a faded brown. The air smelled faintly of marijuana. Half the doors were open, and music drifted out, a combination of Italian pop, American rap, and something that sounded like German opera.

They walked casually down the hall, checking room numbers, until they came to three twenty-two. A skinny girl in a tie-dyed T-shirt and tiny shorts sat on her bed reading a textbook, while a joint smoldered in the ashtray next to her. She had a square face with hints of acne scars on her cheeks.

"Dominique?" Aidan asked.

She looked up. "I told Elise I don't want to talk to you."

They stepped inside, and Liam closed the door behind them. "It's not your choice. We're interested in Vanina Andreadi. What do you know about her?"

Dominique put down her textbook. "Why should I talk to you? She's a monster, and I hate her."

That's a good thing, Liam thought. "Well, then, if she's been doing bad things, you'll want her to get punished, won't you?"

She sat up. "Bad things? What kind of bad things?"

"Why don't you tell us what you know about her first?"

"We grew up in the same neighborhood in Ajaccio, but as soon as we got here, she wouldn't talk to me again. I'm not pretty enough to be one of her inner circle."

"She's a snob?" Aidan asked.

"Her father was a mechanic, but to see her you would think she grew up like a princess. At the lycée, she was always working with him on cars, getting her fingers grimy. But when her parents died and she went to live with her aunt and uncle, she became a beauty and left all that behind."

A mechanic, Liam noted. That meant she had the skill to place the bomb under Olivier's car. "Any boys she hung around with?" he asked.

"She had a parade of them," Dominique said. "Every boy had his tongue hanging out when she was around. And she liked to know everything that was going on. She made herself the social secretary of every group. She sent out all the e-mails for the football team and a half-dozen other clubs. She even figured out how to send e-mails from other people's addresses. She's a little troublemaker."

She looked up. "Is that how she got caught? Sending those kind of e-mails trying to trick people out of money? Or sexting? Sending men dirty pictures of herself or other girls?"

Liam was surprised at her frankness, but teenagers seemed to be increasingly capable of things he'd never thought of at their age. "How about George Phthalis? Do you know him?"

"Oh, that one! She led him like a dog on a leash. She was always asking him about mechanical things and explosives. Once he even asked her if she was trying to make a bomb, and she just laughed."

"What about Students for a Green Corsica? Was she involved with them?"

"That club? For wannabe revolutionaries? I was surprised Vanina joined it. Usually she doesn't think about anyone but herself. But once that man showed up to talk, Cris Aquaviva's father, she fell for him and suddenly the club was her new favorite. She was always talking about how smart he was, how dedicated, how handsome." She mimed making herself throw up. "Come on. He's my father's age. That's creepy."

She picked up her textbook again. "I have an exam on Monday. Now you have to go away."

"Thank you for your help," Aidan said. He opened the door, and they walked back down the hallway to the exit stair. "That was an interesting conversation."

"I'll say. Vanina is moving rapidly up my list of suspects."

29 – Chill Pill

Aidan navigated as Liam drove from the dormitory into the downtown area of Corte and found a parking place for Agathe's car on a steeply inclined street. Aidan was amused at Liam's difficulty at parallel parking. There were so few things his partner could not excel at. "Want me to do it?" he asked.

"I'll manage," Liam grumbled, swinging the wheel around for a third try.

Living in Philadelphia for so many years, Aidan had perfected the art of parallel parking, and he usually drove when they were in Nice for just that reason. On the fourth try, Liam gave up, leaving the car tilted against the curb, its front bumper jutting toward the street.

"According to the map, Vanina's address should be down this hill and three streets over," Aidan said as they got out of the car. They walked down the cobblestoned street. Brightly colored flowers sprouted from window boxes, and students with backpacks passed them going uphill. He spotted the run-down, three-story building at the address they'd been given, and pointed toward it. "It's over there."

Liam paused for surveillance. The front door was propped open, and American rap music floated out through it. "I hate rap," Aidan said.

"We're not here to quiz her about her musical tastes," Liam said. They climbed the stairs to the third floor, passing the source of the music on two. Liam knocked hard on the door to apartment 3G. There was no answer. "Vanina!" Liam called.

The door across the hall popped open, and an elderly woman, barely three feet tall, looked out. "She's not home," she said. "She went out early." Then she slammed her door closed.

"What do we do now?" Aidan asked. "Stake out the apartment until she gets back?"

"Doesn't seem like a good use of our resources," Liam said. "I guess we should head back to Ajaccio."

"We can call Bonnet and Desjardins and tell them what we found out today," Aidan said as they climbed down the stairs to the street.

"We didn't find anything."

"Of course we did. Dominique told us that Vanina was asking George about bombs, that she knew enough about cars to plant one under Olivier's car, that she had a crush on Nic Aquaviva."

Liam reached the street first and held the door open for Aidan. "It's all hearsay. You heard Dominique—she has a grudge against Vanina. She could be making it all up."

"You can be so goddamned literal sometimes, Liam. You have to use your instincts. That girl knows Vanina is bad news—you saw how quick she was to spin out a bunch of ways the girl could be in trouble."

"Yeah, just like you start making up stories before you have all the facts."

"You're an asshole, you know that?" Aidan strode ahead of Liam toward where they had parked. Behind him, he heard Liam's phone ring, but he didn't stop walking until he had reached the car.

When he looked behind him, Liam was nowhere in sight. Good grief. How could he have gotten lost in such a short time? Or was the big lunk pouting because Aidan had yelled at him? Well, he could find his own way back to the car. He was a damn Navy SEAL, after all. He knew how to navigate.

He crossed his arms over his chest and leaned back against Agathe's car. It was a warm afternoon there in the sun, and beads of sweat appeared on his forehead. Young guys in T-shirts swarmed past, carrying guitars or soccer balls. Girls with perfect makeup strode along to the rhythm of whatever was playing in their earbuds.

Chestnut blossoms glowed in the sun, and tiny brown birds hopped from branch to branch. Watching them, Aidan felt some of his tension evaporate. It was a beautiful Saturday afternoon in the mountains. The air was clear, with feathery cirrus clouds high in the atmosphere. There was no reason to be angry.

A small fluffy dog, the same color as Hayam, romped past on a neon-yellow leash, dragging a middle-aged woman with close-cropped hair and serious dark-rimmed glasses behind. She had the distracted air of a professor, and Aidan wondered what it would be like to return to teaching full-time, to live in a college town like this one, in the country somewhere.

Then Liam rounded the corner at a full gallop. "In the car, now," he said. "Michel's gone missing."

Aidan tried to open the passenger door, but it was locked. "I can't get in until you open the door," he said, all his irritation returning in a fraction of a second.

Liam rushed the driver's door, unlocked it, and jumped in. He started the engine and then reached over to unlock Aidan's door. He had the car in reverse before Aidan was fully in his seat. Aidan pulled the door shut as Liam backed up.

"What happened?" Aidan asked.

"Later. Just get me out of this town."

Aidan fumed, but he opened the map. "Take this street up the hill to that stop sign and turn left. That'll take us around the back side of the town and down to the 623 toward Ajaccio." He waited until Liam had made the turn to ask. "Now will you tell me?"

"Dubois called me as you were running off. Michel slipped out his bedroom window sometime this morning. He must have walked his motorbike away from the house and then hit the road."

"Do his parents have any idea where he went?"

"Not a clue," Liam said, zooming down the lightly wooded street called Caffarone, a bit too fast for Aidan's comfort. He made a couple of quick turns and had to slow down on the Faubourg Scaravaglie—a small commercial district on the outskirts of Corte. But once past it, he accelerated again.

"He probably went to look for Cris," Aidan said, pulling his cell phone from his pocket. "Let me call and see if he's heard from Michel."

"You have his number?" Liam asked.

"Of course."

The call went direct to voice mail, though. Aidan left a message for Cris, that Michel had left his parents' house, perhaps looking for him. "If you hear from him, please let me know."

"One more call," he said to Liam. He pulled up his directory once again and found the number he had entered for Nic Aquaviva's home.

A woman answered. "Madame Aquaviva?" he asked.

"Oui?"

In French, he explained he was a friend of her son Cris, and that he was looking for him. Was he there?

"No, he is with his father. Fishing. He left early this morning, and he will not return until at least four or five o'clock."

Aidan thanked her and said he'd call back later, no message.

"Do you think we should go there and wait for him?" Aidan asked. "Maybe Michel is lurking around somewhere."

Liam shook his head. "We need to go back to Olivier and Agathe. They're the primary clients, after all. We need to make sure they're safe, and see what's going on there. Maybe there are clues at the house."

"A clue! A clue!" Aidan said, pretending to make the noise of a sneeze.

"Nobody likes a smart-ass, Aidan."

"Take a chill pill, Bill," Aidan said. "Or would that be a chilly pilly, Billy?"

Liam kept in touch with no one from his old life beyond his mother, his sisters, and a few old SEAL buddies who still called him

Billy. Everyone else knew him as Liam. Aidan knew the use of the name irritated him.

"That's not my name."

"Oh God, Liam," Aidan said. "Do you have to be such a drama queen?"

"Excuse me? Who's the drama queen in this relationship?"

"That would be you," Aidan said, poking him in the side. "I'm the flexible, easygoing one. You're the one who makes a huge deal out of everything."

"Just be quiet, all right?" Liam said.

Aidan mimed pulling a zipper across his mouth, then sealing it and tossing away the key. Liam grimaced and focused on driving.

The road was narrow and twisting, and Aidan felt his stomach churning if he stared too long at the trees zooming past. Instead he closed his eyes and tried to put himself in Michel's place. He'd had his heart broken a few times, after all. Been there, done that, bought the T-shirt, and wore it out.

When had he been so desperate to go chasing after another boy? What had he done? Long before he had returned to Philadelphia and met Blake, he had taken a short-term teaching job in Prague. It was soon after Eastern Europe had begun opening to Western influences, and everyone wanted to learn English. Aidan taught classes during the day and tutored private clients in the evening. Late at night, he and a friend haunted a gay club, where they danced, drank, and made out with strangers in dark corners.

It was such a crazy time. He and his friend were determined to throw off all the outmoded morals of straight society, and underground Prague was just the place to do it. The clubs were full of men willing to experiment with everything from cross-dressing to water sports to S&M. There were nights when he stumbled from a stranger's bed back to his own apartment for a quick shower and a change of clothes before heading to his classroom.

There was one guy, a German named Claus, who got under his skin. Maybe it was that he was the perfect Aryan, and it felt so transgressive to be a Jew sucking his Nazi dick. Or maybe it was because Claus was so icy cool; even at the moment of climax he could have been ordering a latte at a coffee shop, so blasé was his demeanor.

So Aidan chased him. Whenever he ran into Claus at a club, he latched on to him and persisted until he could take the German home. They must have had sex a half-dozen times before Claus dropped out of the scene.

There were no cell phones back then, no Internet, Facebook, or online dating sites. Hooking up was haphazard. You ran into someone, you connected, you fucked. That was it.

Aidan began to obsess. He asked everyone, but no one knew where the German had gone. He went to the apartment building where Claus lived and buttonholed neighbors. He spent hours one evening watching the apartment windows for signs of life.

It took another boy, a Swiss this time, to push Claus out of his mind. But even so, for the rest of his time in Prague, Aidan kept one eye out for the elusive German, though he never saw him again.

So he understood completely Michel's motivation, and he was sure the boy had gone up to Cargése to ambush Cris. All he had to do was convince Liam of that.

30 – My Little Cabbage

Liam gripped the steering wheel through the twists and turns of the road that led back to Ajaccio. Why did Aidan have to be so irritating? And to accuse him of being a drama queen! He was the least dramatic, most levelheaded person he knew. It was only around Aidan that he occasionally lost his temper.

He focused on the breathing techniques he had learned in the Navy. He was going to be no good to the clients unless he could get his temper under control. He'd deal with Aidan and whatever issues there were between them once they had found Michel Perreau and his father had his contract signed on Monday.

By the time he pulled into the driveway of the Perreaus' home, he felt he had regained his center, and he turned to his partner. "I'm sorry I snapped at you." He reached over for Aidan's hand and squeezed it. "I love you."

"I love you too, sweetheart," Aidan said, squeezing back. "Now let's go figure out what happened to Michel."

Inside they found Olivier pacing the living room, and Paul Dubois looking alternately angry and sheepish. "He snuck out the upstairs window," Dubois said. "He was so quiet. None of us realized he was gone for hours."

"I had no idea he could go out the window like that," Olivier said.

Liam looked at Aidan, but neither of them said anything. In

retrospect, they probably should have told Olivier they'd caught his son sneaking out to meet Cris, or at least warned Dubois the boy could slip away. But they had been more concerned with external threats.

"Did he leave any clue where he might have gone?" Aidan asked.

"His mother is upstairs now," Olivier said. "But I don't believe she has found anything."

They climbed the stairs and found Agathe sorting through papers on her son's desk. "His e-mail is password protected," she said. "I've already tried everything I can think of."

She listed them—his birth date, house numbers, and phone numbers from places they had lived, other significant numbers and words.

"Do you mind if I give it a try?" Aidan asked.

She waved her hand toward the computer, and he sat down. "You have some ideas?" Liam asked. He figured Aidan would try some combination of Michel's and Cris's names or the date they met, though how Aidan knew that, he didn't have a clue.

Aidan tried a couple of things, and none of them worked. Then he said, "Of course!" and began typing again.

Leaning over his shoulder, Liam saw him searching for a French-Corsican dictionary. "You think he's using a password in Corsican?" he asked.

"It's a try," he said. He looked at Agathe. "Neither of you know the language, right?"

"I know just a few words, the same as Olivier."

He spoke as he typed. "So it's pretty safe to assume you wouldn't be able to crack his password."

"But you speak Corsu?" Agathe asked.

Aidan shook his head. "But I think I know it when I hear it."

Liam saw him bring up the dictionary and type in *chou*. "Cabbage?" he asked.

"Yup."

The dictionary entry was *carbusgiu*. Aidan typed something, which Liam assumed was that word, and sure enough, the password was accepted. "How…" Liam began.

"I'll tell you later," Aidan said.

The most recent message was from Cris Aquaviva, sent at 10:00 a.m. Liam's French was improving as he spent more time among French speakers, but he wanted to be sure he understood. "Can you translate, please?" he asked Aidan.

"Sure." Aidan looked over at Agathe, who appeared very stoic. "Cris says he loves Michel very much and has to see him right away. He asks Michel to come up to the harbor at Cargése and meet him by the breakwater."

"Do you think this is true, messieurs?" Agathe asked. "That my son—loves—this other boy?"

Liam looked to Aidan. This was definitely his partner's territory. He expected Aidan to launch into a sensitive discussion of the coming-out process. Instead he said, "I don't think Cris sent this e-mail at all, madame. Look at the time."

He pointed. "According to Cris's mother, he was on the boat

with his father at ten o'clock. I don't believe he could have sent an e-mail from out on the ocean."

"I don't understand."

But Liam did. "This morning we drove up to Corte to look for another student, a girl named Vanina Andreadi. She's involved with the group Students for a Green Corsica, who are opposed to your husband's mine reopening. We believe she might have something to do with the threats against you and your family."

Agathe nodded, but it was clear she wasn't making the connection yet.

"We didn't find her, but we did speak to another student, a girl who knew Vanina. And one of the things she told us was that Vanina had access to the e-mail accounts of many of the other students, and that she knew how to…" He stopped. He had no idea how to explain what he needed to in French.

Aidan took over. "We think she was able to access Cris's e-mail account to send this message to Michel, to lure him out of the house."

"But why?" Agathe asked.

"We don't know yet," Liam said. "But we're going to find out."

They called Olivier and Paul Dubois upstairs and explained the situation to them, without specifically referencing the content of the message or why Vanina might have assumed the two boys were in love.

"I will call the detective from Ménasina. Desjardins," Olivier said. "It's only a few kilometers to Cargése, so he should be able to get an officer there quickly to pick up Michel."

He hurried downstairs to his office, and Dubois followed him, leaving Agathe in Michel's bedroom with Aidan and Liam.

"You did not answer my question," Agathe said. "Though you didn't have to. I knew when I saw them together."

"Michel and Cris?" Aidan asked, and she nodded.

"It will be difficult for my husband to accept. First, that his son is gay. And second, that the boy he loves is the son of this man."

"It takes small steps, madame," Aidan said. "The first of those is to get your son home safely."

By the time they got downstairs, Olivier had spoken to Desjardins, who had agreed to send an officer to the harbor at Cargése. "I want to go there," Olivier said.

Liam shook his head. "Let's wait to hear from the police. This could be a diversion to split you all up and make you more vulnerable."

A half hour later, Desjardins had not called, and Olivier was pacing the living room, growing increasingly agitated. Liam had a lot of experience with clients at moments of high anxiety, and he had trained himself to move in the opposite direction. He became calmer and more Zen-like the more agitated Olivier became. He had learned that if you let the client work off the nervous energy, while keeping him protected, eventually he would wear down.

Finally the phone rang. Olivier had brought the office phone into the living room so that he could use the speaker. "This is Perreau," he said. "Do you have news?"

"We found your son's moto," Desjardins said. "Parked at the side of the breakwater."

"Where is he?"

"One of the fisherman saw him arrive, meet with a young girl, then get on a speedboat with her and leave the harbor."

Liam remembered Vanina from the Auberge des Etudiants. "Can he describe her at all?" he asked.

"Very pretty," Desjardins said. "Large breasts and long, curly black hair."

"Sounds like Vanina Andreadi," Liam said.

"Or many other girls of this island."

"We have another reason to suspect her," Aidan said. He explained about the e-mail message.

On the other end of the line, Desjardins sneezed. When he finished, he said, "I will send someone to look for her."

"I am coming up there," Olivier said.

"Monsieur, we don't even know where they have gone," Desjardins said. "With a fast boat and enough petrol, they could be anywhere."

"I don't care. He is my son."

Liam wondered if Olivier would feel the same way if he knew Michel was gay and that he was in love with Nic Aquaviva's son. Perhaps; perhaps not. He didn't know the man well enough to say.

After Olivier ended the call, Liam said, "I have to object. By separating from your wife, you will spread our resources too thin. I don't know if we can find additional agents to help protect you."

"There are men we can call," Dubois said. "But it is Saturday afternoon. I don't know how easy it will be to reach them."

"Then we will all go to Cargése," Olivier said.

Liam tried to protest. Agathe tried to change her husband's mind. But he was adamant, and everyone finally caved in. "We need some time to prepare," Liam said. "A half hour?"

Olivier agreed, and Liam and Aidan returned to their room. Liam retrieved their guns and began to clean and load his own. Aidan handled the other equipment—the flashlights, the walkie-talkies and so on. Dubois had his own equipment in his car.

Liam finished with his gun and turned to Aidan's. When it was ready, he handed it to his partner, who put on his shoulder holster and slipped the gun into it. Liam did the same.

He was about to hoist the duffle bag when Aidan put a hand on his arm. "I promise to do everything you say. No wisecracks, no arguments. I trust you, and I believe in you completely."

Liam smiled. "You have good instincts, Aidan. Don't ever be afraid to tell me what you think. Let's only promise not to argue."

"You got it." Aidan leaned up to kiss him on the lips.

Liam closed his eyes for a second and focused only on Aidan, on the man he loved, trying to be fully present in the moment. Then he opened his eyes and said, "Let's rock."

Liam carried the duffle out to the living room, where Olivier, Agathe, and Dubois waited. As Dubois opened the front door, Liam's cell phone rang, and he recognized Richard's number. He handed the duffle to Aidan and shepherded everyone out the front door. He didn't speak until the door was closed behind them.

"Hey," he said. "You find out anything else for us?"

"I did, and you're not going to like it," Richard said.

He stepped away from the Perreaus. "What is it?"

"I've got this program I run, takes a couple of days sometimes. I throw all the data I have into it, and it searches for connections. I put all the names you asked me about, along with a bunch of other terms that come to mind. You ever see the movie *The French Connection*?"

Liam struggled to focus. His brain was full of the details of Michel's abduction and plans for the trip to Cargése. He didn't have time for movie trivia. "Can you get to the point please, Richard?"

"The point, mate, is that when I think of Corsica, I think of that movie, which is about these two New York City cops trying to crack a French heroin smuggling ring. This ring, see, was run by some blokes from the Corsican mafia. So I hear Corsica, and I throw the word 'mafia' into my search for your girl Vanina."

Liam's heart skipped a beat, because he could already see what was coming.

"And I got a hit," Richard continued. "Her uncle, Alberto Andreadi, the one what adopted her after her father got run over by a bus? He's a big cheese in whatever's left of the Corsican Mafia."

31 – Spinning a Story

Aidan tried not to let his irritation show as Liam walked away to take his call in private. It was his common practice, after all. "Let's get organized," he said to the group. "Liam will ride with Monsieur Perreau, I'll go with Dr. Perreau, and Paul, you can follow in your car. With all three vehicles in Cargése, we'll have a lot of flexibility."

He put the duffle in Olivier's trunk, and they were all ready to go when Liam walked out the front door. Olivier locked the door behind them, and they got into the BMW. Aidan was curious to know who Liam had spoken to but knew he'd have to wait to get his partner alone to find out.

Agathe didn't speak to Aidan until they were well on their way into the hills above Ajaccio. She gripped the steering wheel and asked, "Did you know about my son when you saw him?"

Aidan leaned back against his seat. "We make initial impressions of our clients," he said. "Primarily so that we can understand how they may react in times of crisis. We looked at his relationship with you and his father and what we saw is the way a typical college student acts. Until…"

She looked over at him.

"Tuesday night. He slipped out of his bedroom window, probably the same way he got out this morning. We followed him up the hill behind your house and watched as Cris Aquaviva arrived."

She nodded and faced forward.

"We owe you a great apology, madame," he said. "We should have told you about his escape route as soon as we discovered it. Perhaps if we had, we would have averted our current danger. But at the time we thought we were protecting his privacy. That it should be his decision to tell you, not ours."

"I had some idea," she said, still concentrating on her driving. "But I could not act, because I knew my husband's opinions. In some ways, he is very backward. His world, the one of mining, is a very macho one, few women, no homosexuals. I think sometimes he believes they are not quite human."

"I hope that getting to know Liam and me will help him see that there are many possibilities for Michel," Aidan said.

"Yes, perhaps that will be the one small bright spot in this very cloudy episode."

They drove the rest of the way in silence, their car sandwiched in the middle of the convoy. Aidan forced himself to control his impatience to know about Liam's phone call for the hour it took to drive to Cargése.

It was midafternoon by the time the convoy approached the town. The view of the harbor from the top of the cliff was beautiful. To one side was the square white box of the Greek Orthodox church, surmounted by a pergola with a wraparound balcony. On the other stood the white and sandstone Catholic church, its roof a series of curves and arches and a tall cross at the very top.

In between lay a hodgepodge of pale gray and white houses with sloped roofs of coral tiles. The harbor lay before them with a breakwater shaped like a gooseneck that reminded him of the French Riviera, though the foliage was much sparser and the paddle cactus more threatening.

The three cars lined up before the dockmaster's office. Aidan left Agathe with Dubois and joined Olivier and Liam at the water's edge with Desjardins.

"I found a photograph of Vanina Andreadi," he said. "The fisherman who noticed Michel Perreau leave this morning identified her as the woman with him."

"Have you learned anything more about her?" Liam asked.

Desjardins shook his head. "Just what we already knew. That she is a student at the university." He turned to Olivier. "We aren't even sure how she knew your son."

"Michel has always been secretive about his friends," Olivier said.

"Do you recognize the name Alberto Andreadi?" Liam asked.

Desjardins turned his attention to him. "Andreadi is a common last name in Corsica. But yes, I know the man you speak of."

"He's Vanina's uncle," Liam said. "Her father's brother. When her father died, her aunt and uncle adopted her."

"Who is this man?" Olivier asked.

Desjardins shook his head. "This is not good. He is a dangerous criminal, involved with the Union Corse." To Liam and Aidan he added, "It is our equivalent of La Cosa Nostra of Italy, what you call the Mafia."

That must have been what Liam learned when he took the call as they were leaving Ajaccio, Aidan realized. How frustrating it must have been for Liam to be stuck in a car with the client for an hour, unable to follow up on that piece of information without worrying the client beside him.

Olivier stared at the police detective. "Do you mean the Union Corse has been behind these threats all along? But why? They never asked for money."

"I do not know, monsieur. But I must confer with my colleagues." He sketched a brief bow and said, "I will be back with you shortly." He walked toward his car, pulling his cell phone from his pocket.

"I don't understand what is happening," Olivier said.

"Perhaps we should go back to Ajaccio," Aidan said. "You and your wife will be more comfortable there, and we'll wait to see what the police discover."

Olivier shook his head. "No. I must wait here. But I must tell my wife." He turned and walked across the rough pavement toward Agathe's car, where she stood in conversation with Paul Dubois.

"Did Richard tell you anything else?" Aidan asked.

Liam looked at him. "How did you know I heard from Richard?"

"You got a call just before we left Ajaccio. I presume that's when you heard that Vanina's uncle was a mafioso. And you had to hear it from Richard, because as far as I know, you haven't given Vanina's name to Louis." He paused. "And if you knew before then and didn't tell me…"

"You're right. Richard has some weird program that figured out this Alberto Andreadi was Vanina's uncle and that he was a criminal."

"It makes sense," Aidan said, remembering their conversation with Dominique.

"What? As far as I can see, none of this makes sense."

"Dominique said after her father died and she was adopted by her aunt and uncle, Vanina changed from being a little grease monkey to a beauty queen."

"That's hardly relevant at this point, Aidan."

"Of course it is. Her father died when she was young. So it's logical that she begins looking for new father figures. I'll bet her uncle treated her like a little princess, so that's who she became. Then she crushed on Nic Aquaviva, who's old enough to be her dad."

A fishing boat approached the entrance to the breakwater, sending ripples of blue-green water against the shore and disturbing the feeding of a flock of gulls, who took flight.

"And?" Liam asked.

"And she started doing things to please Nic Aquaviva. Helping out with Students for a Green Corse. Maybe even sending those threatening e-mails to Olivier Perreau. She has the computer skills. She asked George Phthalis about making bombs, so we know she was interested in that topic. And she knew her way around cars, enough to plant the bomb in a way that would frighten Olivier."

The noise of the boat's engine was loud, and in order to keep speaking quietly, they had to step farther away from the water. "What about the mine bombing?" Liam asked.

"Suppose Vanina convinced George to let her prepare a picnic," Aidan said. He held up his right hand, palm out. "I know, I'm spinning a story here, but let me try. She brought everything herself and met him at the mine on Friday."

"That part's believable," Liam admitted.

"I don't know what happened next. Maybe she asked George for help, and he fumbled the bomb somehow. Or she planted it and left, and he discovered it and tried to disable it. Somehow the bomb went off. She cleaned up the picnic stuff, missing the ice cream wrapper, and she left. Mission accomplished. Mine destroyed, blame on George."

"Even if I grant you all that, then what?" Liam asked. "How did we get from there to here?"

"I don't know," Aidan said. He turned toward the water, shading his brow against the bright sun. "But isn't that Cris Aquaviva on the bow of that boat?"

32 – Mixed Signals

Liam recognized Cris on the bow of the fishing boat as it made its turn into the marina. He understood what Michel saw in him—with the light behind him, the boy looked more than ever like a man, his faded, sweat-stained T-shirt clinging to his pecs, his muscular thighs ready to burst through his denim cutoffs.

He calculated where the boat would tie up, and he was waiting there to accept the bow line Cris tossed. He tied it around a cleat, then did the same with the stern line.

"Why are you here?" Cris asked when his father cut the engine.

"Did you send an e-mail to Michel this morning?" Liam asked.

Cris shook his head. "We never use e-mail. Only phone and text. And besides, I was on this boat all morning, and there's no Internet out in the ocean."

"That's what we thought," Liam said as Desjardins approached. The police detective, whose white shirt was looking much less crisp thanks to the heat and humidity, repeated the same questions and got the same answers.

"I don't understand," Cris said. His father appeared behind him, both of them still on the boat's bow, standing beside a wriggling pile of fish and lobsters. Liam noted how much they resembled each other—both had the same dark hair with a slight curl, the same coal-black eyes. Same build, same ruddy skin tanned by work in the sun.

"Someone sent Michel an e-mail this morning from your

account," Liam said. "The message asked him to meet you here, at the harbor, at noon. We believe Vanina Andreadi hacked your e-mail account and sent the message herself."

Cris looked confused. "Vanina? Why? She hardly knows Michel."

"That's what we're trying to figure out. Michel snuck out of his parents' house and rode his motorbike up here. He met Vanina around noon and left with her in a speedboat. That's the last anyone has seen or heard of him."

Cris pulled his cell from the front pocket of his cutoff shorts. "I can get a signal here. Let me call him." He dialed the number, held the phone to his ear. "It goes right to voice mail," he said. "Michel, it's Cris. I'm at the harbor in Cargése. Call me right away."

He ended the call. "Just in case, I'll text him too," he said. While his fingers darted over the phone's keys, Liam turned to Desjardins. "Were you able to reach Vanina's uncle?"

The detective gave a typical Gallic shrug. "Andreadi is not at home, but we spoke to his wife. She said the girl showed up this morning, crying because she had tried to impress a man, and she had made a big mess of it."

"Did she mention Monsieur Aquaviva by name?" Liam asked.

Desjardins shook his head.

"My son?" Nic asked.

"Not your son, but you, monsieur. We believe now that Mademoiselle Andreadi may have orchestrated the threats against Monsieur Perreau and his family as a way to gain your affection."

"I thought she was in earnest," Nic said. "We did talk often, about environmental threats and the need for action. But I had no idea she would take things so far."

"The aunt says Vanina had a long conversation with her uncle, who then made some phone calls. It is likely she obtained her uncle's assistance in her activities."

"Was he involved from the start, do you think?" Liam asked.

Desjardins shook his head. "Not according to the aunt."

Liam heard the sound of kids calling "Papa!" and turned to look up the curving footpath that led from the town down to the harbor. A pretty, dark-haired woman in her forties, the kind who had probably once been quite a beauty, stepped easily along the path. Three dark-haired kids on bicycles—two boys and a girl—were her advance guard.

"I called your mother and asked her to come help unload the boat," Nic said to Cris as they watched the two boys race each other along the breakwater. As soon as they arrived, Nic put them to work on the boat's foredeck.

His wife and daughter followed, and quickly the whole family was working together smoothly. Liam looked around for Aidan and saw him up by the dock master's office, where he, Olivier, Agathe, and Paul Dubois were clustered in the shade.

Aidan stepped forward to meet him as he got close, then continued back up to the office with him. "What happens now?" he asked.

Liam shrugged. "Don't know. Desjardins will have to mount a

search for Michel. I have no idea what kind of boats the police here have."

Olivier, Agathe, and Dubois turned to face them as they approached. "Have the police told you anything?" Liam asked.

"This gangster, he has a boat," Olivier said. "Desjardins says the police have checked where he keeps it, and it's gone. I asked him, is it the same kind of boat that picked up Michel? He said there are many boats of the same type all along the coast."

It was clear from Olivier's tone that he didn't think much of the investigative abilities of the Corsican police. From their vantage point, Liam saw a white boat approaching the harbor at top speed. "We have our binoculars?" he asked Aidan.

"In the duffle. It's in Olivier's trunk."

With all the time they'd been standing around, Liam thought, as he accepted the key from Olivier and loped toward the car, Aidan could at least have gotten things set up. What did he think he was doing?

He reached the car and popped the trunk lid, zipping open the duffle quickly. He had trained Aidan how he liked things packed—always in a particular order, so he could find things easily. At least his partner had mastered that skill. He grabbed the binoculars and raised them to his eyes.

The approaching boat belonged to the police. So Desjardins had managed to call in some help.

Then he took a deep breath. None of this was Aidan's fault; they were partners, and it was up to Liam to behave that way, instead of like a spoiled child. Or a drama queen, he thought grimly.

He returned to the group beside the dock master's office. "Police boat," he said. "I guess they'll search for Michel."

"Only one boat!" Olivier said.

Liam put a hand on his shoulder. "I'm sure they have others working out of Ajaccio."

"Still, it's not enough. I'm going to talk to him."

He stalked toward Desjardins, and Liam looked back toward the fishing boat. He noticed the youngest Aquaviva, the girl, was already heading up to town on her bicycle, a load of packages in the basket of her bicycle. One of the boys was almost ready to leave.

He watched the Aquaviva family work together in harmony, Nic passing the spiny lobsters with banded claws to his wife, who weighed them and marked them with a tag. She handed them to Cris, who packaged them in brown paper and ice and handed them to his brother. When the lobsters had all been taken care of, they moved quickly to the fish, sorting, cleaning, and packaging.

If only he and Aidan could work so smoothly together, he thought. He'd worked with many teams in the Navy and the SEALs, and there had been a whole lot less angst and aggravation among the members there.

It couldn't simply be the presence of testosterone in their relationship, unmediated by female hormones. For most of his military career, he'd been surrounded by men, with only the occasional contact with women—drivers, pilots, even artillery specialists. He'd had no problem with women in combat.

Aidan wasn't a trained soldier, as Liam's male and female teammates had been in the military. They had a common grounding in technique and commands. You instinctively knew how your buddy would react, because you'd both been broken down and rebuilt in the same way. Aidan was a fast learner, and as his strength and conditioning grew and he gained more experience in the field, he became an increasingly reliable partner, but he'd never be a soldier.

He kept gnawing at the question. Was all the friction between them because he and Aidan were gay? Was there some drama gene Liam had been repressing all these years?

While they waited for Desjardins to confer with the arriving police and for the Aquavivas to finish unloading their boat, he thought back to his years with the SEALs. No one had ever accused him of being a drama queen, even in jest. He'd have beaten the man to a pulp over the accusation.

Sure, guys tossed around a million derogatory terms among themselves, but always in the way of brothers. It was something Liam had missed as a kid, having only sisters. Then, as a teenager, he was shy, filled with an unspoken rage against his father that he was afraid to let out in public. Add to that his confusion over his sexuality—why did his dick get hard when he thought about other boys? Why didn't he have the same desperate desire to get into a girl's panties as the rest of the boys in his high school seemed to have?

Though he'd been a star athlete, Liam never felt like he fit in. Even in basic training with the Navy, he'd kept to himself. It was only after going through the BUD/S training and becoming a SEAL that he finally felt part of a group. Just one of the guys.

By then, of course, he knew he was gay. He wasn't stupid, and there were more examples in the media to show him you didn't have to dress like Liberace to like sucking dick. Even so, he'd had no intention of coming out to his teammates, because he knew that would destroy the only human connections he had.

Things changed, though, and eventually he did come out, back when to do so spelled the end of his military career. He accepted it and moved on, met Aidan, fell in love, and…became a drama queen? He was back to the same question. Why were things so different?

Then he looked at Aidan. He had his arm around Agathe's shoulders and was speaking to her in low tones. Probably counseling her about how to deal with her son, he thought. His heart flooded with warmth, and he realized why it was that he got so dramatic with Aidan, worried about him, argued with him, strove desperately to protect him.

It was love, pure and simple. Though of course he cared about his fellow SEALs, thought of them as his brothers, it wasn't the same thing. Not at all.

It was about four thirty by then, and Liam calculated that the sun would set in about two hours. He watched as the last of Cris's brothers took off on his bike, and Nic hosed down the boat's deck. When he was finished, Cris and his parents walked up to the office. All of them smelled like fish, and they ducked into the two washrooms.

When they all returned, cleaned up, Nic spoke to Olivier. "I would like to help you look for your son. I have a boat, and I know these waters, better probably than the police."

Olivier stared at him. "Why?"

"You have a son; I have a son. If it were Cris who was missing…"

He left the question unfinished. Liam thought Olivier's answer would probably have been to walk away, and he hoped the client felt at least a bit ashamed by the other man's generous offer. "I can come with you," Liam offered. "I was in the US Navy. I know my way around boats."

"Liam," Aidan said.

"You stay here with Dr. Perreau," Liam said. "I know what I'm doing."

"You don't need to remain here," Mrs. Aquaviva said. She held her hand out to Agathe. "I am Chjara. You will come up to my home, please. We can wait there."

"Fine," Olivier said. "Let's get moving, then, before we lose the light."

"I'll tell Desjardins," Liam said. "Figure out how to coordinate with him."

As Olivier followed Nic, Liam strode over to the police detective. "Aquaviva has offered to take Perreau out to help with the search." As Desjardins started to argue, he said, "It'll get him out of your hair. I'll go with him and make sure they stay out of trouble. How can we stay in contact with your search team?"

Desjardins called over an officer who accompanied Liam to

Nic's fishing boat. *L'Ange de la Mer* was about twenty meters long, light blue, with a pair of outboard engines at the stern. Good for fishing, but they'd be outgunned by any well-equipped speedboat. But at least they could do some reconnaissance, free up the police from checking certain parts of the coast.

Nic and the officer shared contact information as Liam prowled the boat. It was in good repair, satisfactory for his purposes. He hopped back onshore and returned to Olivier's car. He opened the duffle bag on the trunk and shared the contents with Aidan.

"You're sure about this?" Aidan asked.

"Very sure. I'll be fine—we're just scouting, and we'll be back by dark. And I'm depending on you to keep Agathe calm up at the Aquaviva house."

"I'll do my best."

Liam wanted very much to kiss his partner—but that would be unprofessional. He settled for putting his arm around Aidan's shoulders in a manly hug and whispering in his ear, "I love you."

He didn't have to wait for Aidan's response; he already knew what it would be. He shouldered the half-empty duffle and hurried back to Aquaviva's boat.

33 – Through the Maquis

With a mixture of love, determination, and fear, Aidan watched Liam hurry down along the breakwater. Aidan hated any part of an assignment that separated him from Liam, especially where there was danger involved. Liam was too principled and too strong-willed. He would take risks to do what he thought was right, and that scared the hell out of Aidan, especially if he couldn't be by his partner's side.

He turned to the two women, put on a smile, and asked, "Shall we go?"

They left Olivier's car at the marina, to be there when he and Liam returned. Chjara rode with Agathe, to give her directions, and Paul Dubois would follow in his car. "Cris, why don't you ride with me and Paul?" Aidan asked. He opened the back door of Dubois's car and ushered Cris inside, then slipped in beside him.

"If you know anything you haven't told us, now's the time," he said in a low voice.

"I don't," Cris insisted. "Vanina and Michel are in the same program, but she's a year behind him. And she…well, she only goes for guys she know will respond to her."

"You?"

He shook his head. "She's only nice to me because she likes my papa. For a while she had a thing for the coach of the football team. Always hanging around the team volunteering to do things like take pictures, put them up on the web page, e-mail the team, and so on."

"Her friend Dominique said she knew how to break into e-mail accounts that belonged to other people."

"I don't know about that. But she's very sneaky."

Agathe pulled up in front of a single-story house with a terracotta roof. Brightly painted tin lizards crawled the front wall, and when he saw Aidan looking at them, Cris said, "My mother makes them and sells them in town. She is very talented."

Dubois elected to remain outside, and Aidan and Cris followed the two women up the stone pathway. Chjara took Agathe by the arm and led her into the house. "We'll have some tea," she said. "I make it a special way. Very relaxing."

The house was small but cozy, and Aidan saw that someone, most likely Chjara, had an eye for color and design. He felt comfortable there immediately. Aidan and Agathe sat at the kitchen table while Chjara bustled around the old porcelain stove, boiling water and then steeping tea leaves with some special herbs.

Cris brought out a set of four cups and saucers, not fancy but decorated with twining vines and flowers, and then sat with them. Chjara carried the copper teakettle to the table and poured tea for everyone, then sat down.

No one seemed to have anything to say. Aidan was about to speak, to break the silence, when they heard a car pull up out front. Cris jumped up and returned a moment later. "It's the flic," he said. He opened the front door, and Bruno Desjardins entered.

"An officer passed by your home earlier today, madame," he said to Agathe. "He found this note there." As he handed it to her, he said, "Do not worry, it is a reproduction."

Aidan looked over her shoulder. It was a ransom demand, for a half-million euros, to ensure Michel's safe return. The Perreaus were warned not to contact the police, which was to Aidan like closing the barn door after the cows had run away.

The final line said further instructions would be forthcoming. Agathe's shoulders sagged, and Aidan took her hand.

"This information has been conveyed to your husband via police radio, madame," Desjardins said to Agathe.

She looked up at him. "We cannot pay this. Even if my husband were to sell the rights to the mine completely to Outremer, I doubt we would realize a sum this large."

Desjardins nodded. "That is what your husband indicated. Even so, we must wait for the kidnappers to make the next move. They have not given us any way to contact them, to negotiate."

"What will they do with my son?" Agathe asked, and she began to cry.

Aidan released her hand as Chjara took Agathe in her arms, stroking her hair and murmuring to her. Aidan looked across at Cris, whose eyes were wild.

Desjardins stood. "I am sorry to have to deliver such dark news. I return now to Ajaccio, where we will pursue the connection between the young woman and her uncle in hopes they will lead us to your son. As soon as we receive any information, it will be relayed to you."

Cris stood and walked the detective back to the front door. He waited there for a while, watching the policeman's car leave, as Aidan remained at the table. Liam always said he was better at dealing with emotional situations, but he could not imagine what Agathe was going through.

He spared a moment of pity for Liam, stuck on a boat in the middle of the ocean with a desperate client and the client's worst enemy, all of them on what was probably an impossible quest.

Cris seemed reluctant to return to the drama in the kitchen, so Aidan walked to the front door. "Why don't you show me around the area," he said. "We can get some fresh air, and Paul Dubois will keep an eye on Madame la Docteur."

Cris nodded and pushed open the door. Aidan stopped at Dubois's car to fill him in, and then he and Cris began walking down the country road in the direction of the sea.

"Not much more daylight," Aidan said, just to make conversation.

"Another hour or so," Cris said. He turned to Aidan. "Do you think they will kill him?"

"Liam and I will do everything we can to keep that from happening."

Cris nodded, and both of them were silent for a while, walking beside tall chestnut trees as the air cooled around them. Birds chirped, and in the distance a motorcycle droned.

"Sometimes I look at Michel, and I can't imagine my life without him," Cris said. "And other times I wonder if he is just a crush, if we will both meet other people after university and our lives change."

"Either is possible," Aidan said. "I know couples who met in college who are still together, still in love. And I know guys who go through boyfriends like newspaper. Fresh today, stale tomorrow. It all depends on the two men involved."

Cris nodded, and they walked on. Then without warning, his cell phone vibrated in his hand. "It's a text from Michel!" he said.

He pulled up the message screen. Aidan saw the text Cris had sent to Michel earlier in the day, followed by *passé la casc arrêt dans une crique aidez-moi.*

He didn't know the words *casc* and *crique*, and without them he could make no sense of the message. "What does it mean?"

"Michel and I have a special place, a few kilometers up the coast from the harbor. There is a waterfall there, *un casc*, with a cave behind. Michel and I go there to…" He blushed.

"Oh, I get it. So Michel is trying to say his kidnappers took him past this place?"

"Yes. On the boat."

"And what's this word?" He pointed at *crique*. Given all the watery references, he was tempted to think it meant creek but didn't want to assume.

"It means a little piece of water surrounded by mountains. A small bay."

Aidan looked at the message again. "Michel was taken from the harbor in a speedboat," he said. "He's telling us he passed this waterfall place, so that means the boat was heading north along the coast?"

"Yes, that is it."

"And 'arrêt,' that means stop," Aidan continued. "So the boat is now stopped in a small bay somewhere?"

"Yes, yes, and he needs me to help him." Cris pressed his lips together, thinking. "There aren't many places around here where you can get a phone signal from a boat," he said. "The cliffs are just too high. I know; I've tried many times, in many places."

"Does that mean you know where he is? Or was?"

"Maybe. My father has some charts we can look at. Come with me."

They hurried back to the house, to a rough wooden table outside the garage. "Wait here," Cris said, and he went into the garage. Aidan heard him rummaging, then cursing, then a sound of triumph. When he walked out, he carried a large spiral-bound book.

"Here is the coastline around Cargése," he said, opening the book to a page of nautical charts. "Do you know what time Michel left the harbor?"

"About noon, we think."

"Any idea what kind of boat?"

"Just a speedboat. I don't know anything more."

Cris scribbled a couple of notes. He went into the garage and returned a moment later with a compass. "I haven't seen one of those since I was a kid," Aidan said.

"With this, we can figure out how far they could have gone from the harbor at Cargése," he said. He placed the point of the compass at the harbor and drew a large circle.

"That's a lot of ground to cover," Aidan said, his heart sinking.

"Not so. We know they went north, past the waterfall, which is here." He pointed at a place on the chart. "And there are only a few places where he could get a cell signal. All this area here, this is ocean. No signals there. And these headlands?" He pointed to an area on the map. "They block any signals."

He peered at the map and then pointed. "There is only one place I know you can get a signal. A tiny cove on the far side of the peninsula, which I found once when I was out on my father's boat with some friends."

Aidan looked at the map. A finger of land stuck out into the ocean, creating a protected harbor. "There is a cell tower here," Cris said, pointing. "You see, there is a direct line from the tower."

"We have to get this information to the police," Aidan said. He dug in his pockets for Desjardins's card, found it and his cell phone, and then dialed, but the call went right to voice mail. He left a brief message, then looked up at Cris. "Is there any way to reach your father's boat so I could talk to Liam?"

"The radio in the harbormaster's office," Cris said. He looked down at his watch. "But it is already closed. The only other radios are on boats at the harbor, and we would have to find someone with a boat, convince him to help us, and then get down there. And even then, we don't have the best technology here. My father might be out of range of the harbor."

"Is there any way to get to this place by land?" Aidan asked, pointing at the tiny inlet. It looked like the closest road was something called the Promenade du Pontiglione, and he didn't know enough about the scale of the map to estimate how far it was.

"I think so, yes," Cris said. "We would have to travel by road for several kilometers, and then walk perhaps two kilometers through scrub and low, rocky hills."

"I want to head over there and take a look, if it's not too far or too difficult to reach. I hate standing around doing nothing, and if you're correct about the cell phone signal, maybe we'll find the boat there."

Then Aidan felt a pang of doubt. Maybe this was just a fool's errand. It seemed like they were making some very big assumptions.

"I think we've made a good guess." Cris straightened up, then stretched his right foot against the wall of the house. "It's possible, of course, that they have continued ahead, but it will be dark soon and unless you know the coast well, it is dangerous to travel at night. If the people running the boat who have Michel are from Ajaccio, and they prefer to stay in this area…well, then they are probably at this cove until morning."

"Can you write down the directions, in case Liam comes back before we return? I don't want him to worry."

"Certainly." Cris found a blank piece of paper stuck in the back of the book of charts and wrote out the coordinates of the cove.

Aidan carried the paper out to where Dubois sat in his car, and handed it to him. "Cris thinks he might know where the kidnappers could be," he said. "He's going to show it to me."

"What about your partner?" Dubois asked.

"We have no way to get hold of him. If he comes back before we do, give this to him and tell him what time we left."

"You don't want me to come with you?"

Aidan shook his head. "Someone's got to stay here with Dr. Perreau. We don't know what these people will do when they discover the police are already involved. They may come after her."

He opened the backseat of the car and retrieved his share of the contents of the duffle, then loaded them into a day pack they had brought along.

"Be careful," Dubois called.

Aidan gave him a brief wave and walked back to where Cris straddled his motorbike. He handed a spare helmet to Aidan, and as soon as Aidan was settled behind him, he took off along the winding road, up through the village and then down a small road through scrub. Aidan smelled the maquis, the fragrant underbrush, as he tracked the progress of the setting sun, hoping for every extra second of daylight they could get.

He kept second-guessing himself. What if this was a waste of time? What if Vanina's uncle and his associates came after Dr. Perreau while he and Cris were running through the countryside? Could Dubois hold them off by himself? Would Liam be angry that he'd gone off on what could be a wild-goose chase?

But he remembered what Liam had always said: trust your instincts. And his told him this was where he belonged, on a motorbike going too fast along a country road in the middle of an unfamiliar island, relying on a love-struck teenager as his guide. The road bumped beneath them, and Cris struggled to retain control of the bike. The adult inside Aidan's head urged him to tell the boy to slow down. But the teenager who lived in there too reveled in the exhilaration.

They arrived at a main road and turned onto it. The pavement was less bumpy, and Aidan's heart only jumped when Cris darted around an ancient truck moving at a crawl.

Within a few minutes, Cris began to slow, as if looking for landmarks. Finally he brought the bike to a halt. "I think this is as close as we can get by road," he said. "The cove should be about two kilometers in that direction." He pointed toward the horizon, where the sun's last rays were baking the ground.

Aidan didn't like the hesitancy in Cris's tone, but he had to show some faith. "Then let's get moving," he said.

The first quarter of a mile was easy, and they made good progress, avoiding boulders and large bushes. The air was cool, though still humid, and they had the light of the setting sun to guide them. Cris led and Aidan followed. He couldn't help noticing the continuation of his regular pattern—first trailing along behind Blake, then Liam, and now this college boy.

Then the land began to slope upward in a series of rolling hills. Cris was as sure-footed as a goat, but Aidan stumbled now and then, unleashing a flood of pebbles beneath his feet. They climbed small slopes and threaded their way between foothills, keeping in the general direction of the ocean.

Aidan wished he had the same kind of internal pedometer Liam had, always aware of where he was and how far he'd gone. But then, there were many, many ways in which he wasn't like Liam. He stopped at a clearing and retrieved his phone from the day pack. He held it up high—but could get no signal.

He put the phone in his pocket and slung the pack over his shoulder again as they began to climb a low mountain before them. Aidan's calves twinged, and he was glad he had continued his regular workouts with Liam. Cris, with the energy of youth and the strength of a footballer, didn't flag.

They crested the mountain after a ten-minute climb, only to discover there was yet another between them and the sea. Aidan smelled the salt water—or was that the tang of his own sweat? He wiped his forehead, then held his phone up once again, and this time caught a faint signal, a single bar that disappeared quickly.

He followed Cris sideways down the mountainside. At the base, there was no time to rest; they had to jump a narrow gully and begin to climb again. Another fifteen minutes later and Cris reached the crest of the mountain and waited for Aidan to catch up.

"Down there," he said, pointing.

The view was almost vertiginous, and Aidan was glad he had no fear of heights. Red stone cliffs led downward to the crashing sea. And in one small inlet, a powerboat rocked at anchor.

"You think that's the boat?" Cris asked.

"Is there any other reason why a boat would be anchored here?" Aidan asked, looking around. There was only a tiny sand beach, and the waves all around the area looked high and dangerous.

"There are many better beaches," Cris said.

"That's our answer, then. How close do you think we can get?"

"They say that in Corsica you must be part goat to navigate these cliffs," Cris said. He formed his right hand into a point and placed it against his forehead. "Fortunately you have me to lead you."

Before they began to descend, Aidan tried for a cell signal again. He was surprised to see the full bars show up on his phone. "You were right about the signal," he said to Cris. "I'm going to call Liam."

His call went right to voice mail, which probably meant Liam was out of range, wherever he was. Just in case he could get the message while still out on the boat, he left the coordinates Cris had given him. "There's a powerboat moored down there. Cris and I are going down to investigate. I'll call you again when I can."

Cris went first, carefully placing his feet between the boulders, checking each step for loose stones, verifying handholds. Aidan was worried they would be very visible targets as they began their descent, with the last sunlight shining directly at them. But the rockiness of the cliffs acted in their favor, often camouflaging them from view from below.

The sun continued to sink, and Aidan realized it would almost certainly be gone by the time they reached the beach—if indeed they could get that far before they lost the light. How would they climb back up the mountain in the dark? He had a good flashlight in the pack on his back, but it would be too conspicuous to use that to guide their way. Anyone looking up from the boat would see the tiny beam of light, and he and Cris would be perfect targets for a long-range rifle.

The climb down took longer than Aidan had anticipated. By the time they reached a low slope that led to the beach, his arms and legs were stiff and his body was drenched in sweat. The sun was behind an offshore pile of rock, highlighting the surface of the water with a golden gleam that provided just enough light for them to climb down the slope and collapse on the sand.

Aidan rummaged in the day pack and pulled out his binoculars. In the low light, he could make out the white powerboat—an expensive sport-fishing boat with towering poles. Focusing carefully, he made out a man silhouetted in the light of the interior bridge. Then the man turned the light out.

"How will we know if Michel is on the boat?" Cris asked.

"I don't know," Aidan said. "Let's see if we can get another angle on it."

They were camouflaged by the darkness as they crept along the beach. As the mountain above them curved around, they got their first look at the stern of the boat, where its name had been painted on the transom in a curling script.

La Petite Vanina.

34 – LA PETITE VANINA

"How much longer do you think we can stay out?" Liam asked Nic. The sun was sinking quickly below the horizon, and a cool wind was picking up. Back in the SEALs, such conditions would be no problem, because he'd know his team and their qualifications. But Nic Aquaviva was an unknown quantity, and so was his boat. The man was clearly a competent mariner, but he'd been fishing all day, and Liam saw his exhaustion reflected in the extra seconds he took when a wave pushed them off course.

The boat was old, and its twin engines sounded to Liam like they could use a good tune-up. If they conked out, *L'Ange* could be smashed against the towering, rocky cliffs along the shoreline.

"We will have to turn back soon," Nic said.

Then Liam's phone buzzed in his pocket. "We can get a signal this far out?" he asked as he pulled it out.

"There are a few small places along the coast," Nic said.

Liam's display read *one missed call: Aidan*. And one message. He clicked the button to hear the message, and when he was finished, the first thing that came to his mind was *you idiot!*

He took a deep breath, pushing out his immediate anger and pulling in quietude. He held the phone up to Nic, pressed the Replay button, and said, "Listen to this."

Nic listened, then said, "I know that place. It's not far from here."

Without asking either Liam or Olivier for permission, the Corsican set the coordinates into his loran and accelerated the engine.

"Not too loud!" Liam yelled at him. "We want to creep up."

Nic nodded. "When we get close," he said.

Olivier approached them. "Have you found something?"

"We might know where the boat is." Liam looked back at his phone, ready to call Desjardins and relay the information, in case Aidan had been unable to do so, but the cellular signal was lost again.

Olivier pressed his hand against Liam's shoulder. "Where? Is my son there?"

"Nic is taking us there now," Liam said. "Remember, we're not the police. We're just looking for information."

Liam saw it was going to be difficult to restrain Olivier if he felt his son was close and in danger. Must be nice, he thought grumpily to himself. To have a father who cared so much.

Then again, Michel had secrets that might change the relationship between them forever. What if something happened to out Michel while they were searching for the boy? Would his father change his tone? Tell them to return to Cargése? Or maybe it wouldn't matter at all.

He had no idea how his own father would have reacted to the news that his only son was gay. By the time his father died, Liam was still uncertain about his sexuality; he'd moved beyond anonymous blowjobs in bars but wasn't ready to acknowledge, even to himself, that he'd live the rest of his life as one of his father's drunken epithets—fairy, faggot, cocksucker, butt fucker. With the barest hint of a smile he remembered hearing those words from his father's mouth and wondering what they meant. As a Catholic school teenager he had little real knowledge of sex and certainly knew nothing about the ways men could provide each other pleasure.

Olivier's insistent pleading brought him back to the present. Outing Michel wasn't Liam's decision to make. His only responsibility was to keep his clients safe. "You'll have to trust us," Liam said quietly as the boat's engines moved down to idle. "I've spent years training for any kind of situation, and I'm determined to protect Michel."

Olivier swallowed hard and nodded.

"The cove is just around there," Nic said, pointing to a tall, rocky headland. "I will turn off the engine, and we can ride the current enough to see inside."

Liam looked around. There was no beach to speak of on the shoreline, just a series of red stone cliffs that slanted directly to the water's edge. Ahead of them, a rocky point with a jagged shore pierced the water like an angry knife. Based on his knowledge of the geology of such areas, Liam knew there had to be similar jags just beneath the water's surface. Nic had better be a damn good boatman to steer clear of all the obstacles, especially with no engine.

Olivier joined him at the bow of the boat. Liam slung his night-vision goggles around his neck and gripped the rail, waiting for the motion of the water to push them forward. A wave crashed against the stern with a loud splash, and the cold salt spray felt refreshing.

Nic was at the helm, struggling to keep the boat off the rocks.

With a creak and a roll, they rounded the point. A few hundred feet away, Liam saw a white sportfish at anchor in the protected bay, rolling back and forth with the motion of the incoming tide. The beach was a rough half-moon, with dark sand a few meters deep. The inner cliffs were less jagged than those that faced the sea; a goat could climb them easily.

He had spent years around boats and could recognize most brands by sight. The boat ahead of him was a 60-foot Hatteras, about ten years old.

His brain churned with scenarios. First, was Michel on the boat? Alive and well, or injured? How many men were on the Hatteras with him? Were they armed, and if so, with what kind of weapons? The boat was anchored stem and stern, indicating the captain intended to lie low—given the condition of the shoreline, probably until the morning.

He had no doubt he could get on board. He'd swam through more dangerous waters; he had the skill and the stealth to approach the boat from the water and then use either the dive platform at the stern or the rails along the gunwales to hoist himself up.

He would have to wait and watch, and answer a few of his questions before he could plan further.

"Is that it? Is that the boat?" Olivier asked, grasping the side wall of the cabin.

"I'm not sure," Liam said. "Could simply be tourists making their way up the coast, looking for a quiet spot to anchor. But Aidan sent us here for a reason."

"What are you going to do? How will you rescue my son?"

Liam put a hand on the man's upper arm. "Monsieur Perreau. We don't even know for sure your son is on the boat. I know you're upset, but please, give me a chance to make some observations and formulate a plan."

Olivier looked like he was going to bluster—but then he took a deep breath. "I will wait," he said.

Liam raised the night-vision goggles to his eyes and scanned the Hatteras. He was able to see two figures on the deck—a man and a woman. When the woman turned in profile, she revealed a mass of curly hair gathered at her neck. That could be Vanina, he thought.

The man with her was older and bulkier. Perhaps her uncle? But Liam couldn't be sure.

He scanned the rest of the boat. Someone sat in the fighting chair at the stern, and it looked like the person was restrained somehow.

By then, the indicators were too strong. This had to be the right boat, the one with Michel on board. A man stepped out of the cabin, taller and larger than the man with Vanina. He spoke to Michel, then went back inside.

So there were at least three people with Michel, perhaps more. Liam had to assume they would be armed.

His phone buzzed again—this time with the signal for an incoming call. When he pulled the phone out, his partner's face on the display glowed in the darkness. "Aidan? Where are you?"

"On the beach, at the coordinates I told you about," Aidan said.

"Where are you?"

"Just offshore, in Nic's boat. I got the coordinates. But what the hell are you doing down there?"

"We wanted to make sure it was the right boat. It has to be, Liam. It's called *La Petite Vanina*."

"Is Cris with you?"

"Yes."

Again, Liam was tempted to curse, and again he took a deep breath. "Hold tight. I'm calling Desjardins."

He ended the call with a savage punch of the appropriate button. Then he called Bruno Desjardins. As he waited for the call to connect, he noticed his right foot was tapping impatiently against the deck. He forced it to be still.

"Desjardins." The Frenchman's voice was curt.

"We found the boat." Liam gave the policeman the coordinates. "I can see Michel being held in the fighting chair at the stern. At least three people are on the boat with him, maybe more."

Desjardins cursed in French, including a couple of terms Liam filed in his brain for further use. "The night is black," Desjardins said. "And these are very dangerous shores. If I send the police out there now, it would have to be with engines roaring and lights flashing. I do not wish to push these men, because we don't know how desperate they are. I believe we will have to wait until morning."

"What time is dawn?"

"Hold on." Desjardins returned to the phone a moment later with the time. "We will have a boat within range by sunrise. You will let me know if there is any change."

Liam hated to wait that long, but he recognized the wisdom inherent in the decision. "Will do." He hung up and dialed Aidan again. "The police won't be able to get here until dawn. How was the trip coming down the mountain?"

"Tough. Cris is a great guide, though I doubt he could manage the climb at night."

"Any other way off the beach besides a climb?"

"Nope. I had Cris scope it out. The only way is back up the mountain or off the beach."

"Find a place to hide where you can stay until dawn. Don't do anything without hearing from me first, all right?"

"Yes, sir," Aidan said, and Liam heard the snarky tone.

"I mean it, Aidan." He lowered his voice and strove to remove the anger from his tone. "I love you too much to have you risk doing something stupid."

He heard his partner take a deep breath. "I love you just as much. You make the same promise to me."

This was what he hated about working with his lover. This conflict of duty—protect Aidan, protect himself, protect the client. Which came first? With his index and second finger twined behind his back, Liam said, "Promise," and then ended the call.

"What is the plan?" Olivier asked.

"We wait for dawn," Liam said. "The police will get a boat here, and they'll take over."

"But what about my son?"

"He'll have to wait."

"You have a gun," Olivier said, nodding toward the GLOCK nestled firmly at Liam's waist. "We will motor up to them and demand they release him."

"You don't think they have guns themselves?" Liam asked. "This is the Union Corse we're talking about. Can you be that naïve?"

Immediately he regretted lashing out at the client. "I'm sorry, monsieur," he said. "I understand your impatience. But we must wait—either until the police arrive, or until we receive another demand from them."

"The anchor," Nic called from the helm. "We need to set the anchor, or we will be pushed too far away."

"Is the water shallow enough here?" Liam called.

"I have navigated us to the best position," Nic called. "But you must hurry."

Liam scrambled to the bow of the ship, where he found the heavy anchor. He lifted it over the gunwale and let it sink into the water. He waited, holding onto the hoist, as the chain unraveled. The rattling of the chain ceased, and then he felt the boat begin to strain against the anchor.

It held. He looked around the boat. It was a day fisher; it would be hard to find a place for any of them to bed down for the night. That was all right for him; he could go up to twenty-four hours without sleep with no effect on his performance. But the two older men wouldn't have the same stamina or conditioning.

He was puzzling that out when his cell rang. "What is it, Aidan?"

"I waded out into the water to see if I could hear anything," his partner said. "Just like you taught me, moving with the current, keeping my profile low."

Liam felt his blood pressure rise once again. Why couldn't his partner follow even the simplest instructions? Even as the words formed in his head, though, he recognized the term he'd used—partner. He had to trust that Aidan knew what he was doing, knew how to take precautions to protect himself and the boy who was with him. And he had to trust the training he'd given Aidan—which it was clear his partner had remembered. "And did you?" Liam asked.

"Yeah. Andreadi and Vanina were arguing. They were speaking a mixture of French and Corsican, so it took me a while to figure out what they were saying. But I'm certain Andreadi knows the police are involved now, despite the instructions in the message he left at the Perreaus' house."

Liam's immediate reaction was a series of curses he'd learned in the Navy—added with the new ones in French he'd learned from Desjardins. But to give voice to them would only add to the agitation Olivier Perreau felt, and might even make Aidan think Liam was cursing at him. He took a deep breath. "Where are you now?"

"Back onshore," Aidan said. "I brought a pair of swim trunks with me in my pack, and a towel. So I'm nice and dry again."

Liam had a momentary vision of Aidan naked, pausing for a moment to show off his trim, hairy body to Cris's admiring eyes, and jealousy surged through him. Then he remembered he was the one

Aidan accused of being an exhibitionist, because he liked to be naked and didn't mind showing off his body. Aidan had probably hidden behind a rock to change into and out of his bathing suit anyway.

Unless Cris had been waiting for him with the towel…

He forced himself back to the present. "If Andreadi believes Olivier deliberately disobeyed his orders about involving the police, we're in trouble." He took a deep breath. "Anything more?"

"It gets worse. From what I understood, Vanina only wanted to impress Nic with her devotion to the environment. It was her uncle's idea to kidnap Michel and ask for the ransom—he told her that if she took all of Olivier's money, he wouldn't be able to proceed. Andreadi wants to kill Michel and dump his body, and then get out of here. He says the money isn't worth the danger, but Vanina is trying to convince him to stick to the original plan. Liam, what are we going to do?"

Liam took a moment to phrase his thoughts. "You know I trust you and your instincts when it comes to dealing with people," he said. "And you continue to impress me with your ability to think outside the box. You did well, going out to the boat and snooping. But now you've got to listen to me. These are very dangerous people, and we need to tread very carefully. Don't do anything without checking with me first." He hesitated, then added, "Please, Aidan?"

"I understand," Aidan said. "Poor Michel. He must be scared out of his wits."

"I know. But if we go in there half-assed, the danger skyrockets for him, and for us." He ended the call and stood there, staring out at the night.

Was this why the military didn't want gay men in combat? Or women? Because love gets in the way of tactical decisions? Liam couldn't help worrying about Aidan, over there on the beach, motivated as much by his human concern for a lovesick boy in great danger as he was by his responsibility to the mission and to his partner. If it came down to a choice, who would he save? Aidan or Michel? Aidan or Olivier? Or even, if the dice rolled that way, Aidan or Nic Aquaviva, who willingly put himself in harm's way to help another man's son?

35 – The Mission

Liam stared at the stars for long time as *L'Ange de la Mer* rocked back and forth in the rough tide. The chilly air raised goose bumps on his upper arms, and his nostrils swelled with the tang of salt and seaweed. When he turned back, he saw Nic had left the helm and joined Olivier at the bow of the boat with Liam.

"What have you learned?" Olivier asked.

Liam wasn't going to tell the client about Andreadi's argument with his niece or the possibility that Michel might not survive the night. He made the only decision he knew he could live with. "I'm going to get closer." He turned to Nic. "You have any kind of waterproof pouch on this boat?"

"Of course."

Liam followed him toward the helm, retrieving the duffle bag. Good. Aidan had packed well. He found a pair of swim trunks and kicked off his shoes and khakis, remembering his own concern about Aidan being naked in front of Cris. Nic and Olivier were both straight, though out of a bit of uncharacteristic modesty he turned his back to them as he slid off his jockstrap and stepped into the trunks.

He focused on what he knew. Nic had a chart of the area that indicated the water in the cove had an average depth of about ten feet, shallowing gradually toward the shore. He could slip into the water soundlessly and swim beneath the surface until he neared the Hatteras. The boat had long, teardrop-shaped windows on either side and he would have to make sure no one saw him from the salon. He couldn't be sure until he reached the boat whether he could climb onto the dive platform at the stern or hoist himself up and over the protective rail along the boat's gunwales.

Once on board, he'd have to find a way to subdue the crew and rescue Michel. Out of the bounds of his normal work as a bodyguard, but a mission any SEAL should be able to accomplish.

He felt a strange exhilaration course through his body, as if he had been waiting since his discharge for just such a chance. It was a relief, he had to admit, not to have to worry about Aidan, who was safe onshore. Liam had been on his own for so long before Aidan stumbled into his life, and though he loved his partner deeply, he was at heart still a solitary man, particularly when it came to paramilitary operations like this. With no one to worry about but himself, he could devote his full attention to the mission and dismiss those lingering doubts about who he would protect first—Aidan or the client—in case of danger.

When Nic returned with the pouch, he slotted his GLOCK into it and sealed it. He strapped it around his waist and slung the waterproof night-vision goggles around his neck.

"Be careful," Nic said.

"Please take care of my son," Olivier said.

"Yes to both of you," Liam said. He sat on the stern and stuck his legs into the water. The cold was a bit of a shock, but no worse than he'd expected. And then he was overboard, striking out for the powerboat, keeping his profile low and silent in the water.

He closed his mind to everything but the plan. He would reach the Hatteras and tread water while he evaluated the best way on board. Then disable each of the people guarding Michel, untie him, and take control of the boat.

The waves were stronger than he had anticipated, and he fought the outgoing tide, shifting his course as necessary, until he was only a meter away from the Hatteras. He surfaced, settled into a float, and observed.

Vanina and her uncle were at the helm up on the flying bridge. She was crying, and he was speaking to her in a voice too low for Liam to understand, but the intent was clear. She had lost the argument, and he was calming her down. Liam pulled the night-vision goggles up, uncapped the lenses, and began to scan the Hatteras.

He discovered there were four people on board: Vanina, her uncle, Michel, and a younger man assigned to guard him. Liam waited until the guard had gone inside the cabin to hoist himself out of the ocean, water cascading from his head and shoulders, using one of the fenders hanging alongside for support. He slung his legs over the gunwale.

He waited alongside the salon on the side deck until the guard stepped out onto the stern. In a quick move, he wrapped his arm around the man's neck in the sleeper hold, pressed one hand against the jugular vein, the other on the carotid artery. Within seconds, the oxygen flow to guard's brain shut down, and he slid into unconsciousness.

Liam released his hold, and the man collapsed to the deck. Michel twisted around in the fighting seat and saw Liam, who raised a finger to his lips. The boy nodded, though his eyes were wide. His wrists were tied to the arms of the fighting chair, his legs bound to the post that held the chair up.

With a dock line from the midship cleat, Liam bound the guard's hands and feet, then grabbed the man's shoulders and dragged him into the main salon. It was simply equipped, with an L-shaped bench along two sides, usable for seating as well as sleeping. He stuffed a towel from the galley into the man's mouth so he couldn't cry out if he awoke.

A pair of framed eight-by-ten photos were the only decoration, shots of someone, presumably the boat's owner, at a dockside weighing station beside an enormous fish. A low table was firmly affixed to the deck, with a shallow rail around it to keep items from sliding off in rough weather. The other corner was a basic galley, with a large freezer.

He wedged the guard between the table and the bench. He looked around the galley for a moment, then grabbed a knife and another towel. Then he stepped carefully back to the exit door. Everything looked quiet; Michel remained tied to his chair, facing out to sea.

He retrieved the gun from its pouch once more and stepped out onto the stern, his senses attuned to the environment around him. He heard a creak from above and recognized that it wasn't a typical movement of the boat. He swiveled around to face a man at the top of the ladder to the flying bridge.

He was middle-aged and stocky, with a fringe of white hair around a bald head, and he was silhouetted against the light from the flying bridge. The man aimed a handgun at Liam and fired.

Acting completely on instinct, Liam shifted position back against the bulkhead, raised his GLOCK, and fired at the man, aiming for body mass. Liam's brain registered everything in slow motion: the staccato bursts of gunfire, the searing pain in his upper arm, the way the man staggered backward on the flying bridge, then slumped to the deck.

Up on the deck above him, he heard Vanina's sobs. He tried to raise his right arm, but it wouldn't move; the bullet must have pierced a nerve. Shit. Blood was seeping from the wound and dripping down his arm. He wrapped the galley towel around his arm, creating a quick tourniquet.

He stepped over to Michel and used the knife to slice through the gag around the young man's mouth, working awkwardly with his left hand.

"Vanina!" Michel cried as soon as he could. "Up there!"

Liam was so tired he was moving slowly, his reflexes drained by the pain and nerve damage in his arm. He looked above him to see Vanina, framed just as her uncle had been, in the light from the cockpit. Though tears stained her face, she looked incongruously beautiful, her curly black hair flowing around her shoulders. She held her uncle's bloody gun in both hands, hiccupped once, aimed directly at Liam, and fired once. He summoned all his strength to shift sideways, trying to avoid her aim and draw her down the ladder to the deck.

A fraction of a second later, he heard another shot. Then Vanina swayed at the top of the ladder and dropped the gun, which banged down a couple of rungs and landed on the deck. "Gotcha, bitch!" Liam heard Aidan crow from somewhere in the water.

Vanina grabbed for the handrail and missed, and then toppled the six feet or so to the deck beside Liam. He noted the way her head was twisted to the side, her eyes wide open and staring up at the stars.

Liam was shivering as he slid to the deck beside her. He knew he had to get up and untie Michel, then radio the police. But he couldn't move, and he closed his eyes, just for a second.

36 – Secrets

After he shot Vanina, Aidan held the gun up high out of the water and splashed forward, eventually swimming the last few feet in a modified crawl, keeping one arm out of the water, glad for the moves Liam had taught him, both in the water and at the shooting range, where his partner had been impressed at Aidan's natural ability.

He reached the boat and climbed up the dive ladder. He saw Michel still strapped to the fighting chair, and Liam and Vanina sprawled beside each other on the blood-spattered deck. From the twist of the girl's neck, he knew she was dead.

"Liam!" he cried in what was almost an animal howl. He scrambled across the deck and raised Liam's head to his lap. His partner opened his eyes for a second and smiled, then passed out again.

"Stay with me, sweetheart," Aidan said, his heart racing. He unwrapped the towel from Liam's bicep and shifted his partner so he could examine the bullet wound in the light. It was a through-and-through shot, so he knew the bullet wasn't inside Liam anymore.

"Cris! Call your father!" he yelled out to the beach. "We need the police here, and an ambulance."

He stripped off his wet shirt and used it to fashion a fresh tourniquet for Liam's arm. As he did, he heard an engine strike up, and a powerful searchlight turned on the Hatteras. "Talk to me,

Liam," he said, slapping his partner's cheek lightly.

"What?" Liam looked up at him, groggy.

"You've lost a lot of blood. You need to hold on until we get you to shore, and get an ambulance."

Nic pulled *L'Ange de la Mer* up beside the Hatteras and cut the engine. As he shouted instructions to Olivier to toss out the bumpers and tie the two boats together, Aidan heard a loud splashing in the water. He raised his head to see Cris clamber up the dive ladder as the Hatteras rocked in the tide. As soon as he was on deck, he dashed to Michel and began to untie him.

Once Michel was free, he and Cris locked lips and arms, passion combined with tension and relief. Aidan used a life vest as a pillow for Liam's head and then stood. He hurried into the galley, searching for something to give Liam to drink. He found a bottle of a power drink, heavy on the electrolytes, and returned to Liam with it.

Olivier and Nic stood together on the deck of Nic's boat, both of them staring at their sons. "We need to get Liam to a hospital!" Aidan said. "Come on, move!" He knelt down beside Liam again and uncapped the bottle. "Sweetheart? Wake up. You need some fluids." He held up the bottle as Liam opened his eyes. "See? Electrolytes. You taught me the body needs these in a crisis."

"Good to see," Liam rasped, taking shallow breaths between phrases, "that you listened to something."

Cris and Michel pulled apart, and from the deck of *L'Ange de la Mer*, Nic said, "The Hatteras is the faster boat. I will take her helm. Cristo, you follow in *L'Ange*. Let's go!"

The two boats rocked in the current, the bumpers between them taking most of the impact. Aidan's heart pounded as he struggled to drizzle liquid into Liam's mouth. There was no way Liam was going to die, not when their lives were going so well. Losing Liam would be a thousand times worse than being dumped by Blake. His relationship back in Philadelphia had been on life support, and when Blake pulled the plug, it had been a mercy killing.

Liam swallowed, and Aidan wiped the edge of his partner's lip with his fingertip. Liam was his heart and soul, and he didn't know if he could go on living if Liam wasn't by his side. "A few more drops?" he asked, and when Liam smiled and nodded, Aidan felt almost dizzy.

Nic jumped onto the side deck of the Hatteras and stepped along until he reached the bow. Aidan heard the grinding noise of the bow anchor reeling in, and he willed the process to hurry.

"Come with me," Cris said, taking Michel's hand. He jumped onto his father's boat, pulling Michel behind him. They landed beside Olivier, who stood there gripping the rail.

"Papa," Michel said.

As Aidan looked up, Olivier stared at his son, openmouthed.

Liam coughed, and Aidan lifted his head and wiped the dribble from his partner's lips. "Hold on, baby. We're almost on our way."

"Want to sleep," Liam said.

"If you have a concussion, you should stay awake," Aidan said.

Liam shook his head and then groaned. "Shot in the arm, not the head," he said. He coughed again. "Just gonna close my eyes."

"I'll hold you," Aidan said. "You sleep. I'll be right here."

Liam closed his eyes and shifted his head to rest sideways on Aidan's thigh. Cradling his partner's head in his lap, Aidan watched as Nic followed the side deck once more, now back to the anchor at the stern. He saw Michel move around his father and begin untying the rope that connected the two boats. He knew Liam would say his first responsibility was to the client, that Aidan should push him off to the side and get out there and help. But he couldn't. No matter what contract he'd signed or who paid him, his first loyalty would always be to Liam.

As Michel finally got the rope untied and began pulling in the bumpers, Olivier stumbled past him and made an awkward leap over the railing from Nic's boat onto the Hatteras. Then the boats were separated, and Cris moved to the helm of his father's boat. Aidan's last view of *L'Ange de la Mer* was as Cris backed carefully through the narrow gap in the spiky rocks, and Michel stood at the stern, staring at his father.

Nic stowed the stern anchor, then stepped past Aidan. "We will get underway as soon as Cristo has cleared the rocks. How is your partner?" he asked.

Aidan looked down and passed his index finger across Liam's stubbled chin. "He's resting. But I'm worried that he's lost a lot of blood. I want to get him back to the harbor and into an ambulance."

"Leave that to me," Nic said as he climbed the ladder to the flying bridge. "This boat can do thirty knots when she gets going." When he reached the top, though, he stopped, holding the ladder rails with both hands. "There is a man up here!"

Aidan looked up, remembering the first series of shots he had heard as he was wading toward the boat from the shore. He knew he should get up, check the man Liam had shot, see if there was anything he could do.

"Go," Olivier said, sliding to the deck. "I will watch over Liam."

It was what Liam would do, Aidan thought. And what if the man wasn't dead, if he tried to interfere with Nic's navigation? The most important thing to him was to get Liam to shore, and he couldn't let anything, or anyone, stand in the way.

He looked up. Nic had stepped around the man on the deck of the flying bridge, and Aidan saw the man's foot, encased in a garish yellow track shoe, hanging just above. He capped the bottle of energy drink, rose, and began to climb the ladder as Nic started the engine of the Hatteras. He found the body of a fifty-something man sprawled on the deck of the flying bridge, and as Nic followed Cris out of the protected cove, Aidan felt the man's neck for a pulse.

There was none. Aidan refused to feel pity for the man, who'd shot Liam. If the bullet had struck just a few inches closer to his heart, his partner might be the dead one. As Nic moved the sportfish slowly toward the narrow channel between the headland and the spiky rock, Aidan grabbed the man under his arms and pulled him to the side of the boat. He locked him into a safe position with a combination of rope and seat cushions.

Once the Hatteras breached the cove, Nic gunned the engine and headed for the open ocean. They quickly lost the two boys in the slow-moving fishing boat behind them.

The Hatteras moved so quickly Aidan had trouble keeping his balance; he grabbed the side rail to steady himself. Was Liam all right? He had to get back down there. But he had work to do first. He found a roll of paper towels in a locker and wiped up the blood on the deck so there was no danger he or Nic would slide right off the flying bridge.

No matter how he tried to dry them, his hands remained faintly slippery, the coppery stink of the blood merging with the salt spray. He climbed back down the bloody ladder, where he checked on Liam once again. His partner appeared to be sleeping, his respiration shallow but steady. Olivier sat beside him, his body keeping Liam wedged against the bulkhead.

Aidan stepped into the main salon, where a deeply tanned man in his thirties struggled against his bindings. He had managed to spit enough of the gag out of his mouth that he could speak. "Don't kill me, please!" he gasped in French, his voice raw. "I am innocent." He wouldn't shut up, continuing to babble about how he had nothing to do with anything on the boat.

"Save it for the police," Aidan grumbled, making sure the guard's bindings held. He was tempted to stuff the gag back in the man's mouth, but there was no alarm he could raise now.

Exhausted, Aidan stood up, balancing himself against the cabin wall as he stepped back toward the stern. When he got outside, he slumped on the deck beside Liam and Olivier. He felt Liam's pulse; it was strong. His partner's eyelids fluttered, but he didn't wake.

We are both going to sleep for a long time when this is over, Aidan thought, stroking the rough knuckles on Liam's hand. You and me, beside each other in that big bed you say is too comfortable for you. We haven't had enough time together in Nice to make that apartment our own, but we will.

Above him, he heard Nic on the radio, trying to raise the police and get an ambulance to Cargése. Angry waves slapped at the sides of the boat as they rushed through the ocean. Clouds moved overhead, blocking and then revealing stars. Aidan remembered spending nights in the desert with Liam, soon after they met, sheltered by these very same stars. He sent them a brief prayer asking them to guide Nic's hand as he led them back to Cargése.

When he looked at Olivier, he saw the man watching him, and he was suddenly conscious of the intimacy he and Liam shared, the way he held his partner's hand, the way he stroked Liam's short blond hair.

Olivier appeared shell-shocked, and no wonder, after all that had happened that day. "Everything will be well, monsieur," Aidan said. "Your son is safe, and I believe soon we will understand everything about the threats against your family and your company."

"You have a father?" Olivier asked, and it took Aidan a moment to process the question, which appeared to have come out of the blue.

"Yes," Aidan said. "He passed away about six years ago."

"Did he know?"

Aidan's brain wasn't firing on all cylinders. Did his father know what? That he was dying? Then he looked at Olivier's face once again, and he understood. "Some men are better at keeping secrets than others," he said. "Me? I was not so good. My parents knew about my life when I was a college student." He paused. "But some, like Liam? His father is dead, and he doesn't discuss his life with his mother, back in the United States."

"You are the braver of the two," Olivier said.

Again, Aidan was confused. Bravery? That was one of the characteristics he admired most in Liam. His partner could face any danger with a cool head.

Olivier appeared lost in thought, and Aidan considered what the client might have meant by bravery. As early as high school, Aidan had admired the effeminate gay boys he knew, even while being frightened to associate with them. They faced the world as who they were, unable to hide, and they developed courage as a result.

The sportfish crested a wave and bounced hard, and Liam stirred, tried to get up. "It's okay, sweetheart," Aidan said, wiping a bit of salt spray from his partner's forehead. "Just a little turbulence. But you and me, together, we can beat anything."

Liam smiled and closed his eyes again, and Aidan looked up to see Olivier watching them closely.

"You love each other very much," Olivier said.

Aidan nodded. "He's all I want in the world. This job, being bodyguards? It's his life. I'd be just as happy in a classroom somewhere—and I'd be even happier knowing he wasn't putting himself in danger."

"My wife, she has made sacrifices for me," Olivier said. "Leaving France so I could bring this old mine back to life."

"It's what we do for the ones we love," Aidan said. "Like your son. Michel is the same boy you loved and worried about before you knew."

"Yes," Olivier said. "And it is not a major surprise, after all. His mother…she had her suspicions. I chose to ignore them."

"He's a good kid. He's smart and loyal. You and Dr. Perreau did a good job with him."

"I hope so," Olivier said.

The boat turned quickly and breached a wave, and a geyser of salt water erupted onto the stern, soaking them all. Aidan looked around for a dry cloth to wipe Liam's face, but there was nothing. He could have gotten up and searched the salon, but he didn't want to leave Liam unprotected. What if the next wave got into his mouth and choked him? Or he rolled against the deck and hurt something else?

Why was it taking so long to get back to Cargése, when Nic had said the boat could move so quickly? Nic wasn't lost, was he? There was no sign of the boys in the fishing boat behind them. They were well offshore, and Aidan couldn't see any lights on the coastal cliffs. What if…

He stopped himself. He was spinning another story, one that would only serve to worry him. He had to trust the boat, trust Nic, trust that the stars above would watch out for him and Liam and bring them safe to harbor.

37 – WATERWORKS

When he heard Nic cut the boat's engine, Aidan realized they were approaching Cargése harbor. He took Liam's wrist and felt his pulse; it was still strong, and he was breathing easily, though Aidan worried about how much blood he'd lost, and hoped there would be no permanent damage to his arm.

The flashing blue and white lights on the shore lit up the night sky like a carnival. At least three police cars and an ambulance were lined up along the breakwater. He, Liam, and Olivier were all soaked from the rogue waves. His clothes were cold and clammy against his skin.

As Nic navigated them to a berth beside the breakwater, Aidan lifted Liam's head from his lap and positioned his partner carefully against the wall. Then he stood up, his legs a bit shaky, and found the stern line in a loose coil. When Nic pulled the boat close, Aidan tossed the line to a uniformed policeman on the dock.

Olivier stood behind him, and Aidan stepped carefully along the side deck to reach the bow. Once the flic had the stern line tied around a metal post, Aidan tossed him the bow line. As soon as the boat was secured, Desjardins was first on board, followed quickly by two white-coated EMTs.

In the flickering light, Aidan saw Paul Dubois standing well back from the water's edge, with Agathe Perreau and Chjara Aquaviva.

He scrambled back along the side deck as the EMTs stepped on board. Liam was awake again and groggy, trying to sit up. One of the EMTs stood behind him, the other at his legs, and the two of them expertly lifted him. A flic onshore steadied the stretcher for them, and they stepped easily from the stern to land, resting Liam on the stretcher.

Aidan tried to jump off and follow them, but Desjardins placed a hand on his arm. "A few moments, please, monsieur. Then I will see you are transported to the hospital."

Aidan reached across to the shore, his hand outstretched. Liam turned his head toward the boat and lifted his good arm so that their fingertips touched. "I love you, sweetheart," Aidan said. "I'll see you soon."

Liam murmured something, and his hand dropped back to the stretcher. Then the EMTs headed for the ambulance, and Aidan turned back to the detective.

"Now, you will please tell me what happened here," Desjardins said.

Aidan was exhausted, his polo shirt and khakis clung to him like a second skin, and he felt an uncomfortable itch at his groin. But he knew there was still work to be done. "Alberto Andreadi is up on the flying bridge," he said, pointing. "That's his niece Vanina over there. Both of them are dead. There's another man tied up in the salon."

"Come with me," Desjardins said. They stepped off the boat, followed by Nic and Olivier. Uniformed officers and crime scene technicians swarmed the sportfish, collecting evidence, bodies, and the captive man. Nic and Olivier were reunited with their wives, then separated again and held off to the side waiting to be questioned.

Desjardins and Aidan sat on a wrought-iron bench at the water's edge. The night wind was cold, and Aidan shivered. Desjardins called for a blanket for him, and when it arrived, Aidan wrapped it gratefully around his shoulders.

He went through everything that had happened from the time Desjardins had left Cargése earlier that day. As he was reciting the story of the hurried trip back from the inlet, *L'Ange de la Mer* returned to the harbor, and Aidan saw Michel standing next to Cris by the helm.

Aidan desperately wanted to take a hot shower and curl up under the covers for a good night's sleep. But he wouldn't be able to do that until he saw that Liam was all right.

"Are we finished?" Aidan asked. "I really want to get to the hospital."

"I will speak to you more tomorrow," Desjardins said.

Aidan stood up, the blanket still wrapped around his shoulders, and walked toward Dubois and the two women. Chjara held out a bundle of clothing. "You are about my son's size," she said. "I thought you would need something dry."

"Thank you," Aidan said. The warmth of the sweatpants and T-shirt felt so good against his cold, damp flesh.

He hurried toward the dock master's office, but, finding it and the restrooms locked, he stepped behind the building to change. He felt a bit like Liam, stripping naked outdoors, but he was very grateful to get the soggy clothes off and slip into the fresh ones.

He emerged wearing a pair of heavy cotton sweatpants and a long-sleeved T-shirt with the name of Cris's college football team emblazoned on it. His shoes were soaked, but he'd slipped on a pair of heavy socks, which were good enough for walking.

"I will drive you to Notre-Dame de la Misericorde hospital in Ajaccio," Agathe said. "I know the staff there, and I will make sure your partner gets the care he needs."

Aidan thanked her and followed her to her car. He saw Desjardins speaking to Olivier Perreau as they walked away.

"I do not know how to say how grateful we are," Agathe said once they were on the road back to the capital. "That you have protected us from these monsters, that you have retrieved our son."

"It's our job," Aidan said. "And knowing you are all safe is a very sweet reward."

"But it is more than that," Agathe said. "You've shown our son to us, made us see him as a young man now, not the little boy we raised." She hesitated. "And shown my husband that there is a way Michel can be happy."

"I hope he will be," Aidan said. "His road won't be easy. It's hard for first love to sustain itself for many years—and when it ends, there's great pain. But life is full of unexpected changes, and with your love and support I'm sure Michel will succeed."

He sat back against the seat and closed his eyes for just a moment. But when he reopened them, Agathe was pulling into the parking lot at the hospital. "Now we shall see how they treat Monsieur McCullough," she said.

He followed her into the emergency room entrance, where she announced herself to the nurse on duty, and they were immediately led to a curtained bed where Liam was sitting up in a hospital gown. Aidan was so glad to see him that tears flooded his eyes, and he rushed forward.

Liam wrapped his left arm around Aidan's shoulders. "No need for waterworks," he said. "I'll be fine."

Agathe picked up the chart at the foot of the bed and reviewed it. "There may be a bit of damage to the nerve in the upper arm," she said. "But with luck it will repair itself in time. They've given him the appropriate antibiotics, and I know the doctor who treated him." She smiled. "You're going to heal," she said to Liam.

Liam's wet clothes were in a plastic bag on the bedside table. "You can be discharged soon, but you cannot wear those wet things. I will get you something," Agathe said, and she stepped away.

Aidan leaned over and kissed his partner on the lips, closing his eyes and inhaling Liam's scent. Liam's lips were dry but hungry for Aidan's, and they remained together until they heard Agathe return with a pair of hospital scrubs.

Liam stood, holding on to the bed for balance, and Aidan helped him step into the pale green pants, then slip off the gown. The scrub shirt was tight against Liam's pecs, his nipple rings pressing against the fabric. Then Agathe led them to the checkout area. As they filled out the appropriate forms, her cell phone rang.

She pulled the phone from her purse and stepped away, and Aidan remembered that was Liam's characteristic gesture when receiving a call as well.

Agathe returned when she was finished. "My husband and son are on their way home. We will meet them there."

Agathe drove them back up the winding roads toward the Rue des Magnolias, and for the first time, Aidan felt like he could sit back and be a tourist. The night was dark, with only the car's headlights for illumination, but instead of finding the darkness menacing, Aidan found it peaceful and romantic. In the backseat he snuggled next to Liam, squeezing his partner's hand.

By the time they reached the house, it was after midnight. Liam was still a bit unsteady, so Aidan helped him out of the car and up the stone pathway. As they reached the front door, Michel and Olivier pulled up in Olivier's car. Aidan wondered what the drive had been like for father and son.

Michel hopped out of the car and rushed to his mother, embracing her. "My sweet boy," Agathe said, stroking his back. "We're so glad to have you back."

Michel snuffled something into her shoulder, and the two of them walked inside. Behind them, Olivier beeped his car locked, and Aidan led Liam down the hall. After Liam finished in the bathroom, Aidan went in there himself, then hung their wet clothes over the shower rail to dry.

When he returned to the bedroom, Liam was sitting on the edge of the bed. "A hell of a day," he said and yawned.

"Not one I'd like to repeat again soon." Aidan closed the bedroom door behind him, then helped Liam remove the hospital scrubs. As he knelt before Liam, tugging at the waistband of the pants, his hand grazed Liam's half-hard dick.

"Don't get any ideas," Liam said, smiling. "I'm exhausted."

Even so, his dick stiffened at Aidan's touch. "Hey, I'm not the one getting hard," Aidan said.

As he said that, though, both he and Liam looked down and saw that Aidan's erection had begun to blossom, and they laughed. "Tomorrow," Aidan said. "Right now all I want to do is cuddle up next to you and sleep for hours."

"Sounds good to me." Aidan helped Liam into bed, then stripped down and joined him. Liam was asleep quickly, his skill at dozing anywhere kicking in. Aidan sat up and watched him breathe, then looked around. It wasn't the apartment in Nice, which they were still settling into. It wasn't the little house behind the Bar Mamounia in Tunis, where they had first become a couple.

But Aidan was learning that he carried his home within him, as long as Liam was beside him. They had slept together in desert tents, in a resort villa on the island of Djerba, in a restored monastery on the Mediterranean coast, and in a poolside guest house surrounded by olive groves.

Aidan slid down beneath the covers, curling his body against Liam's, and even in his sleep Liam wrapped a protective arm around Aidan. This was where he belonged, he thought. Beside this man, for richer or poorer, in sickness and in health, all those marriage vows he'd thought were forbidden to men like him and Liam.

The world was changing, though, often one heart at a time, as with Olivier Perreau. The next day, they'd return to Nice. Who knew where the next case would take them? Or what danger it would put them in? But as long as he had Liam by his side, Aidan knew he could face anything.

38 – Quicksand

The whole house slept in the next morning. Sunday was Maria's day off, so it was Agathe who woke first and began preparing breakfast. It was nearly ten by the time Aidan and Liam went out to the kitchen. Olivier was there, but Michel was still asleep.

"At least I think he is," Agathe said. "I didn't check his bedroom."

"I don't think he'll need to sneak away again," Aidan said.

Agathe proved herself to be an expert at making crepes, and she kept preparing them as Michel arrived, rubbing the sleep from his eyes.

"You will go back to the university today?" Olivier asked him.

"Yes, Papa," Michel said. "After breakfast."

"And you, messieurs?" Olivier asked. "You will return to France?"

"Desjardins said last night he wanted to speak to us again," Aidan said. "We'll have to talk to him and then see what flight we can get."

The Perreaus' phone rang a few minutes later. Olivier answered. "Yes, Detective," he said. "We are all here. Good, then we will expect you within the hour."

He hung up and then joined his wife at the sink, taking the dishes from her and loading the dishwasher.

"My father the engineer," Michel said, nodding his head toward them. "He must load the dishes exactly to achieve the maximum load for the machine."

"And so that each dish has an equal chance to be washed," Agathe added, and she and her son both laughed.

Olivier said, "At least I know you are both listening."

Aidan and Liam stood and thanked Agathe for the breakfast. Liam went back to the bedroom, while Aidan retrieved their sea-crusted clothes from the bathroom, still damp and needing a good wash.

When he joined Liam in the bedroom, he found his partner sitting on the bed. "Desjardins has both our guns," he said. "I hope he'll bring them back this morning. It'll be hell to get them back to Nice otherwise."

"It's Sunday," Aidan said. "I'm not sure he can get all the ballistics tests finished."

"You're right. Fuck."

"Did Louis say when they're moving to Nice?" Aidan asked.

Liam cocked his head and stared at him, as if not following the direction of the conversation. "Because maybe Desjardins can hand them over to someone in the US consulate, who can get them sent to Louis. If he's not in Nice yet, then he could pass them on to someone there."

"Complicated. But that may be what we end up doing." Liam looked at him. "How do you feel about that? Louis and Hassan moving to Nice?"

"I'm happy," Aidan said, folding dirty clothes to put into their duffle bags. "Aren't you? They're our friends."

"It feels weird to me," Liam said. "You think maybe they're following us?"

Aidan stared at him. "Oh, I get it. You're still thinking about that comment Louis made to you." He sat on the bed next to his partner. "Didn't you ever look at some guy and think about having sex with him? Just because he was cute, or had his shirt off, or because he looked at you?"

"You're the only man for me, Aidan."

"You don't have to pretend to me, Liam. I think about sex with other guys, even though I have you. It doesn't mean I'm going to act on it, but I'm human. Even if we've just made love, if I see some hunk who rocks my boat, I get hard. I'm sure you do too."

"Not everybody is as sex-crazed as you are." Liam crossed his arms over his chest, though Aidan noticed he was favoring his right one, the one with the bandages.

"I'm not sex-crazed." He tickled his hand up Liam's thigh. "I'm just a guy. Like you."

Liam pushed his hand away, though halfheartedly.

"You want to fuck them, don't you?" Aidan asked. "That's what this is about. You want to do Louis, or Hassan, or both of them, and it freaks you out."

Liam stood up and stalked to the bureau, where Aidan had tossed the bags they'd taken to Cargése the day before, and began to unpack them.

"I love you, Liam," Aidan said, still sitting on the bed. "And I love having sex with you. But they're two different things."

Liam turned back to him. "How can you think that?"

Aidan shrugged. "I don't know, I just do. Would I be jealous if you had sex with Louis or Hassan? Hell, yes. Would I want to join in?" He hesitated. How would he feel about that? "You know I'm an only child, and I don't like to share. But if it was something you wanted…"

"Right now I just want to get this gear repacked," Liam said.

"Fine." Aidan helped him, and though it took a couple of minutes for the tension in the room to dissipate, eventually they were working together as smoothly as ever.

They were almost finished by the time Desjardins arrived. He had another officer and a tape recorder with him, and he ushered each one of them into Olivier's office to take their official statements. "May I go first?" Michel asked him. "I'd like to be able to go back up to the university when we're finished."

Desjardins looked amused at Michel's impertinence, but Aidan assumed he was cutting the kid some slack after his kidnapping. "As you wish," he said with a small nod.

He led the boy into Olivier's office and shut the door. "I'll see when we can get a flight back to Nice," Aidan said, leaving Liam and the two Perreaus in the kitchen. He found an Air France flight at 4:10 that afternoon, which would get them back to Nice just before five, and he made two reservations. He had to dig into the armoire for their passports, and once he was finished, he started packing.

He was almost finished by the time Liam appeared in the

doorway. "I'm finished with Desjardins. Your turn."

"You get the guns back from him?"

Liam shook his head. "But he knows somebody in the American consulate, and he said he'll see they get shipped back to Nice by the end of the week."

When he walked out to the living room, Michel was embracing his parents. "I go back to the university now," he said. "Thank you for everything. I'm sorry I was stupid and put you and Liam in danger."

"Cris told me about an old Corsican proverb," Aidan said. "If you walk through the waterfall, don't complain if you get wet." He smiled. "Growing up and coming out, they're both like walking through a waterfall. As long as you come out the other side, you've done a good job."

"And what about the parents?" Olivier said. "We get wet at the same time."

"That is the price of parenthood," Agathe said. "Drive safely, mon petit."

He kissed both parents and walked out, his pack slung over one shoulder. "Monsieur?" Desjardins said from the doorway to Olivier's office. Aidan joined him there and retraced the things he'd done over the past few days. Since Desjardins knew it already, the conversation passed quickly, with only occasional requests for elaboration. Even so, it was nearly two in the afternoon by the time Desjardins was ready to move on to Agathe and Olivier.

"You have our contact information in Nice," Liam said to

Desjardins. He already had their duffle bags stacked in the living room.

"Yes. And I will make sure your weapons are returned to you."

There was a flurry of hand-shaking and cheek-kissing, and then a cab pulled up in the semicircular driveway to take Aidan and Liam to the airport. "I'm going to take a nap," Liam said when they were ensconced in the backseat of the cab. "Wake me when we get there."

Liam was asleep within a minute, and Aidan's mind wandered as the cab descended toward the city, flitting from topic to topic like one of the butterflies by the roadside. He hoped there wouldn't be any permanent damage to Liam's arm. He wondered when Louis and Hassan would arrive in Nice and how the four of them would get along. How Michel and Cris would adapt to being out of the closet to their families, and what they'd both do after graduating.

When the cab pulled into the airport entrance, Aidan nudged Liam. "We're here."

Liam was awake instantly. "Nice nap."

"You can have another on the plane." They moved smoothly through the check-in procedure, and Liam napped again on the hard plastic chair at the gate. Once they were in their seats, he was out again, only this time Aidan slept too, both of them waking to the announcement that they would be landing shortly at the Aéroport Nice Côte d'Azur.

"As soon as we get back to the apartment, I'm going to get in bed and sleep until tomorrow morning," Liam said, then yawned.

"Oh, you mean the bed that's like quicksand," Aidan said

teasingly. "The one you just sink into. I thought you didn't like it."

"As long as you're in the bed beside me, I'll survive," Liam said. The plane taxied to a stop, and the warning lights went off. Liam stood up and reached his hand down to Aidan. "Come on, let's go home."

If you enjoyed this book, I hope you'll continue with the next book in the series, *The Noblest Vengeance*. Aidan and Liam must fly to Istanbul to protect Aidan's distant cousins, and both of them will learn more about themselves and others.

Thanks for reading! I'd love to stay in touch with you. Subscribe to one or more of my newsletters: Gay Mystery and Adventure, Gay Romance or Golden Retriever Mysteries and I promise I won't spam you!

Follow me at Goodreads to see what I'm reading, and my author page at Facebook where I post news and giveaways.

If you liked this book, please consider posting a brief review at your vendor, at Goodreads and in reader groups. Even a short review help other readers discover books they might like. Thanks!

Dedication

To Marc: You might think I'm crazy, but all I want is you.

Acknowledgments

Chris Kling, author of the amazing *Circle of Bones*, helped me a great deal with powerboat details, and Victoria Allman provided important suggestions about Corsica. Sharon Potts, Chris Jackson, and Miriam Auerbach gave me useful advice about the writing here. I'm always grateful to my editor, Maryam Salim, who has been a continuing source of inspiration and support, and to everyone at Loose Id who helped these books blossom.

Zoë Sharp's terrific books about Charlie Fox inspired me to write a bodyguard book of my own. As always, I owe a debt of gratitude to all the baristas at Starbucks who kept me fueled with caffeine as I wrote, plotted, edited, and groaned in frustration.

Thanks to all the fans, bloggers, and reviewers who have supported my writing, both in mystery and in romance.

Thanks too to the professional groups that have helped me learn to write better, to make contacts in the world of writing, and to promote my work, and the librarians who first encouraged my love of books.

I'm also grateful to Broward College, where I teach, for the sabbatical term off that allowed me to get so much writing done, as well as to the many wonderful writers and teachers I work with.

About the Author

A native of Bucks County, PA, Neil is a graduate of the University of Pennsylvania, Columbia University and Florida International University, where he received his MFA in creative writing. He lives in South Florida with his husband and two rambunctious golden retrievers. He is a four-time finalist for the Lambda Literary Award in Best Gay Mystery and Best Gay Romance.

A professor of English at Broward College's South Campus, he has written and edited many other books; details can be found at his website, **http://www.mahubooks.com**. He is also past president of the Florida chapter of Mystery Writers of America.

www.ingramcontent.com/pod-product-compliance
Lightning Source LLC
LaVergne TN
LVHW011944060526
838201LV00061B/4200